THE USUR]

WILLA MUIR (1890–1970), born Will:
feminist author and translator, marrie
She wrote about her own life and career in *Belonging: A Memoir*,
published in 1968. She is known to have written four novels. The
first two, *Imagined Corners* and *Mrs Ritchie* were first published in
1931 and 1935 respectively, and republished in a single volume
together with some of her feminist essays in 1996 as *Imagined Selves*,
edited by Kirsty Allen. Her third novel *Mrs Muttoe and the Top
Storey*, written 1938–1940, remains unpublished. *The Usurpers*, her
fourth novel, is published here for the first time. It was written in
the early 1950s and grew out of her experiences in Prague in the
years leading up to the Communist takeover of Czechoslovakia in
1948. In that time Edwin Muir was the Director of the British
Institute, the lecturing and teaching branch of the British Council
in Prague.

Under the guise of Utopians in Slavomania, *The Usurpers* offers
acute, humorous and sometimes acerbic observations on relations
among the British themselves in Prague (the city is never named)
and between them and their Czech friends and those in the
Czechoslovak establishment who were suspicious of the British
presence, and depicts, largely through the actions and conversation of its characters, a deteriorating political environment in
which the lives of many Slavomanians and even some of the
Utopians are increasingly under threat.

The non-publication of the *The Usurpers* in the 1950s may have
been partly due to political pressure, at a time when the government grant-in-aid to the British Council was being called in
question. It was to have been published under the pen-name
"Alexander Cory" and Willa Muir herself withdrew it after she was
publicly identified as the author.

The Introduction explores these and other issues surrounding *The
Usurpers*. It is written by Jim Potts who has long been an admirer
of the work of both Willa and Edwin Muir and who was himself
the Director of the British Council in Prague some forty years
after the Muirs were there.

Other works of fiction from Colenso Books

The life and death of Hangman Thomas (2016),
Corfiot tales (2017), *What price honour? – The convict* (2020, two
novellas), all by Konstantinos Theotokis,
translated from the Greek by J. M. Q. Davies

The placebo by Lawrence Durrell (2018, in conjunction
with The Durrell Library of Corfu)

This spinning world: 43 stories from far and wide by Jim Potts (2019)

Stay with me by Louisa AdjoaParker (2020, short stories)

Life Term by Mark Allen (2021, a novel)

Before The Fire by Leslie Retallick (2021, a novel)

Kalamas and Acheron: Rivers of Hades by Christophoros Milionis
(2021, short stories) and
Keratochori: my life in the furnace by Panayotis Tranoulis
(2023, a novel)
both translated from the Greek by Marjorie Chambers

And my mother's bitter tears by Demetrius Toteras (2023, a novel)

———— ————

Volumes of poetry by Jim Potts from Colenso Books

Reading the signs (2020)

Words on the table (2021)

The latter includes a substantial section entitled
"Facing off the Thought Police", with many poems
arising from the author's experiences in Czechoslovakia,
and also a "Postscript on Czechoslovakia" in prose.

THE USURPERS

by

WILLA MUIR

*(a hitherto unpublished satirical novel
written in the early nineteen-fifties)*

EDITED BY
ANTHONY HIRST AND JIM POTTS

INTRODUCED BY JIM POTTS

COLENSO BOOKS
2023

First published March 2023
by
COLENSO BOOKS
68 Palatine Road, London N16 8ST
colensobooks@gmail.com

ISBN 978-1-912788-27-9

CONTENTS

ACKNOWLEDGEMENTS

We are very grateful to Kenneth Ross, representing The Estate of Willa Muir, for permission to publish this novel, and for his patience during the long time it has taken to prepare it for publication.

We thank the University of St Andrews Library, Department of Special Collections for providing a copy of the typescript which is described as follows: 'Typescript of a novel "The Usurpers" by Willa Muir under the pseudonym Alexander Croy. Apparently unpublished, the note "corrected" appears by the title.' It is held in the Library's Archive Collections/Papers of Willa Muir, and the Reference Number is ms38466/2/9.

We thank the National Galleries of Scotland for permission to reproduce the portrait painting of Willa Muir which appears on the front cover. It is entitled *Willa Anderson, Mrs Edwin Muir, 1890–1970* and was donated in 1970 by the artist, Nigel Isaacs.

We are grateful to Michelle McGaughey who retyped the novel in electronic format, and to Catie Gladstone, who, after our initial editing, proofread the text, constantly comparing it with the original typescript and offering much useful advice.

Anthony Hirst & Jim Potts
February 2023

INTRODUCTION

BY

JIM POTTS

I have long been an admirer of the novels and other writings of Willa Muir and of the poetry of her husband, Edwin Muir. Their translations — primarily the work of Willa — of the writings of Franz Kafka influenced me profoundly at an early age. It was the Muirs' translation of Kafka's *Metamorphosis*, in the 1961 Penguin edition, that inspired me to write an essay on ethical issues related to the cruel treatment and fate of the transformed Gregor Samsa, and the lessons we can potentially learn about our attitudes towards those who suffer from "locked-in syndrome", severe strokes, comas, or incurable disabilities which block their powers of communication. I wrote the essay for the Oxford University entrance examinations. I feel certain that it was this that led to the offer of a place to read English. The same enthusiasm contributed, much later, to my eagerness to accept a posting to Prague when the opportunity arose. I was there from April 1986 until the end of 1989 as the Director (Representative) of the British Council, Czechoslovakia, and Cultural Attaché at the British Embassy in Prague.

Edwin Muir was the Director of the British Institute in Prague from 1945 to 1948, the Institute being the major wing of the British Council there, responsible for most of the educational activities and cultural events. Edwin's account of their Prague years can be found in *An Autobiography*[1] and in his poetry collection *The Labyrinth*;[2] and Willa's in *Belonging: A Memoir*[3] and in the unpublished diary

[1] London: Hogarth Press, 1954.
[2] London: Faber and Faber, 1949.
[3] London: Hogarth Press, 1968

she kept while in Prague, which she described as "the only diary I have ever kept".[4]

I was drawn to the Muirs' writings about Prague and Czechoslovakia when I myself was writing an account (unpublished) from what one might call "the other end of the tunnel". They were writing in the time leading up to, and immediately after, the Communist Party's seizure of power — the Coup, or Putsch, of late February, 1948; I was writing primarily about the years leading up to the collapse of Central European Communism, the fall of the Berlin Wall and the Czechoslovak "Velvet Revolution" of November 1989, although I did also discuss events of the period 1947–1950.

Later, when I learned about Willa's unpublished novel *The Usurpers* I was eager to read it and obtained a copy of the typescript from Special Collections in the Library of the University of St Andrews. Drawing extensively on her Prague diaries the novel reached its present form in early 1952 and was submitted unsuccessfully to publishers under the pen-name Alexander Croy.

Label from the front cover of the typescript

[4] *Belonging*, page 239. The Prague diary is in the University of St Andrews Library Department of Special Collections, ref. ms384666/5/2, /3 & /4.

The supposedly imaginary country in which this humorous satirical novel is set is called "Slavomania", which clearly stands for Czechoslovakia; and the main British protagonists are working for the "Utopian Cultural Mission" or the "College" attached to it, clearly based on the British Council and Institute respectively, "Utopia" standing for the United Kingdom. The fictional names of the two nations are heavily ironical. Other characters include the Ambassador and staff at the Utopian Embassy in a city which is never named, but can only be Prague.

In her Journal from the early 1950s (quite different from the Prague diary as there a long gaps between entries), Willa describes, in February 1952, the final stages in the gestation of the novel:

> Vast gap of more than a year, because I began to write my book again and have therefore written nothing else. It is finished but not revised. (The Usurpers)
>
> I think, whiles,[5] it's very good; surprised that I could have thought it out at all; then, whiles, that it's disjointed, ill put together, lacking proportion and style.
>
> I had a fit of black despair and resentment when I had finished it, just because Edwin let it lie for days before reading it, I know he was tired and busy, but I had wanted him to show enthusiasm and interest; he *never said a word* about it, not even regretting that he couldn't read it, because his eyes hurt, or he had other work, or what-not. Had he regretted not reading it, had he said: I'm sorry I can't get at it yet, I should have been appeased, for I think I am reasonable. It was his apparent utter indifference that got me down; I could see how little value he attached to the *expectations* he might have of it, how little real importance he felt it would have. Perhaps he is right, thought I; this book I have been dreaming myself into, with such

[5] Scots dialect for "at times".

enthusiasm and delight, is really a very second-rate production: it won't matter to anyone. It made me suicidal for some hours, until I got the better of it.

Once convinced that you are utterly unimportant, you think suicide doesn't matter. Nothing matters.

Well, it is now lying about, that book, waiting again for Edwin to make suggestions, which he said he would like to make. It has been waiting for ten days, since he read it. I shall begin going over it myself; I can't wait. If I wait, I grow resentful again, and it's not worth while letting one's own vanity swell things up until one weeps with hurt pride. The only thing is to depend on oneself, although I shrink from looking at the book again.[6]

She did go through it again, making cuts, and wrote almost three months later:

I did go over the book, cutting out my excess of emotional statement: all the "alls" and the "veries" and some of the descriptive adverbs; more important, I excised bits here and there that weren't strictly necessary. The result I think is shapely. When Edwin did look at it, he had no suggestions to offer; I had done what he thought needed doing.

In writing a book I attend far more to the construction, the sequence of incidents, the feeling conveyed, than to the style, although I am not aware of neglecting the style. I was surprised to find how many clumsinesses I had left in the book, and how many superfluous bits of explanation and elaboration. They are pretty well out now, and it will have to rest, as it is.

Ella Jameson has sent it for typing. I suggested (1) Macmillans (2) Hamish Hamilton (3) Chatto and Windus.

I sent it off from Woodstock, where we went on holiday, first with Rex and Barbara, then with Flora and Joan. [...]

In a dumb way, I had hoped Flora would read the ms,

[6] Journal, 22 February 1952. St Andrews ref. ms38466/5.

but she cried that I wasn't to expect her to read handwritten stuff. Anyhow, I knew she wasn't well — a bad cold — and I didn't let resentment come up this time, although *again* I felt how little importance other people expect to find in anything I write. I must have been damned splurgy in the books I put out when I was young. But this one isn't a splurge.[7]

The outcome of the submission of *The Usurpers* and the reason for her decision to withdraw it are recorded by Willa exactly six months later:

I have withdrawn my ms, because of a letter from Marjorie Williams identifying me as the writer. Also, all the publishers it was offered to turned it down perhaps afraid of libel.[8]

Much has been made of the fear of libel, and it is possible that others intervened to persuade the publishing houses to reject the novel. Was it really considered potentially libellous at the time, or simply too damaging an exposure of the increasingly hostile relationships, jealousies and suspicious attitudes within and between a British Council office and its teaching institute in those tense, uncertain times? Was it too political and provocative to be published in a period when the Council's budget was under continual threat of stringent financial retrenchment measures and savage cuts, prior to the Drogheda Report to the government in July 1953 (a summary was made public in April 1954), and in the wake of a relentlessly hostile Beaverbrook Press campaign which seemed intent on its abolition? Willa's husband, Edwin (who continued to work for the British Council), may have had his own reservations about the wisdom of publishing such a novel, and he didn't always give her the support she

[7] Journal, 14 April 1952, St Andrews ref. ms38466/5.
[8] Journal, 14 October 1952, *ibid.*

expected. As we have seen, he seemed indifferent to Willa's draft and didn't even bother to read it for some time.

In all the years it has lain unpublished, a number of critics and biographers have read the typescript of *The Usurpers*, and have in my view paid too much attention to its relation to the real circumstances out of which it was written.

Kirsty Anne Allen calls it "a profoundly flawed work of fiction", a "novel which fails to be fiction", and suggests that "the parallels" between characters in the novel and real people "are numerous and scurrilous".[9] Aileen Christianson finds that the "conflation of Edwin's problems with Czechoslovakia's perhaps shows one of the roots of the unsatisfactory nature of the fictionalising of their experiences into *The Usurpers*."[10]

In a 2015 article Margery Palmer McCulloch writes as follows:

> The examination of Willa Muir's personal journals of the time suggest how external tensions can transform daily reporting of events into creative texts in their own right, while her conscious attempt to convert such experience into fictional narratives raises artistic questions of distance and of impersonality.[11]
>
> [...]
>
> In her Prague journals [...] there are times when she appears to be involving herself too closely and emotionally with the internal difficulties of Institute staff and their families. This emotional empathy was also problematical when she decided to write a novel based on her and

---

[9] "The Life and Work of Willa Muir, 1890–1955", unpublished PhD thesis, University of St Andrews, 1967, pages 460 and 451.

[10] *Moving in circles: Willa Muir's Writings* (Edinburgh: Word Power Books, 2007), page 151.

[11] "Edwin and Willa Muir in Prague; a case study in twentieth-century archival and creative writings", *Textus* 3, September–December 2015, page 57 (from the Abstract).

> Edwin's experiences in Prague in the late 1940s (*The Usurpers*) [...] In addition, her attempt to disguise setting and characters through changes of names and places was artificially clumsy and unconvincing.[12]

I do not agree at all with these judgements of *The Usurpers*. A work of fiction should be judged in its own terms and on its own merits. Its relation to the author's own experience or to specific persons or events in the real world have no bearing on its literary merit. Unlike Edwin Muir, and perhaps the authors just cited, I have read *The Usurpers* with great pleasure a number of times, and regard it as a masterpiece of fiction. I can, though, happily agree with Christianson when she says that the novel could be used "as the basis for a screenplay for a political film or television series about the warring British community in the imploding post-war Czechoslovakia".[13] One only has to think of the BBC's 1987 adaptation of Olivia Manning's *Balkan Trilogy* as *Fortunes of War* to see the potential.

I had originally planned to append to this Introduction a substantial list identifying the possible sources for many of the fictional of characters in the novel, both British and Czech, but this now seems unnecessary and irrelevant here. Those who are interested will find some possible identifications in the writings of Aileen Christianson and Kirsty Anne Allen cited in the footnotes.

I find it extraordinary that a novel as good as *The Usurpers*, by an author critically esteemed for many of her other writings, has been left unpublished for over seventy years, and I am very happy to have been instrumental in finally bringing it into the light and making it available for all to read.

January 2023

---

[12] "Edwin and Willa Muir in Prague", page 69.
[13] *Moving in Circles*, pages 153–154.

THE

USURPERS

*If a man sees himself in a dream being made
into an official, that is bad; death is close at hand.*

From The Egyptian Book of Dreams,
quoted by the B.B.C.

This story is a pattern seen in a field of probability.
The characters, the action, the country in which
the story is set, are all to be regarded as imaginary.

Chapter I

For once in his life Archibald Edgar Bower entered a room without wondering whether his arrival had passed unnoticed. He was too angry to care. From the very end of the street — a long street — he had heard the din made by the Students' Party, and the nearer his car came to the portal of the Mission's palace the more cacophonous, the more compromising, the more personally insulting had seemed the noise exploding through every one of a dozen tall, shining windows. Although on his way to an appointment in the Ambassador Hotel, he had stopped the car and almost run up the broad, shallow marble steps, right through the anteroom, the library, the buffet room, and now paused, just inside the doorway of the great ballroom, to recover his breath if not his temper, a short stocky figure in a dinner-jacket, his eyes glittering behind thick-lensed spectacles.

However formidable he might feel, Mr Bower did not look formidable, not at first sight, anyhow. But none of those present gave him a first let alone a second glance; they were all too busy watching Bob Owen waving his arms beneath the tinkling chandelier as he brayed, bleated, and hissed at herds and flocks and gaggles of students, who brayed back at him, or bleated, or hissed, and rushed into different corners of the ballroom. Had Venus herself risen from a scalloped shell just inside the doorway she would have received little attention at that moment. From behind his spectacles Mr Bower focussed a glare on Bob Owen's back, yet if Bob's shoulder-blades wriggled it was not because he was conscious of disapproval.

Mere speech could not have been heard, and Mr Bower was not the man to shout.

He primmed his lips and breathed deeply as his anger

3

sank to meet old resentments that made room for it. In Mr Bower's experience the stupidity of other people was matched only by their malevolence, and this outrage to his dignity was another instance of both. The word "outrageous" had begun to articulate itself in his consciousness when Jamesina Russell, peering in her short-sighted, kindly manner, came from behind the buffet and spoke at his shoulder.

"It's you, is it, Mr Bower?" she said. "I'm sorry I didn't notice you coming in. How nice of you to look in on our party. The students are enjoying themselves, aren't they?"

Mr Bower's lips moved soundlessly and his self-controlled expression grew more wooden. Jamesina sensed that he was displeased and her persuasiveness came suddenly to life.

"It's a dreadful noise, I know," she said in her soft voice, "but they're young, after all, and only think what they've been through! Poor things, they had such a time in the Occupation. They disliked and distrusted everyone when we first came. If you only knew the difficulty we had in getting, them to stop being formal and awkward! We couldn't get a smile out of them at all. They *would* click their heels and bow from the waist and stand huffily on their dignity. They were terribly suspicious and self-conscious, Mr Bower, and no wonder. And now, look at them! Just look at them!"

Jamesina beamed at the room. "It was a great surprise to them to find that we are the kind of people who don't mind making fools of ourselves in parlour games. And, of course, they adore Bob. Bob can do anything with them . . . Excuse me, that game's finishing, and I'll be needed at the buffet. The buffet is a great success, by the way; we'll do more than pay expenses, we'll have a good bit left over."

It would not do to let Mrs Russell slide away like that, thinking she had said the last word.

"I suppose your husband is here somewhere?" said Mr Bower, quite sharply.

"Martin? Why, of course. I think he's somewhere in the library with two or three of his seminar students."

Mr Bower shelved Mrs Russell for the moment; perhaps she was merely stupid and not malevolent; time would tell. Owen, drifting with the chattering crowd towards the buffet-room had at last observed him, and Owen must be dealt with. He stood waiting in silence.

"Oh, hello, Mr Bower," said Bob Owen. "Glad you've come in. Good party, isn't it?"

"I heard the noise," stated Mr Bower distantly, "from the very end of the street."

"Oh, that farmyard game *is* a bit rowdy," returned Bob airily, with his crooked grin, "but we'll have some decent singing in a minute — the choir, you know. The choir's getting on famously, we're going to sing some early Utopian songs and rounds. Perhaps you'd like to sit up on the dais and hear us?"

Owen had certainly been drinking, Mr Bower decided. He shot a side-glance at the students streaming past him to the buffet, flushed and merry. Had they been drinking too?

"What drinks are you serving at the buffet?"

"Oh, would you like some coffee? Jamesina's handing out coffee now. Come along and I'll get you a cup."

"No thank you. What other drinks are you serving?"

"Oh, some wine, red wine, and a little beer. But there's very little left; if you want some, better come along now."

"No thank you," repeated Mr Bower. "I'm afraid I can't stay; I have an appointment. Why aren't you in a dinner jacket?"

Bob Owen's beaky face sharpened. The lock of fair hair on his brow suddenly looked draggled, as if he had been half-drowned.

5

"This is supposed to be an informal party, you know. Our usual Students' Party. We dress for dances, but not for this."

"I think you owe it to your position to put on a black tie," said Mr Bower. "We must go into all this at a Staff Conference, tomorrow, if possible. I may say that I thoroughly disapprove, thoroughly disapprove, of what you call an informal party."

"Oh, come, I say!" protested Bob. "You haven't seen us . . ."

"I have heard quite sufficient. I suppose Mr Russell is here?"

"Yes, yes. Yes, of course. I saw him not long ago. But, look here . . ."

"Bob! Bob!" came a yell from the other end of the ballroom where the grand piano stood and a cluster of performers was gathering. Iris Owen came slithering across the polished floor, also calling out: "Bob! Bob! The choir!"

"Do wait and hear the choir," pleaded Bob, in a last attempt to save the good name of the party.

"Oh, good evening, Mr Bower. You're just in time to hear the choir," said Mrs Owen, a thin, dark, pretty but nervous-looking girl. "We're just about ready, Bob, except for Kosina. Have you seen him?"

"There he is!" Bob was darting off. "Got your 'cello, Kosina? That's right. Oh, Martin, here's Mr Bower asking for you."

Bob escaped on the instant — he was a gifted escaper — and the baulked Mr Bower turned to greet Martin Russell, who was Bob's immediate chief and nominally responsible for this so-called entertainment.

"Good evening," said Russell, smiling, "it was very good of you to come."

Mr Bower quailed a little, but his face remained

wooden.

"Er, yes . . . good evening, Martin," he said, feeling angry with himself. He must learn to control that fluttering in the pit of his stomach whenever he met Russell. If only the man did not look so like his father-in-law.

"You'll sit up on the dais to hear the choir, Martin, won't you?" put in Iris Owen. "And you too, Mr Bower?"

Mr Bower could at least lead the way on to the long dais, where ceremonial arm-chairs were being set out, and he did so; but he had an uncomfortable sense of being shepherded. Still, he reminded himself, he was the most important person in the room. He, Archibald Edgar Bower, was the Chief of the Utopian Cultural Mission to Slavomania, while Martin Russell was merely the head of a lecturing and teaching branch. In a way, it was quite fitting that he should be the only person present who was properly dressed in a dinner jacket — although he must bring the matter up at a Staff Conference next day. All functions of the Mission must be conducted on the highest level, the very highest level.

He gave a quick sideways glance at Russell, and peevishly noted again the resemblance to Victoria's father; the same mild, thoughtful eyes retreating behind high cheek-bones, the same lofty forehead. Indeed, Russell's forehead was even higher than his father-in-law's; one could not believe it meant anything, there was so much bone. And the shock of grey hair was too theatrically impressive.

The string orchestra now struck up bravely, and Mr Bower composed himself to lend a critical ear. "Here's a programme," said Russell, thrusting a somewhat smudgy hectographed sheet into his hands.

Under cover of the applause that followed this prelude he remarked: "A little ragged, don't you think, Martin?"

"Well, perhaps. But not so bad, considering. They haven't had much time to practise. Been sitting University

7

examinations for weeks, you know."

Mr Bower's face became even more expressionless. Apparently he disliked references to the University. His anger was still turning slowly within him, sinking deeper down, and he was in a mood to be captious, even pettish.

"We ought to be able to provide concerts here on the very highest level," he commented. "This is an excellent hall for such a purpose."

"I think the chandelier might get in the way," said Russell. "I find it catches all the sounds and lets them drop among the audience at rather irregular intervals."

Mr Bower permitted himself a small smile, which vanished almost as soon as born. For the choir was now bursting into rollicking song:

> He who would an alehouse keep
> Must have three things in store,
> A chamber with a feather-bed,
> A chimney and a hey nonny-no,
> hey nonny-no, hey nonny nonny-no.

Martin Russell laughed. Mr Bower looked at his programme, where the words of the song stared impudently at him. He pursed his lips and sat very stiffly. When that number was finished, he rose to his feet.

"I fear I must go now. Collins is waiting for me at his hotel."

"Oh, ah, Collins?" said Martin Russell, applauding vigorously. "Collins?" he asked again, as if he had never heard the name before.

"My new Deputy. He arrived last night."

"Oh yes, I'd forgotten about him."

Mr Bower, knowing that this was probably true, since Russell was notoriously absent-minded, felt an unexpected rush of patronising affection for such a child-like, unworldly, bookish creature. Quite unworldly, of course. He really did not understand that this so-called Students' Party was an outrage. This reflection made it possible for Mr Bower to say good-night in a friendly manner. He managed to bring out quite casually what he had been fearing to say: "By the way, Martin, I think we'd better have a Staff Conference tomorrow. It will be a good opportunity to introduce Collins to the office. We can discuss our programme of social functions. Would eleven o'clock be convenient for you?"

"Yes, I think so, oh yes." Russell looked vague.

"I'll send a chit to your secretary in the morning," said Mr Bower, and on this firm note descended to his waiting car.

Behind him, the University students of Slavomania's capital cheered again and again, until Bob conducted a repetition of the rollicking song. All present, including Martin Russell, joined happily in singing it, and their hey-nonny-noes pursued Mr Bower's car until it turned a corner and threaded its way into the Square, the principal street of the city.

CHAPTER II

Victoria Bower had had the Collinses on her hands for long enough. Maisie Collins was so *fussy*. In Mrs Bower's vocabulary this word cloaked, like charity, a multitude of sins committed by other people; its connotation widened and shifted a little every time it recurred, and as the evening wore on it recurred to her mind at shorter and shorter intervals. The ladylike droop of Mrs Collins's shoulders as she deplored the delicate nervous constitution of her husband, her son and herself, the account of the frightful sufferings endured on a long journey by such sensitive creatures, the hint gently conveyed that Paris was really the Collinses' spiritual home and that it was insensate of the Organisation to throw them away on Slavomania, irritated Mrs Bower all the more because she had already reached a high level of irritation during the afternoon drive, the tea and the dinner. Why on earth had Arch wanted her to shepherd the Collinses for so long?

"I can't think why Arch hasn't turned up yet," she said, looking for the tenth time at her wrist-watch. "He *told* me he'd be here by nine o'clock. Of course, the Ambassador may have kept him longer than he expected, and that would make him late for everything."

Mention of the Ambassador seemed to revive the drooping Mrs Collins.

"I suppose relations with the Embassy must be very close in a place like this," she suggested, inclining her head a little to one side so that her drop ear-rings wobbled.

"Well, you would think so, wouldn't you?" returned Mrs Bower, thankfully venting her acrimony. "I must say, neither the Ambassador nor Lady Thring has been more than just civil. Arch does his best; he keeps running up to consult the

Ambassador on *everything*; but he gets no thanks for it, if you ask me. You *would* think, as you say, that in a place of this kind Utopians would be at least neighbourly. Of course, we haven't been here very long yet, but all the same . . ."

Here Victoria Bower paused guiltily; was she being indiscreet again? Arch was so absurdly secretive. Too cautious by half. Why, why, why had he insisted that Collins was to be kept away from the office all day?

"Of course," she went on hastily, "the Ambassador naturally enough didn't like Rigg, the man who was here before us, you know, who seems to have left such a mess behind him. Arch has to clear it all up. I'm sure I don't know why the Organisation always has to pick on Arch to clear up other people's messes, but there it is. And I suppose we'll just have to live Rigg down."

"Mr Bower must have a great deal to do," said Mrs Collins, "holding such an important position."

Horatio Collins cleared his throat and leaned forward with boyish eagerness. "Er . . . this is just where I shall come in useful, Mrs Bower," he said, showing a fine crowd of pointed teeth. "I shall try to take a lot of the work off Mr Bower's shoulders."

It was a pity, thought Victoria Bower, that he had such a rasping voice, a voice which got on one's nerves as much as his wife's plaintive accents. Oh, why didn't Arch come?

"There's one thing: we have a very good building for our Mission," she said aloud. "An old baroque palace. You'll like it, Mr Collins."

"Yes, I've been *rather* wondering all day when I should see it," said Mr Collins, looking magnanimous.

"You'll see only too much of it. Arch seems to spend his whole life there," retorted Mrs Bower. "But he said that today he'd have to be away from it most of the time; he had a lot of people to see, at the Ministry of Education and the

Foreign Office, besides running up to our Embassy and goodness knows what else. He couldn't even come home for lunch, I shall be thankful when he's able to relax a little; I don't see why he should work himself to death."

"I shall certainly do my best to keep him alive," promised Mr Collins, rising to his feet and striding about with his hands in his trouser pockets. "Er . . . would you mind, Mrs Bower, if I smoked my pipe?"

"Oh, Bob!" protested Mrs Collins. "Not in a dinner jacket!"

"Of course I don't mind. I like to see a man smoking a pipe."

This sentiment fitted exactly into Mr Collins's mental image of The Manly Utopian, a picture which he reflected with fair accuracy as he stood filling the pipe. He looked, in fact, very like an advertisement for pipe tobacco in any pre-war Utopian magazine. His face was handsome enough in that style, with a good, slightly aquiline nose, a squarish chin and a high narrow forehead; he was fairly tall, held himself straight and had an engaging boyish manner although he was nearly forty. One did not notice his teeth so much when they were clenched upon the pipe-stem. Maisie Collins glanced up at him and thought to herself: "Well, at any rate, Bob *looks* like a gentleman." It was with a renewal of sympathy that she turned to Mrs Bower: "I suppose it *is* difficult beginning Social Life in a new place. We've never had to do it before; we've been in Jamaica ever since we were married. And, of course, there we knew everybody and everybody knew us."

"You're lucky, then," said Mrs Bower. "I've had nothing but changes. You belong to Jamaica, don't you?"

"Well, our people — Bob's and mine — have been there for generations. But, of course, we went to school and college in Utopia."

"Oh, so did I. My father was a missionary in India, you see. So, of course . . ."

Like a buoy marking the fairway, the phrase "of course" guided their conversation through the shallows. Meanwhile, Mr Bower's car was parking in front of the hotel among an array of cars belonging to other important people, such as diplomats, Press correspondents and black marketeers. He had to push his way through the crowded foyer, and so did not notice a tall young Third Secretary of the Utopian Embassy taking cover behind a friend, murmuring, as he passed: "The world's prize bore, don't want him to see me." But Mr Bower had the lift to himself; and as he was wafted up, a motion that soothed him, he decided to play the Communist card. From what he had seen of Collins, he was fairly sure of his man. Still, he wanted to be quite sure.

The corridors of the Ambassador Hotel were intricate, yet not so intricate as to defeat Mr Bower. In three minutes he had found the door of the Collinses' sitting-room and crossed the threshold.

For a moment or two he stood there, smiling, holding both forearms out not quite in front of his body and with fingers extended.

"Oh, there you are, Arch!" called Mrs Bower, and on that releasing phrase he came forward with short tripping steps, tilting his face up a little as he smiled.

Horatio Collins's hands were out of his trouser pockets on the instant, grasping and presenting a chair to his Chief, who sank into it and dropped his hands wearily on the arms,

"Well, here I am," he said. "A little late, I fear. I have had a great deal to do today."

He raised his hands and dropped them again to show how exhausted he was.

"Would you like a drink?" said Mr Collins, in his most manly manner. "A spot of brandy? I can ring for it."

"No thank you," said Mr Bower. Then, tilting his head again and smiling with a hint of deprecation: "But, do you know, would it be possible, could I have a cup of tea, do you think?"

"Oh yes, of course we can have tea. Ring the bell, Bob."

"The tea in this hotel is quite good."

"It must be UNRRA[1] tea, I suppose."

Although she had herself contributed to these encouraging cries, Mrs Bower was not deflected from her grievances.

"I can't believe that you need to work so late, Arch. Nobody else would dream of doing it. What good do you imagine it's going to do the mission if you work yourself to death?"

I have had a most interesting day," said Mr Bower. "Really, a most interesting day."

"Was the Ambassador . . . ?" began Mrs Bower. Her husband checked her with lifted hand.

"No, not the Ambassador, although I did go up to see him; I felt I had to report something of what I had learned. No, the Ministry of Education, it was."

"I thought you told me you didn't like the men at the Ministry of Education?"

"Well, two of them I should perhaps call hostile. Yes, definitely hostile and obstructive."

Mr Bower pursed his lips and put his finger-tips together. "But there is a third man, Doctor Dushki, who appreciates very much the points I have been pressing in Committee. This Committee," he explained to Mr Collins, "supervises the so-called Utopian Grammar School."

"Oh, is there a Utopian School?" cried Mr Collins.

"So-called. It used to deserve its name, I believe. But now it is a State school and has ceased to be Utopian in anything

1 United Nations Relief and Rehabilitation Administration

but name, although we still subsidise it. Doctor Dushki has been associating himself with me in handling the Committee, and today, after our meeting, I had a long and confidential interview with him. In his private room. He is quite an important man, the head of a department. And in the course of this interview he enlightened me on the position of affairs — considerably enlightened me."

He looked from one to another of his audience in stating this remarkable fact, and then announced, "It appears that the headmistress of the Utopian Grammar School is a member of the Communist Party."

Scandalised ejaculations were uttered, Mr Collins rose and began to stride up and down the room, fiercely sucking his pipe.

"My predecessor, Rigg," went on Mr Bower, turning his eyes up and the corners of his mouth down, "was of course a member of the Committee that appointed her. I need say no more about Rigg at present than that I am not surprised at his appointing a woman who is doing her best to sabotage the school."

"Oh, Arch!" protested Mrs Bower, "how can you say that about her? It's Doctor Marsakova, isn't it? I thought she was such a nice little woman."

"I shall only point out, Victoria, that it is too easy for us to be deceived in foreigners. Doctor Dushki assures me that really cultured Slavomanes, with a good knowledge of Utopian, who want their children to enjoy the same advantages they had themselves, in the days when the Utopian Grammar School was a most exclusive establishment, catering only for the best families — he assures me that these people cannot get their children into the school at all, because the headmistress is filling up all the places with ragamuffins from the gutter."

"But that's only what Doctor Dushki says," persisted Mrs

Bower. Just like Arch to be cautious in the wrong place and rash in the wrong place, she was thinking with dismay. Holding back when he should push forward and pushing forward when he should hold back. "Don't you believe everything *he* says, either!"

"I do not believe everything that anyone says," returned her spouse, a little huffily. "But I am inclined to believe Doctor Dushki in such a matter as this. Besides . . ." He paused, and then, as if making up his mind to spill every bean, added: "This is all, of course, highly confidential. The fact that the headmistress of our school should be a Communist is only one strand in the web of intrigue which the Communists are spinning."

"Did Doctor Dushki say that?" queried Mrs Bower.

Mr Bower ignored the interruption.

"In this country the Communists are in key positions. The Minister of the Interior is a Communist, so is the Minister of Information. The one controls the police, the other all broadcasting and film news. Each of them is dismissing, one by one, all non-Communists in his Ministry, and replacing them by Party members. The police force is being filled with Communists! The wireless is entirely in the hands of Communists! Doctor Dushki regards this as very sinister, and so do I."

"Very sinister indeed!" cried Mr Collins.

"There is a deliberate purge of Government services. A secret purge. A web of intrigue."

"Can't the Government do something about it, then?" asked Mrs Bower tartly.

"Steps will certainly be taken, Doctor Dushki assures me . . ." Here Mr Bower pursed up his mouth again and looked secretive.

"But *you're* not going to be pushed into taking any steps, Arch, I hope?"

"My dear Victoria, I need no pushing. The Utopian Cultural Mission may not be political, but it is entirely on the side of law and order. I think we can say so much. You agree with me, Collins?"

Mr Collins came to a standstill and said, "Most certainly I agree! What is needed everywhere is more discipline. All this red scum . . ." he waved his pipe towards the window, "all this atheism! The lower orders getting out of hand! Decidedly I agree!"

"Ah!" said Mr Bower, laying down his tea-cup as if it were a trump card, "I thought I could count on your support."

But Mr Collins, having been wound up, was not so easily unwound. "Subversive elements!" he went on, "Spoiled, selfish, godless . . ."

Mr Bower cut him short: "We shall find ways and means of countering them," he said. "The first thing, in my opinion, is to get rid of Doctor Marsakova."

"And how are you going to do that?" enquired Mrs Bower, even more tartly than before.

"There are ways and means, Victoria, ways and means."

Mr Bower's eyes glittered behind his glasses. He rose from his chair. "And now, perhaps, the ladies will excuse us? You and I, Collins, must go into conference together."

"Certainly, certainly," said Mr Collins, striding this time towards an inner door which he flung open. "We can have this room to ourselves, if you don't mind its being a bedroom."

"If Mrs Collins will pray excuse me?"

Mr Bower tripped after his new Deputy and vanished with him into the cul-de-sac.

The expression on Mrs Bower's face seemed to intimate that she it was who should have been prayed to excuse him. But her fretful look sprang from uneasiness, even from dread. She had been sorely tried all day, and now what she was most deeply afraid of seemed to be taking substantial shape: her husband's tendency to assume that he was ringed in by hostile forces, and to act precipitately on that assumption. "Arch will have another nervous breakdown," was how she put it to herself.

Bravely, however, she set herself to take up again the white woman's burden of making conversation, and in this she was greatly helped by Mrs Collins. Without asking direct questions as Mrs Bower did, Maisie Collins was skilled in eliciting, most politely, all the information she wanted. She had been assuming, for instance, that the Bowers belonged to Grade One of the service, and was now gratified to learn that they were still only Grade Two, like the Collinses themselves. Her manner towards Mrs Bower altered subtly. After all, Victoria Bower was not really a *lady*.

"We shall have to organise the Social Life of the Mission between us, I suppose? I hope I shall be able to be of great use to you."

"I shall be thankful for any help," said the downright Mrs Bower. "I've been to several receptions already and it's time I gave one myself."

"Oh, I *love* receptions!"

"Well, when we do give one, I shan't know half the people at it. I shall have to invite all the Doctor Dushkis and Shudkis and their wives. Aren't the names here awful? Of course, we have Rigg's invitation list to go on, but from what I can gather he went in mainly for petting parties. At least, so Jamesina Russell tells me. Oh, you don't know her, of course; her husband's in charge of the College." Not without malice Mrs Bower added: "They're Grade Two as well."

"Oh, three Grade Two families! How lovely."

"They've been here for two years already, and they must know much more about the Slavomanes than we do. I keep telling Arch . . ."

Here Mrs Bower made one of her guilty pauses. To cover her momentary confusion she looked at her wrist-watch and said, "I do hope Arch doesn't keep you too long out of your bedroom. By the way, I notice you call your husband Bob. I thought his name was Horatio?"

"Horatio is a family name. So, of course, he had to have it. But everybody has always called him Bob, from the time when he was a little boy."

Mrs Bower now took a step which she had been shirking. "It seems to me that it would be more friendly if we called one another by our Christian names, wouldn't it? May I call you Maisie, and will you call me Victoria? And Mr Collins won't mind being called Bob, do you think?"

"I know he would prefer it, thank you very much, Victoria. And so should I."

Privately, however, Mrs Collins decided that nothing should induce her and Bob to call the Chief by a name so vulgar as Arch.

Presently Mr Bower and Mr Collins came back.

"God dig you good den, fair ladies," cried Mr Collins. "We hope you are both feeling gruntled?"

"You seem very pleased with yourselves," said Mrs Bower. "Have you settled all the affairs of the universe?"

"We have had a very satisfactory conference," said Mr Bower, with a shade of reserve in his manner. He hovered beside his wife, but did not sit down.

"So have we," said Victoria. "We've agreed to call each other by our Christian names, Arch. I hope you don't mind, Bob?"

"I am delighted," protested Mr Collins. "Bob's your Uncle from now on. All will go merry as a marriage bell."[2]

"I'm sure I hope so," said Mrs Bower, rising to her feet

[2] Collins is adapting a line from the first stanza of Byron's poem "The Eve of Waterloo": "All went merry as a marriage bell".

20

in answer to her husband's unspoken suggestion.

"I am certain of it," said Mr Collins, waving his pipe. "We're going to have no more Riggery, either in the office or elsewhere, isn't that so, Bower?"

Maisie Collins noted that her dear sensitive husband had avoided the obnoxious name. She smiled upon him.

"Riggery?" she said. "What's that, Bob?"

"The Chief's excellent term for the infection spread around by the late unlamented Rigg. Riggery-Pokery, in fact."

Mr Bower looked uneasily at his wife. "Shall we be going, my dear?" he asked. "I shall pick you up, then, Collins, tomorrow morning at about nine o'clock."

"Right you are," returned his Deputy, looking more manly than ever. "Then we shall smite the Philistines hip and thigh."[3]

Mr Bower said nothing.

---

[3] Collins is alluding to the Old Testament: "And he [Sampson] smote them [the Philistines] hip and thigh with a great slaughter" (Judges 15.8, Authorized Version).

CHAPTER III

Archibald Bower was an ambitious man of the kind that does not lie long in bed of a morning. In summer he was fond of saying that he rose with the sun. But it was now November in Slavomania, and he had to anticipate the sun in getting up.

By night the recalcitrant forces within himself, which by day he could more or less control, had things all their own way, so that his sleep was uneasy and haunted by monsters. Nothing in the world was so welcome to him as his early morning tea, which he drank quickly, in gulps; as it went down, the monstrous shapes usually shrank and receded into their fastness, and Mr Bower was his own man again, able to rise from the helpless horizontal position, to brace and buckle himself for the day.

Yet on this morning, even while he was shaving, the horrid shapes were still haunting him. He had had a bad night and his hand was not quite steady. He should not have allowed himself to be so angry at the Students' Party. One should never allow personal feeling to get the upper hand; it was regrettable. And he was a little afraid that perhaps he had betrayed too much personal feeling in describing to Collins the Riggery pervading the Mission. Today it would be advisable to be cool and distant to Collins. Yes. He must remain quite impersonal. Yes. He must be very much the Head of the Mission.

At this point a strong bubble of resentment rose from the depths and burst on the surface. After all, he *was* the Head of the Mission, and it was infuriating to have the Slavomanes behaving as if Martin Russell were the more important official. And not only the Slavomanes. The Ambassador.

Mr Bower, angrily eliminating the thick, dark growth

from his chin, cut himself.

"Dear, dear," he said aloud, hunting for a piece of sticking-plaster. "Dear, dear. This will never do."

Patching his wound, he began to be sorry for himself. It was most unfair that he should inherit from Rigg such a legacy of disapproval. The Ambassador was most unfair. Not to say rude. A good Ambassador would never permit himself to be so childish. And spiteful. For he *had* been spiteful when he said: "I suppose you know the University is thinking of giving Russell an honorary degree?"

The University, of course, knew nothing yet about Archibald Edgar Bower. He must give a course of lectures there himself. Methods of analysing the Utopian Language. Yes. With all the newest graphs and diagrams. Something quite solid and up-to-date. Lectures which could later be published.

Mr Bower's face grew wooden and immobile again and he went on shaving, very carefully. His mind was busy planning that course of lectures, with bold, keen sweeps, and in the process, somehow, all inconvenient personal feeling was eliminated, so that when he had finished shaving he was, if not serene, at least calm. He was back on the highest level, where logical patterns were not blurred by emotion.

Now was the time to consider again his Master Plan. He put on his shoes, an overcoat and a thick scarf and stepped out for his brisk walk round the garden. As compared with a long walk on a summer morning, the turn or two round the garden was not inspiring; one had not that sense of marching into an illimitable future; but the crispness of the air and the frost underfoot cleared one's head and helped one's mind to remain cool.

The Master Plan. Yes. He had it clear now. Things were always much clearer in one's mind than when they came to be set down on paper, but, all the same, he thought that he would now be able to draw up that Report for which Headquarters were pressing him. He must only guard against being shaken out of the lucid calm in which he found himself at the present moment, and the Report would practically write itself.

Firstly, an analysis of the existing situation. The Mission had little or no prestige, thanks to Rigg. The College, although functioning in the same building, had dissociated itself, probably in self-defense, from the Mission and had come to be regarded as a separate body.

Secondly, suggestions for curing this evil. The prestige of the whole Mission must be built up, and the rift closed between Mission and College. This could best be done — no, achieved — best be achieved by an overall process of centralization and reorganisation.

Mr Bower paused here in his survey, and also in his walk, fascinated by the words "centralization and reorganisation", which he repeated twice, like an incantation, before going on.

As he trotted along the path he saw in his mind a diagram of the new Cultural Centre he wished to organise. It was an impeccably regular diagram radiating from a single central point — the Head of the Mission — with an inner ring of specialist officers fanning out to a wider ring of secretaries and typists. It seemed to him beautiful. It was simple, logical, and, above all, economical.

Centralization and reorganisation, then, directed towards creating a single Cultural Centre staffed by specialist officers. The College, as such, would cease to exist; it would be integrated into the Cultural Centre instead of remaining a separate body.

Thirdly, the saving in administrative expenses by this re-grouping would be considerable. Duplication of services, such as typists and messengers, would be eliminated.

Lecturing staff could be reduced, also teaching classes; all the lectures needed could well be given, on the very highest level, by the specialist officers.

No. Headquarters could not fail to be impressed by the Plan, even should they not accept it in its entirety, thought Mr Bower, stepping out briskly. At that moment, however, he must not permit doubts to disturb his equanimity. Of course it would be accepted.

Having thus accomplished the not uncommon feat of satisfying personal desires by abstracting them into an apparently impersonal scheme, Mr Bower cleared the caked snow off his shoes on the scraper and went indoors to breakfast.

There was no one yet in the dining-room, and he was still able to maintain his god-like calm. He stood on the hearth-rug, clean-shaven, brushed, spectacled and befittingly clad, behind a two-days-old copy of the Utopian Times, unmistakably a man of weight and importance, so calm and assured that he barely lowered the paper when his wife, late as usual, came in carrying the letters.

Victoria Bower perceived at once that her husband's defenses were up, and as she had no reason to believe that the man behind them was infallible she felt uneasy. This made her voice sound sharp as she said: "It looks as if one of these letters is from our landlady. I know her sprawling writing. What's she up to now?"

"H'm," said Mr Bower, guardedly. He laid the letter down beside his cup, unopened.

"Aren't you going to read it?"

Mr Bower rustled the Utopian Times. It was the thin-paper air-mail edition, and it rustled well.

"You never listen to a word I say, Arch. Aren't you going to read that letter?"

Had Mr Bower been a frank man, he would have

answered: "Not if I can help it."

"Er . . ." he said, "yes, I suppose so."

This should have silenced Mrs Bower, but did not.

"Well, read it then," she retorted. "I want to know what's happening. Is she going to sell the house over our heads?"

With a reserved air Mr Bower picked up the envelope, slit it neatly open with a knife and extracted a letter covered with large and temperamental characters. He read it through, carefully folded it again and stowed it in a vest pocket.

"Well?" demanded his wife.

"She has sold the house," admitted Mr Bower.

"Well!" Mrs Bower's tone had sharpened still more. "Can't you do something about it? Are we to be turned out?"

"Give me some more tea, will you, my dear?" said Mr Bower, maintaining his calm.

Mrs Bower could not refuse to pour out the tea, but she wielded the tea-pot with ferociously direct action.

"What are you going to do about it?" she persisted.

"There is no need to worry, Victoria. The contract she made with Rigg holds good for us as well. It was a contract with the Organisation, not a personal contract with Rigg, whatever she may choose to think."

"Do you mean that the new owner has just got to let us go on staying here?"

"I see no reason to think otherwise."

"Well, I only hope you're right. Hadn't you better make sure of it? Can't the people at the Foreign Office do anything?"

"I shall consult the Foreign Office in the matter," said Mr Bower. "After all, I am the Head of a Mission."

"You mean the Foreign Office is bound to find you a house? How do you know they wouldn't just let you live in a hotel?"

"Leave it to me, Victoria, if you please."

"A hotel would be simply dreadful with two children. We *must* have a house with a garden," said Mrs Bower, fretfully. "And the Collinses will be wanting a house too."

"Collins will have to see the Foreign Office about that himself. He won't be able to afford the Ambassador Hotel for very long," said Mr Bower, drawing a fine red herring before his wife's nose.

"Why, won't the Organisation pay his hotel bills?"

"Under the new dispensation, which has just come into force, hotel bills are paid in full for a fortnight only. After that, a certain proportion of the hotel bills, for six weeks, I think. After that, Collins is supposed to pay the bills himself — unless I make some arrangement."

"And they have a suite of three rooms! And you've no idea how fussy Maisie Collins is. I shouldn't wonder if the hotel were to turn nasty and refuse to keep them. You should just have heard her yesterday complaining about little Francis's supper . . ."

Mr Bower put up the Utopian Times again and gradually resumed his lucid calm. But this time it was mellower than before, as if irradiated by a freshly switched-on bulb in some concealed lighting system. For he had just realised that the New Dispensation, as he called it, gave into his hands an excellent bridle for the control of Collins.

And so Bob Collins, hurrying down into the foyer of his hotel like an eager terrier, barking: "Good morrow, good morrow! And how are we today?" was somewhat dashed by the cool reception he got from his Chief. Mr Bower was monosyllabic, distant, even lofty.

"I see you're driving yourself," said the Deputy, unhappily, striving to create a more matey atmosphere.

Mr Bower unbent a little.

"This car is nearly new; I had it sent out for my personal use. So I prefer to keep it in my own garage overnight and drive it to the office myself in the mornings. Of course, during the day I use the chauffeur for official visits."

"Oh yes, of course. Er . . . is there any other car?"

"There is the car which Rigg brought out."

Mr Bower's voice had the tone of distaste with which he always mentioned his predecessor.

"I suppose I could use that?" ventured Collins.

"It is out of action at the moment."

Mr Bower negotiated a corner leading into a very narrow street which was effectively corked by some enormous trucks ahead of him, so that he came to a standstill.

"The traffic seems to be badly regulated here," said Mr Collins, "like everything else."

"This may have become a one-way street overnight," vouchsafed Mr Bower. "They do that kind of thing here without warning. One drives into the usual street and finds there is a fine to pay."

Mr Bower tried to peer past the trucks.

A car behind him hooted angrily.

"Can we back out, do you think?" he asked, dropping the words negligently as if he took no responsibility for them. Yet even this moderate encouragement heartened Mr Collins; perhaps the Chief, after all, was not so unaccountably like the streets that changed character overnight. He twisted round in his seat and his raucous voice sounded masterful as he cried: "Yes. Yes . . . No — No. The car behind's moving up."

"So are the trucks in front," said Mr Bower drily.

"*Eppur si muove,*"[1] went on Mr Collins.

---

[1] Italian for "And yet it moves": words attributed to the physicist and astronomer Galileo (1564–1642). He is supposed to have uttered them after being compelled by the Inquisition (in 1633) to renounce his belief that the earth moves around the sun and not vice versa as the Church maintained. Here Mr Collins' use of the expression to refer to a traffic jam is purely facetious.

"H'm," said Mr Bower.

After that, all his Deputy's attempts to be effusive were received in chill silence. By the time the car pulled up in the courtyard of the palace dedicated to the Utopian Cultural Mission, Mr Collins, somewhat forlornly, was feeling for his pipe.

Once the pipe was in his mouth, however, the Deputy strode noisily enough beside his Chief up marble steps and over parquet flooring.

"These are all Locally Appointed Staff," said Mr Bower, referring to typists as if they were inanimate fixtures, "but here is our Librarian, Mr Bradshaw. Claude, this is Mr Collins, our new Deputy."

Mr Collins took his pipe out of his mouth, hitched one shoulder, pivoted from one leg to the other, and barked: "How do you do?" Then he thrust both hands deep into his trouser pockets, where they found some keys to jingle, and grinned at Claude Bradshaw through the stem of his pipe.

Claude was easy to grin at, being bluff and hearty, with a weather-beaten skin, slightly protuberant, frank blue eyes, and a friendly smile. It was rumoured in the office that he had once been President of the Utopian Bull-dog Breeders' Association, and he certainly had been in the Navy during the last war; perhaps that was why he looked a little like a cross between a sea-dog and a bull-dog.

"Oh, you've come instead of Wilson, have you?" he said in a fruity voice.

Mr Collins gave a nervous giggle.

"Er . . . have I? Yes, I suppose I must have."

"H'm," said Mr Bower. "We have to be getting on, I fear, Claude. You know that there is to be a Staff Conference at eleven o'clock this morning?"

"No, I hadn't heard of it," said Claude, gazing down into Mr Bower's spectacles. "In your room, is it? Right. I'll be there."

Something seemed to have embarrassed Mr Bower, for he breathed uneasily as he led the way out of the library and darted little side-glances at the rows of book-cases. Outside the door he even paused till Collins came up, and confided to him: "Not very bright, Claude, I fear, but a most loyal member of staff. He can be depended on. Quite unlike the rest of them." He trotted on for a few steps and then added: "Er — Wilson was your predecessor here. He couldn't put two sentences together grammatically. He couldn't even spell. His Reports were disgraceful. I had to re-write them all myself."

"Very tiresome," said Mr Collins. Mr Bower became cool and assured again.

"You will meet the rest of the Utopian Staff at the Conference. Until then, I shall be busy in my own room. But you had better meet your Secretary now, Miss . . . ah . . . Miss Finestone. She came out from Utopia only last week; appointed by Headquarters, of course, not Locally Appointed. You and I are entitled to Headquarters Secretaries. I asked her yesterday to have the administration files ready for you in your room. Perhaps you will look over them and consider the suggestions I have made for economies in the running of the office? Headquarters, as you know, are pressing for economies."

In the library two women came warily out from behind one of the book-cases and joined Claude in front of his desk.

"I'm sure Arch spotted us," said Mary Ballard, the Registrar, one-time Captain in the Utopian Women's Army, "when I very nearly sneezed. What's this about a Staff Conference?"

"I'll have to type and deliver chits all round the office, I suppose," commented Mr Bower's Secretary, Mabel Smith. "I say, Claude, what's the new broom like?"

Claude hitched one shoulder, crooked his right arm with a nervous jerk, thrust an imaginary pipe between his teeth, buried his hands in his trouser-pockets and straddled his legs wide apart, pivoting from one to the other. "Er, my dear fellah," he squawked, "I'm the Prison Chaplain, what?"

"Pretty good, Claude, for a first attempt," said the Registrar judicially.

"But not a patch on your Arch," said Arch's Secretary. "That's the best you've ever done, believe me."

"Well, thank you very much," said the Registrar, "I shall have a fond memory to sweeten the day. I must be pushing off now."

"Me, too," said the Secretary. "In another five minutes Arch will have finished locking his skeletons in the cupboard and he'll be ringing his little bell for me."

"What d'you mean, skeletons?" asked Claude.

"Oh, didn't you know? He keeps a Locked Drawer."

"That's where all the files are I can never get my hands on," said the Registrar. "Hallo, there's Martin. Oh, Martin, do come over here a minute. You haven't seen Claude's latest and best. Show the kind gentleman, Claude."

"Show me what?" Martin Russell paused on his way to his room.

"A lovely impersonation of Arch. Go on, Claude." Claude obligingly vanished between two bookcases and then re-appeared in the opening, holding his fore-arms out like flippers, tilting his head a little upwards and sideways, with a small, fixed smile just lifting the corners of his lips. He minced forward with short, tripping steps and said in a hushed but flat voice: "I've come for the corpse," after which he stood immobile until the last, hissing sound had died on the air.

"Brilliant!" said Martin Russell. "Really brilliant, Claude! I congratulate you."

"Gives you quite a turn, doesn't it?" said Mabel, the Secretary. "And it's only too true. This place is getting more and more like a morgue."

"Is it? I haven't noticed that."

"You wouldn't, because the College is still alive. But our side hasn't had a single visitor for the last ten days. People just won't come when all they get is me telling them that Arch is too busy to see anyone and will they make an appointment for several weeks later, please."

"Well," said the Registrar, "we're all going to have fun and games at eleven o'clock today, anyhow. Cheerio, people."

"Staff Conference," said the Secretary, answering the lift of Russell's eyebrows.

"Another Staff Conference? What's in the wind now, I wonder?" said Martin Russell, whose memory retained no trace of the Chief's remarks on the previous evening.

He had been at his desk only five minutes when he got an answer to the question. Bob Owen came in to see him, unsmiling and bleak. The absence of his usual grin made Bob look a different man; his face sharpened to shrillness, his chin became uncertain, his very hair lost its vitality and lay limp.

"Martin," he said, and his voice too was shrill, "have you heard about this Staff Conference?"

Martin Russell picked up his spectacles and put them on to see his Senior Tutor more clearly. A hangover, he decided. "Yes," he answered, "I was just wondering what was in the wind."

"I can tell you that," said Bob Owen, dropping into a chair. "It's me. Listen, Martin . . ."

A sympathetic audience, even of one, had a reviving effect on Bob Owen, and by the time he had finished telling Russell how Arch had looked and what Arch had said at the

Students' Party, he was beginning to feel better, even to enjoy his own fears.

"It's all quite ridiculous, of course," he kept saying. "He's such a *silly* little twerp."

Martin Russell took off his spectacles and laid them on his desk.

"Yes," he said, "at times I feel very sorry for him."

Bob took alarm at once. His voice grew shrill again. "But I tell you he's got his knife in me! And you know what he's like when he gets his knife in anyone. Look what he did to Jack Wilson, for all his war record. He'll do the dirty on me at Headquarters till they send me to a malarial swamp somewhere. And it isn't only me; there's Iris and the kids."

"It certainly isn't only you, Bob," said Martin Russell. "If he has his knife in anyone he has it in all of us. Don't you remember how he abused us all for what he called Riggery, at his first Staff Conference, before he knew anything about us? I think he feels he has to assert his authority, and the only way he knows of doing that is to rebuke and find fault and carp. Wait and see what this second Staff Conference is like. We should give him a chance. He'll probably only recommend us to wear black ties and do everything on the highest level. Anyhow, the Students' Party was rather on the noisy side last night, wasn't it?"

"They did get a bit out of hand," admitted Bob. "But how they enjoyed themselves! And wasn't the choir good?"

"The choir was a great success. You're building it up very well. Arch is bound to appreciate the work you're doing with that choir and the orchestra, whatever he may say about black ties."

Meanwhile Mr Bower, secure in his room, had put his landlady's letter into the Locked Drawer and fingered the draft of his Master Plan, which lay in the same receptacle. Later in the day he would begin to draw up his Report. The

Staff Conference, however, claimed his attention first; it must be conducted, of course, on the same lofty, impersonal level as the lucid Master Plan. Absolutely impersonal . . .

CHAPTER IV

No one, afterwards, was able to give a full report of all that Mr Bower said at his second Staff Conference. After introducing Mr Collins, who sat at his side behind a small table on which were laid some sheets of paper apparently containing the heads of his address, since he consulted them from time to time, Mr Bower spoke into a solidly resistant medium which could not be described as empty air but which isolated the speaker as if he were in a vacuum. Mr Bower looked at no one; he seemed to be gazing at a point in the farther wall; and no one, except Claude and at first Martin Russell, looked at him.

"Things cannot go on as they have been doing," said Mr Bower, and then proceeded to make what Russell considered an unfair attack on the Students' Party and, still worse, on the activities of the College in general. "Amateur boy-scoutery and girl-guidery," said Mr Bower. Martin Russell found himself, against his will, growing angry, and as he made an effort to keep his eyes on Mr Bower's face he got the impression that it was a talking mask, that there was no human being behind it. One could not see the eyes for the glittering lenses of the spectacles; the face was doughy, as if no blood ran beneath its sallow integument; the nose might have been a bit of putty dabbed on and pressed down with a heavy thumb; the small mouth was primmed, with the corners sourly turned down. At this point Russell heard his own name. Mr Bower was saying that of course these strictures did not apply to Mr Russell, whose work at the University was on the very highest level and could serve as an example to all. They were fortunate in having amongst them a man who was a recognised expert in literature, a real specialist.

Martin Russell lowered his eyes and ceased to hear what Mr Bower said. Bob Owen told him later that Mr Bower forbade anyone to tinker with lectures on literature while Mr Russell was available, since amateurish work on any subject was not to be tolerated. He then went on to announce that he hoped to secure a Music Officer, to raise musical activities to the same high level. This was the point at which Bob Owen ceased to listen. For what later followed Mary, the Registrar, was a source of some information; she averred that Arch hinted at a general pool of typists, of which she herself was to be made Queen; the rest, she said, was just the usual pep talk.

Russell heard nothing of this. When he recovered himself sufficiently to be aware of his surroundings, it was the general atmosphere in the room that took his attention, not the flat, prosing voice of the speaker. The air was charged with hostility, all the more deadly for being mute. It made Martin Russell's spine prickle. He glanced in alarm from one member of the Utopian Staff to another. They were all more or less his friends. Most of them had come to Slavomania when he did, shortly after the liberation over two years ago; together they had shared hardships, lack of food, lack of accommodation, working and eating together in one small room; together they had shared fears and hopes; except for Claude, he thought, they were as good a Staff as one could find anywhere. And, except for Claude, who was gazing at Mr Bower with an appearance of dog-like devotion, they were all sitting with downcast eyes and sullen, closed faces.

Was the damage irreparable? His eyes rested on Jane Lidgard's face, usually so serene; her lips suddenly trembled and she shot a clear blue look of indignation at Mr Bower, then bent her head again and stared at her lap. Involuntarily startled, Russell also looked at Mr Bower, who was still apparently delivering his address to the farther wall, and so became aware of his words.

"Having the privilege and the duty of representing Utopia," Mr Bower was telling the wall, "we must never, I repeat, be guilty of the slightest deviation from the highest standard of conduct; in particular, we must never be guilty of the slightest discourtesy to any Slavomane."

Martin Russell found himself on his feet. "Excuse me, Mr Bower," he said, and noted that Mr Bower started as if awakened from a trance, "I hope you are not suggesting that we are ever discourteous?"

Mr Bower seemed to have a moment's difficulty in re-adjusting his wits.

"Er . . . no, no, Martin," he said, "of course not. Oh, no. I was only enunciating a general principle."

Mr Bower looked like a disconcerted child. Russell hardened his heart and went on: "I should just like to get this quite clear. I do not think, Mr Bower, that you appreciate — perhaps you do not know — that most of us came here in the first place because we *wanted* to come to Slavomania. Because we wished to be of service in some way to the Slavomanes. The last thing that would occur to any of us, I am sure, would be to show discourtesy to any Slavomane."

"Yes . . . er . . . yes, I trust I am aware of that," said Mr Bower.

Russell remained standing.

"The Slavomanes know that we feel goodwill towards them, a goodwill they are beginning to return in full measure, if I may say so. And that is important. For the Slavomanes are mistrustful of people they do not like, or who do not like them. That is probably true of everyone, but it is especially true of Slavomanes. And we represent a democratic way of living and thinking, as you rightly reminded us, and so we must give the Slavomanes only what they are themselves willing to accept. We are not here to impose anything on them, but to exchange, in good-fellowship, whatever they and we can receive. I emphasise this, Mr Bower, because you seem to think that the work of the College is desultory, even frivolous. I think, on the other hand, that it is varied and experimental, because for these two years we have been probing to find out what the Slavomanes want from us. And in my opinion it has been successful. You praised me, Mr Bower, but you should have praised the whole Staff. All the Staff, except myself — I am at fault there — have learned to speak Slavomanian, not an easy language, and have worked devotedly to carry on in spite of difficulties." He did not specify these difficulties but everyone knew he meant Rigg. "We have succeeded in winning real affection from the Slavomanes. They like us. They feel at home in the College. What we have planted has been planted with green fingers . . ."

Here Martin Russell whipped his spectacles off and suddenly sat down. As he said "green fingers" he was all at once aware that Mr Bower did not in the least understand what he meant. There seemed to be no point in going on.

The Conference filed out. Mr Bower trotted after Russell and said: "Er . . . Martin . . . can I have a word with you?" Russell turned and waited until the room was empty and the Chief had carefully shut the door.

"Martin, I wanted to ask you," said Mr Bower, still like a child rather at a loss, "do you think that what I said was too severe?"

"Yes, I do," said Russell.

Mr Bower began to look huffy.

"I am sorry you should take that attitude," he said. From behind his spectacles he seemed to be scrutinising Russell's face, which did not relax its uncompromising expression. Mr Bower's huffiness became offended dignity.

At that moment a rat-tat sounded on the door and it opened to disclose Claude.

"Oh, sorry," said Claude, "I didn't know you had anyone with you. I'll come back again."

"I'm just going," said Russell and went, leaving Claude in possession.

Not wishing to meet anyone, Russell turned aside through a back passage, crammed inexplicably with enormous wooden hat-stands, and let himself into his own room by a small, discreet door opening almost invisibly in one of the walls. The room was a pleasant one, facing the inner courtyard, hung with blue silk shot with gold, which made it look cool in summer and darkly splendid in winter, as now.

Here he sat down behind the ornate desk provided for him and rested his head in his hands. The dislike he felt for Archibald Edgar Bower had made itself shockingly evident. The man had appealed to him for a little sympathy and he had given none. The child had been at a loss, had looked for reassurance, and had not received it. Only too probably he would never again be able to influence Bower in any way. Yet in that moment, when Bower had searched his face, he had found himself incapable of giving the smallest sign of sympathy.

"I *could not* do it," he said aloud, stressing the words with an emphasis unusual for him.

By the time he went home for luncheon he had a raging headache.

"One of my headaches," he said to Jamesina, who looked concerned and brought out aspirin.

"We've had another Staff Conference," he added, as if this were sufficient explanation

"Was it as bad as the first one?"

"Worse if anything. The air was thick with hostility; you

41

could feel it like a thunder-cloud."

"Oh dear," said Jamesina. "Was Arch very abusive?"

"He was outrageous," said Martin Russell, fortifying himself with indignation.

"Oh, I don't know," said Jamesina, "he seems to me a very commonplace little man. A weak little man, of course, and so he hits out all round to protect himself. But such an ordinary little man! How could he be outrageous? You all take him too seriously, I'm sure. I don't think he should be taken so seriously."

CHAPTER V

Martin Russell felt more cheerful next morning; his headache had gone and he was inclined to believe Jamesina's suggestion that he had been making a mountain out of a mole-hill. So he refused to be rattled when Claude button-holed him in the library with one of his silly stories, looking very bull-doggish. "Another straw, old boy, to show which way the wind's blowing," said Claude in a stage whisper. "D'you know what happened yesterday when we were all at the Staff Conference? A man came walking as cool as you please through the library and said to little Tanya there —" he jerked a thumb towards an extremely pretty girl who was cataloguing books in a corner — "'How long have you been working here?' And when she said: 'six months', he asked her: 'And do you like your job?' And she said: 'Yes, I do, very much.' And d'you know what he said to her?" Claude prodded the words into Martin's waistcoat with a thick forefinger. "'Make the most of it, then, for you won't be here long!' And then he stalked off. Another of these Communist snoopers!"

"Probably only a sex-mad lunatic," said Russell. "If you take on such pretty girls, Claude, you must expect them to get more or less veiled proposals. Where you find them all, you old ruffian, I don't know; but I notice that the library is always swarming with pretty girls who are supposed to be your assistants."

This was banter of the kind Claude enjoyed, and Russell smiled to himself as he went away. One of these days he really must tell Claude that *The Waste Land* should not be catalogued under Agriculture; he had always meant to do it, but hated spoiling a good joke. And Claude was altogether a good joke, the old rascal, with his eyes popping out of his head at imaginary Communists.

Still, the Communists were becoming rather a bogey in the country; there was a lot of wild talk. Why not go round to see Dick for five minutes and find out what the real situation was? Dick would be in his office; he always came in at some ungodly hour in the morning, even before the cleaners.

Major Zelezny, known to everyone as Dick, since his Christian name was some Slavomane equivalent of Richard, was Liaison Officer between the Utopian Cultural Mission and the Government of Slavomania. He was one of the busiest people in the building. His office, at the far end of a flight of rooms, had another separate entrance, a back stair running down to the inner courtyard, which was much used by Slavomane ex-soldiers who had served in Utopia during the war and by their Utopian wives. Dick had been a war-time Liaison Officer in Utopia, and he was still devoting himself, with single-minded passion, to strengthening ties between his own country and his late Allies. It was said that he was organising the men into an ex-Service legion; he had certainly organised a club for their wives with Lady Thring as active patroness, and he was running Utopian Societies all over the country. His immediate work — handling Slavomane officials for the Mission in all relevant Government Departments — would in itself have been a full-time job for any other man.

"Hello, Dick, how goes it?" said Russell at his door. "Could you spare me five minutes, I wonder?"

"Fifteen, my dear Martin, if you like. Do sit down."

Dick lifted a bundle of correspondence from his other chair. His small office was piled high with bundles of papers; but although the general effect was untidy, Russell noted with some envy that Dick's bundles were in themselves orderly.

"I suppose you can put your hand on anything the moment you want it? I only wish I could."

"More or less," said Dick.

"That's what it is to have a gift for organisation. Well, look here, Dick, I need a little organising. I'm all behindhand in my knowledge of the political situation. How is it shaping? There's been a lot of tension, I know, but I have the impression that things are a little easier. Only there's so much wild talk flying around. What do you think?"

"Things are easier, yes, in a way. You're quite right there."

Dick had a ready warmth which came more than half-way to meet people, so that they found him charming, and his pleasant baritone voice perfectly conveyed his innate kindliness.

Russell went on probing until he got the information that things were easier only because more people were allowing themselves to hope, not because the Communists had slackened their efforts.

"We're hoping that the Social Democrats' Congress, which is due in a fortnight, will vote down the pro-Communist faction. It's going to be a fight, I can tell you; but I think we're going to win it. And if we win it, Martin, we shall have turned the corner. It's like seeing light at the end of a long tunnel."

"Would you say, then, that the Communist influence is waning?"

"I think so. They're shouting about getting fifty-one percent of the votes at the spring elections, but I shall be surprised if they get more than thirty. You can almost tell that they're losing by the terrific efforts Agitprop is making."

"What's Agitprop?"

"The Communists' propaganda department. Agitprop is very active just now ... It's trying to get in among my Societies at the moment." Dick squirmed round and picked up the bundle of papers he had cleared off the chair.

"Look here. This is my correspondence with our newest Utopian Society, in Skrs. I've just been running through it. I'm pretty certain that the Secretary, a man calling himself Spalek, is a Communist agent. He actually came here once to see me and insinuated that he could pass on military information if I was interested. Skrs is near the frontier, you see. I turned him down, of course, and I've been doing my best ever since to persuade the committee to get rid of him. And I think they're going to do it, but it's a slow job persuading them. I have to keep quoting their constitution at them. And I'm beginning to suspect that some of them are under Spalek's thumb. There seems to be a possibility that he has encouraged a few of them to collect arms. That would have to be stopped at once, of course, and I shall probably have to go there myself and make a row . . . Well, that's Agitprop."

"Did you hear about the man who came into the library yesterday and put the wind up Claude?"

Dick listened to the story, but, unlike Russell, he did not laugh.

"It might quite well have been a harmless lunatic, but equally well it might have been a weak-minded Communist. Of course they've got an eye on us. They would like to make us out to be a nest of spies."

"Do they want to discredit us?"

"Nothing would suit them better. Have you seen any film shows recently?"

"No. Why?"

"Oh, you should watch the news-reels. They have to do something to counteract your activities, you know, Martin. And people *will* go to see Utopian films. So they try to make up for it in the news-reels. Any shots of Utopia which appear show only ruins and war devastation, or ten-year-old pictures of hunger marchers, or twenty-year-old meetings between old-time politicians. Of course they want to discredit Utopia."

"But people won't believe it."

"Perhaps not, if they notice it. But, you see, it's so indirect, so casual, that they may not be conscious of it. And that's partly why I am starting so many Utopian Societies."

"I see. I wish we had more people to lend you for lectures. But only Bob and Jane are capable of giving a whole lecture in Slavomanian. They're good, though, don't you think?"

"I'm very grateful for them. Especially Jane."

"Isn't Bob so good? I'm surprised to hear that."

"Oh, he's good. Our audience like him. But his stuff isn't so well organised as Jane's."

Russell looked thoughtful for a moment or two, reflecting that organisation of anything wasn't Bob's strong point, worse luck. Then he said: "About this arms business. That's the kind of thing I meant when I said there was wild talk flying around. Talk about arms being secretly collected. Can it be true?"

Dick prodded the table with a pencil.

"It might be Agitprop," he said, finally. "And that would mean, of course, that the Communists are arming themselves behind their own smoke-screen. But I can't be sure."

"People don't really want to start civil war, do they?"

"Well, Martin, this isn't Utopia, you know, but I'm inclined to think that it's just a bluff."

"After all, you Slavomanes have a fine, obstinate core of commonsense."

"Obstinate, yes," said Dick. "Pig-headed is what you should say, Martin. That's why I'm pinning my faith on my own party, the Social Democrats; they have a fine, obstinate core of pig-headed old Trade Union men. But you've no idea how difficult it is to get Slavomanes to trust each other for their own good. They're not like Utopians."

"You're a bit in love with Utopia, aren't you, Dick?"

To Russell's surprise, Dick turned a ripe plum colour and looked confused. For the first time Russell had an inkling of how vulnerable Dick was, and he felt embarrassed.

"I suppose you're going to the Congress yourself?" he asked, hastily.

"Oh, of course. I shall be in what you call the thick of the fight."

"Well, good luck to it. I hope you turn that corner."

"I think we shall . . . Martin, will you and Jamesina be at home tonight?"

"Yes, this is our evening for the Literary Group."

"Can I ring you up at about eight o'clock." Dick was now smiling, an irrepressible smile, it seemed.

"My dear Dick, of course."

"There's something I have to tell you, but it must wait till then."

The telephone rang. Dick listened while a sharp, anxious voice quacked at him. "Better come up to see me at once, then, Mrs Bower," he said, and put back the receiver with a grimace.

"Mrs Bower's milk registration has got all tangled up, and she wants permits for shoes for the children."

"Good Lord," said Russell. "Do you have to do that kind of thing too?"

"I am Mrs Bower's butler and major-domo," said Major Zelezny. "Didn't you know?"

"What would the Mission do without you?" retorted Martin Russell.

He decamped quickly, for he did not wish to meet the lady; he could hear her voice echoing in the distance and an even more penetrating, rather unpleasant male voice putting in some counter-point. The sound of it made him feel prickly, as if a burr were sticking to his skin somewhere. And not even a Communist burr, he thought, as he fled like a youngster round the last doorway, but a burr from Utopia.

The prickly feeling vanished, however, when his secretary came in and said: "Could you see Doctor Mladski just now, Mr Russell?"

"My dear chap," he cried, starting from his chair, "what brings you round here?"

Vladimir Mladski was looking full of mischief, which made him appear even younger than usual. He was in the early thirties, but being a fair Slav with blue eyes and a tautly modelled face he gave the impression of being little older than Russell's students. During the war Russell and he had met in Utopia and taken a liking to each other which was now a warm friendship.

Vladimir carefully deposited in another chair the leather brief-case without which no Slavomane official could allow himself to be seen, hitched up his trouser-legs and seated himself with a ceremoniousness that heightened by contrast, as he intended, the mischievous glee in his eyes.

"Oh," he said, very casually, "I had to visit your Embassy and I thought I would just call in here on my way back."

"Come on, Vladimir," said Russell, laughing, "what have you been up to now? The Foreign Office doesn't usually send its budding diplomats to call on me in my office."

"Aha!" said Vladimir. "Give me a cigarette, Martin. I think this is an occasion for allowing myself one."

"What is it, my dear boy? Is your grateful country going to make you an Ambassador?"

"Oh, sometime, sooner or later," said Vladimir, with a lordly wave of the hand. "But haven't you ever wondered what my grateful country might make *you*?"

"No," said Russell. "I don't suppose the Foreign Office has ever given me a thought."

"Have you really heard nothing, Martin?"

"What is all this about? You look as if you were bursting with top secrets."

"I am," said Vladimir. "And the topmost of top secrets is this. My dear Martin, the University is going to make you an honorary doctor. It was finally settled yesterday. A Ph.D. *honoris causa.*"

Martin Russell, taken completely by surprise, was deeply moved.

"It's too good of them," he said again and again, "much too good of them."

"We are like foxes who have lost their tails," said Vladimir, "we can't be happy until our friends are like ourselves. You always did make fun of us Slavomanes for all being Doctor So-and-so — do you remember? — and now you'll have to be Doctor Russell yourself."

"Oh no," said Russell, "I'm damned if I will! It's an honorary degree, after all, and I needn't wear it all the time. Only on State occasions."

The campaign to secure this honour, it appeared, had been long and arduous, conducted mainly by Russell's colleague, Professor Kodichek, with Vladimir as chief strategist in the background. "You know what academic bodies are like," said Vladimir, "and Slavomane academic bodies are the worst of them. Every department is frightfully jealous and suspicious of every other. So we had to tell the historians that you are a historian — did you never wonder why I was borrowing so many books of yours? — and we have actually persuaded the philologists that you are a kind of philologist. Anyhow, we got round them all, and the vote was unanimous, Martin. Unanimous! Think of that! I am so happy . . . I wanted to be the first to tell you. In fact, I threatened to extradite Kodichek if he told you first. And now it can't be kept dark any longer; you'll hear all about it when you go to your classes today."

"So you've got me this degree on false pretences, have you?"

"That's why we were so afraid of information leaking out. We were almost sure that you would sabotage our campaign if you heard of it."

"My dear boy," said Russell, "I don't know what to say. I really don't know what to say."

"It's an expression of our gratitude for what you have done here," said Vladimir, growing serious. "Our University doesn't give these honours lightly. It is something to be proud of, Martin, and I congratulate you very heartily. Jamesina knows about it, by the way."

"Jamesina!" said Russell, looking stupefied. "How long has she known?"

"Oh, quite a while. I had to get the information about you from *somebody*, hadn't I? We are all very pleased. Your Ambassador, too."

"Does Sir Edward know?"

"I told him it was likely, a few days ago, and I've just left word that it's settled."

"Well, well, well," said Martin Russell, scrabbling with one hand in his shock of grey hair, "what a surprising lot goes on behind my back!"

Doctor Mladski did not reveal by so much as a flicker of an eye his inmost thought at the moment: that if Martin knew more of what went on in the country behind his back he would be still more surprised.

He said aloud: "We'll have to celebrate, of course. What about a little dinner tomorrow night?"

And so Communism was not mentioned. Nor did it get more than a passing mention when Martin Russell went home to discuss the surprising news with his wife.

It was nearly eight o'clock before he remembered Dick.

"Oh, by the way," he said, "I looked in on Dick this morning, and he seems to have some secret on his mind too. He wants to ring us up at about eight o'clock, to tell us something."

"I expect Eleanor's promised to marry him," said Jamesina. "I've been rather waiting for it."

"Eleanor? Are you sure, Jamesina?"

"Certain sure. They've been sitting in each other's pockets at all the parties, for weeks past. Didn't you see them at the Students' Party? I'm very glad of it, for Dick's a lonely creature inside himself."

"His wife and children were killed during the Occupation, weren't they?"

"Two children. Yes. This will mean a new beginning for Dick. Did he look happy?"

"More confused and self-conscious than happy. I told him he was a bit in love with Utopia, you see, and if I had only known I should have said 'in love with a bit of Utopia'. But he's cheerful enough. We were discussing the Communists, and he thinks this country is just about to turn the corner, in a fortnight or so, when the Social Democrats' Congress will vote the fellow-travellers out of office. The Communist influence seems to be waning. All the wild talk is mostly bluff, he thinks. We really don't need to take it seriously, Jamesina."

CHAPTER VI

For the next week or so Martin Russell awoke each morning feeling at peace with the world. Slavomania was now parched with a still, black frost, and out of doors it was difficult to draw breath, but Russell hummed gay little tunes as he buckled on spats and wound a muffler over his ears. Jamesina, too, was happy; her friends Dick and Eleanor were going to be married and her husband was to be publicly honoured by the University. She did not hum tunes, but she fed flocks of birds on her window-sills after breakfast.

It was the more surprising, then, that Russell should daily come home from the office with the beginnings of a headache. The Chief seemed fated to irritate and upset him. He was prepared to blame himself for these spasms of irritation, and on learning from the Staff that Mr Bower had apologised separately to each of them for his remarks at the Staff Conference, he blamed himself more severely than ever because he merely despised Mr Bower for this action instead of approving him. Yet all his self-blame did not prevent him from again feeling irritated and contemptuous at unforeseen moments. And presently the moments condensed into a series of incidents.

The first incident concerned his secretary, Jarmila. She came to him in tears saying that Mr Bower had told her she was to sit in the new Typists' Pool and do any work that was handed to her, instead of being Mr Russell's secretary. Martin Russell, anxious to be fair, went immediately to the Chief's room to enquire into the matter.

"My secretary tells me that she is no longer to be my secretary," he said, as mildly as he could. "I have heard nothing about it, and so I suppose there has been some misunderstanding?"

"H'm," said Mr Bower, looking embarrassed. "Yes, she must have misunderstood the situation, Martin. Of course she is still your secretary. You have first call on her. But Headquarters are pressing for economies, and we have to make the utmost use of the office personnel. She is Locally Appointed, and so we must be able to use her in emergencies, when there is extra work."

"Is she to sit in the Typists' Pool, instead of just outside my room?"

"Er .. er . . . have you any objection, Martin?"

"I need her at hand to protect me from too many visitors, I think. I have no objection to your making use of her; indeed, I know quite well that the work I give her cannot take up all her time."

This was a too magnanimous admission, for in fact Jarmila shared with another girl all the College typing and duplicating as well as Russell's correspondence.

"Er . . . I quite see your point, Martin. I shall consult with Collins and see if we can leave her where she is, on the understanding that she is available for extra work should it prove necessary."

"Thank you," said Russell, not trusting himself to say more.

To his annoyance, the Staff showed no such restraint. The speed at which gossip ran through the building had always surprised him, and in less than an hour's time he found clusters of indignant Staff saying that to meddle with a man's secretary and not even inform him beforehand was an insult. They insisted on telling him, too, that Arch was green with jealousy, because of the honorary degree, and was doing his best to play down the College and diminish the importance of its Director.

"It's probably my own fault," protested Russell, "since I'm always overlooking chits because I won't have an in-tray and an out-tray on my fine rococo desk."

Yet the more he protested, the more loyally the Staff nursed their suspicions. He tried to ignore the affair, to dismiss it as trivial, yet he was left with a feeling of prickliness. Putting things as charitably as possible, he knew that Mr Bower had hedged, had not been quite straight; for he was sure that Jarmila had reported correctly what had been said to her.

A day or two later came the second incident, which was to have many consequences and so could not be dismissed as trivial. Bob Owen came rushing into Russell's room almost hysterical with rage.

"They've pinched our car, Martin!" he cried. "They've pinched the College car!"

By this time Russell did not need to ask who "they" were.

"But how can they?" he said, stupidly enough. "Are you quite sure, Bob?"

"I've just been speaking to Karnet. I asked him to take me to the Interpreters' Class, over in the Ministry of Information, as usual . . ."

Russell nodded. It was a routine engagement. ". . . and he said he couldn't, without Collins's leave. This morning at ten o'clock Collins told him that the cars were pooled and that he was to consider himself under Collins's orders for the future. Collins's!"

"This is really a bit thick," said Russell. "You need the car at once, don't you?"

"If I don't get it, I'll be late. It takes at least twenty minutes by tram, and it's ten minutes to eleven now."

"I'll go to see Bower."

"He's not in the office. Mabel says he went off to the Ministry of Education some time ago."

"Is Collins in the office? Wait a minute; I'll ring him up."

The shattering roar that finally came from the instrument

nearly made Russell jump; he held it away from his eardrum as if it had stung him and said with quiet distaste: "That's you, I suppose, Collins? Russell speaking. My Senior Tutor has to conduct an important class on the other side of the city in ten minutes' time. Will you kindly tell Karnet to get out the car for him? Yes, thank you."

He put the receiver down and looked at Bob Owen. His face was pale.

"There's no point in arguing it out with Collins," he said. "I'll send a stiff minute to Bower. But I'm afraid, Bob, that this is the *fait accompli*."

Mr Bower's answer to the stiff minute was unexpected; he came in person to see Russell, full of explanations, apologies and aspersions on Collins. Rigg's enormous car, it appeared, was in need of what amounted to a new engine, new brake-linings, new big ends, a new horn and what have you; it was uneconomical in petrol and oil; in short, it was a kind of white elephant. "Or, rather," said Mr Bower, making a little joke, "a mauve elephant."

"Yes," said Russell, "I remember his rubbing his hands as he told me he was sure it was the biggest private car in the city."

"The Mission should never have been saddled with such a preposterous vehicle. We have decided to try to sell it. Collins is going to buy himself a car, I believe, but meanwhile we are short of cars. And the obvious course, you will agree, is to pool the two cars we have. But Collins was entirely wrong in the way he set about it. He should have informed you in a proper manner. I can see, Martin," confided Mr Bower, "that Collins is going to be a Problem. And I do not wish you to suffer inconvenience; it is only a matter of re-organisation."

Russell's feelings were mixed. He thought that the Chief was trying to be fair and reasonable, even friendly, and his own hostility subsided.

"Oh, that will be all right," he said. "As long as we can get a car when we need it."

"I could pick you up every morning in my car and bring you to the office," suggested Mr Bower.

Russell agreed to this, and so entered upon what was to become his purgatory. Every morning he settled down beside Mr Bower in the car, and every morning Mr Bower, as he drove, cast aspersions, in a casual, negligent voice, upon some member of the Staff. Most often it was Collins who was castigated. Yet no one escaped accusation or innuendo. And more and more often Mr Bower brought up Bob Owen as a topic. Russell's flesh shrank on his bones whenever he saw the car coming: being a fellow-traveller with Mr Bower was too much of an ordeal.

"Here comes the Black Maria," he would say to Jamesina, as he peered out of the front window.

Sitting beside Mr Bower, however, he tried to overcome his distaste. He preferred to think that Mr Bower was misguided rather than hateful; mistaken, insensitive, unimaginative, over-anxious. A score of adjectives could be provided to account for the Chief's peculiarities. And Russell did his best, by suggestion and rebuttal, to correct mistaken judgements about the Staff.

In especial he did his best to justify the existence of Bob Owen. It was Bob's business to administer the teaching side of the College and to do a good deal of teaching himself. In Russell's opinion he was a first-rate teacher. But the very gifts that inspired his students and made him so popular among young Slavomanes prevented him from settling to details of routine. He relied on a talent for gay improvisation and too often left the rest of the College Staff to repair faults in his administration. Besides, his real passion was for music. He was never so happy as when conducting a choir or training a string orchestra, and would spend hours, which should have been devoted to other matters, in transcribing scores, hunting through the city for gramophone records, or hob-nobbing with Slavomane quartets.

"As an administrator, Bob is rather a round peg in a square hole," said Russell frankly to Bower. "But he's excellent on the social and musical side. He's far and away the most popular member of our Staff."

"H'm," said Mr Bower.

Again Russell's feelings fluctuated. Bower might be an honest, stupid little man trying to do his best according to his lights, or he might be a twister of some kind. Should one admit to a twister that Bob Owen was a bad administrator? Bob himself was convinced that Bower was looking for any opportunity to discredit him.

"And he's an admirable teacher," he added.

"His Book Returns," pronounced Mr Bower, "are in a shocking state of chaos."

Russell relapsed into depressed silence. He felt adrift among uncertainties. Strictures might be deserved; people might be evil; nothing seemed unambiguous.

The same feeling of uncertain confusion was apparently spreading by contagion through the office. As for Bob Owen, he was worse than confused; ever since hearing that a Music Officer might be coming he had been distracted.

Jane Lidgard came in to Russell's room one day to lodge a complaint against Bob.

"We have tried not to bother you, Martin," she said unhappily, "but yesterday was the third time Bob completely forgot about a class. And yesterday it was the Diploma Class. He didn't turn up, and he didn't arrange beforehand for Harold or me to take them, and they had been waiting for twenty minutes before I discovered them."

To Russell's uncertain mind positive evidence of any kind

came as a relief. Bob was clearly in the wrong.

"But that isn't the worst of it," went on Jane. "Arch has somehow got to hear of it already."

"How could he hear about it when I didn't?"

"Well, Mabel says . . ."

Jane hesitated, frowning.

"This is just tittle-tattle, of course," she apologised, "and you know Mabel; she always takes the gloomy view. But Mabel swears that someone in the office is definitely spying for Arch and carrying everything to him."

"I don't believe it for a moment!" Martin Russell brought his hand down on the desk. "What has come over this office? Spying, indeed! What next? Tell Bob to come to see me, will you?"

Bob, when he arrived, produced an excuse which seemed unanswerable. The car which should have been sent as usual to bring him back from the Ministry of Information had not turned up; he had waited some time for it and then taken the tram; but by then it was too late to do anything about the Diploma Class, so he had tried to discover instead what had happened to the car. And Collins had gone off in it, flat-hunting.

Russell knew that this was a credible excuse. He himself, the day before, had failed to get the car to take him to the University; he too had been late for a class. Bower and Collins were clearly in the wrong.

He stared wordlessly at Bob Owen, and in about a minute that susceptible creature lost his somewhat truculent air of conscious innocence and began to look stricken. Perhaps he was remembering the other two occasions, still unexplained, on which he had forgotten a class.

"It occurs to me, Bob," said Russell finally, "that the more complicated the machinery of this office, the less does it produce results. When we had no Collins to organise our transport, we could always get the car when we wanted it."

Bob visibly revived.

"That's because no one was trying to throw a spanner into the works," he said. "I think Arch and Collins are doing it on purpose. They're trying to do the dirty on the College."

"Are you all going crazy? Or am I going crazy?" demanded Russell. "Why on earth should they try to sabotage the College? It's the best asset the Mission has in this city."

"Put like that, it doesn't sound reasonable," agreed Bob. "But I don't think Arch is reasonable about the College. It's not the Mission he's thinking about, really; it's his own blasted little self-importance."

Russell grew tired of protesting against the prejudices of the Staff. "It doesn't do any good," he said to Jamesina, having again asked her for a couple of aspirins. "The whole office is fermenting."

"Can it be," said Jamesina, "that the tension in the country has affected the office?"

"It's odd that you should say that, for I have just been thinking that the feeling in the office is very like the general uncertainty and suspicion in the country at large. Only, in the country it was worse about a month ago and seems easier now, especially since the Social Democrats' Congress; while in the office things are growing worse every day. And as for me, I don't know where I am."

The next incident, however, at least settled Martin Russell's uncertainties. Although it was a small private incident.

Victoria Bower, advised and assisted by Maisie Collins, whom the office now referred to as "Proud Maisie", had issued invitations for her first reception. Mabel Smith, who had the task of filling in and despatching the invitations, reported that it was to be a very high-level affair. The

Utopian Ambassador and his lady were of course invited, and various high-ranking secretaries from the Utopian Embassy and the Slavomane Foreign Office. Naturally, as Mrs Bower had foreseen, all the Doctor Dushkis and Shudkis from the Ministries of Education and Information were on the list, with their wives and daughters, as well as several Professors from the University. As for the Mission Staff — here Proud Maisie had been very firm — only Grade Two had been invited, that is to say, the Collinses and the Russells; the rest were not considered worthy.

Except Major Zelezny. Victoria Bower had insisted on inviting both him and his fiancée, Eleanor, the young Utopian widow of a Slavomane Brigadier-General.

"I know he's only Locally Appointed," she explained to Maisie, "but he's a close personal friend of our Ambassador."

Victoria would have died rather than let Maisie Collins know that she was filled with trepidation about playing hostess to the Ambassador; but she told herself that it was natural enough for her to invite one of his personal friends.

Maisie Collins's eyebrows, however, went up.

"They met in Utopia, you know," insisted Victoria, "during the War."

"Oh, during the War!" said Maisie, as if that might explain any aberration.

So when the Russells arrived at the reception, a little late because they had had to wait until Collins's timetable permitted a car to fetch them, they found friends and acquaintances scattered all over the Bowers' rooms. His Excellency was especially cordial to them and seemed in good spirits. Doctor Mladski's elegant form towered above the crowd. Professor Kodichek with his wife and son enfolded them in comradely affection. Major Zelezny beamed at them, and so did Eleanor, to whom he was going to be married in a week's time, because, as he said, there was no reason why they should wait longer. People pressed forward to congratulate Russell on his doctorate and Dick Zelezny on his engagement. Victoria Bower, handsome in stiff brocade, had lost her usual anxious frown, and Mr Bower himself was tripping from room to room with the fat smile of a contented child.

Martin Russell expanded in this atmosphere. After several cocktails he even went out of his way to congratulate Mr Bower on the party.

"It's a pleasant evening," he said. "A very pleasant evening. Everyone's enjoying it."

"Yes, Martin," said Mr Bower, radiating satisfaction, "I think we can call it a success. And, do you know, when I look round on a company like this and see what can be done, I think I am entitled to be absolutely ruthless." He gazed around him with a sentimental smile, repeating: "Absolutely ruthless."

This phrase, dropped so gently into Russell's mind, had an immediate effect. Russell stared incredulously at Mr Bower, carefully set down his glass on a small table, and turned away. Still with the same blind, incredulous look on his face, he drifted through the rooms, absent-mindedly accepting each cocktail that was offered him and shaking off acquaintances, until he caught sight of Jamesina and Doctor Mladski sitting cosily together on a small sofa in a far corner.

"A queer mixture of people," Doctor Mladski was saying, with his mischievous smile. "Your Mr Bower seems to have fallen among the reactionaries."

"He would, wouldn't he?" said Jamesina. "But there are some Communists here."

She pointed out a distinguished woman novelist and the pretty, young wife of a high official in the Ministry of Information.

"I like these two so much," she confided. "And I know they are both Communists. Probably Arch hasn't realised that respectable people can be Communists in Slavomania . . . Oh, by the way, Vladimir, do you know a woman called Knizhinkova? I've never met her before, but she foisted herself on me tonight and was *so* gushing. And Mila, who was sitting beside me, got up and moved off in the most pointed manner when Knizhinkova bore down on us. Now, why was that? I didn't much care for the woman, but I should like to know about her."

"Ah," said Vladimir. "She's a clever woman, that one. She hits out just like a man."

"What on earth do you mean?"

"She and her husband escaped to Utopia during the Occupation, and spent most of their time there in plotting against the President. You know how we exiles loved one another. And some very bitter satires against them went from hand to hand. But she wrote and published an even more bitter and much better-written satire against the satirists. Oh yes, a clever woman."

"Against the President?" said Jamesina, in horror.

"How law-abiding you Utopians are!" returned Vladimir, his eyes dancing. "A President isn't sacred, Jamesina. I think her husband — or perhaps it was she — had the idea that he would make a much better President."

"How ridiculous! But I understand now why Mila moved off . . . Oh, here's Martin."

Martin Russell, not at all unsteady on his feet, yet to the eye of his wife obviously too full of cocktails, came to a halt in front of them, waved a half-empty glass and said:

"A man can smile and smile and be a villain."

"Come and sit down, Martin," said Jamesina.

"Sit down between us," said Mladski, "and tell us all about it."

"But I've told you," said Martin Russell. "A man can smile and smile and be a villain."

He subsided on to the sofa between them, looked at his glass in surprise, drank off what was in it and handed the empty glass to his wife.

"I have had a flash of illumination," he said, being only a little careful about his syllables. "I can throw an entirely new light on Hamlet. I now really understand Hamlet. Hamlet believed in democracy."

Vladimir Mladski was delighted.

"Have another drink, Martin," he said. "We'll all have another drink. Wait a minute till I get them."

"Not Martin," said Jamesina. "He doesn't need any more cocktails."

"Well, now we can really get down to Hamlet," said Mladski, coming back with full glasses. "What about Hamlet, Martin?"

Martin Russell looked up in bewilderment.

"I thought I had told you. Hamlet had a large, generous, democratic nature. Didn't I tell you? A large, generous, democratic nature." He waved one hand in a large, democratic gesture and warmed to his subject. "The rhythm of organic life is slow, large and peaceful. I once saw a ballet somewhere with the Spirit of Evil in it, and the Spirit of Evil was a cat. Name beginning with K, Jamesina, what was its name?"

Jamesina, laughing, denied knowledge of the cat's name.

"Well, it doesn't matter. What really matters is that its movements were all abrupt and quick; the quick, short, insistent movements of aggression, of purposive evil. Purposive evil comes in quick, short ripples. You do see that, Vladimir, don't you?"

He laid an appealing hand on Mladski's knee.

"Yes, yes, Martin, of course I do," said Mladski.

"Quick, short waves of evil," insisted Martin Russell. "And when these quick waves cut across the large, slow, unsuspicious rhythm of organic life, what is the result?"

He stared at them both in triumph, and announced: "The result is confusion. Uncertainty. Resentment. Suspicion. You don't know where you are. Especially if you don't know what the evil purpose is, Vladimir. You are unwilling to believe that it can be an evil purpose at all. But the whole rhythm of your life is disorganized. You are thrown into confusion. And if you are to resist the evil you must quicken up your own rhythm and so become evil yourself. And if you have a large, generous nature, you don't want to do that. So you are immobilized for a while. As Hamlet was. That's what I keep telling you."

"But, my dear Martin," objected Vladimir, "Hamlet knew already what the evil purpose was. It was already accomplished before the play began. It was a *fait accompli.*"

"Not in Hamlet's mind. He had to convince himself first that it was a *fait accompli.* Of course the evil purpose always tries to present you with a *fait accompli*, so that it can profit from the interval of your confusion. Don't you see, Vladimir, it takes time to recover from the confusion of one's whole nature? And the evil purpose doesn't want you to have time to recover. It strikes quickly. Hamlet needed time, I tell you. He had to have time, for he had to change the whole course of his nature. But my point is that he was first thrown into confusion. Baffled confusion," repeated Russell, sagely. "That explains a lot doesn't it, Vladimir? Look at the baffled confusion in this democratic country."

"I have been looking at nothing else for some time," said Vladimir, staring into his glass as he twirled it in his fingers.

"Well, there you are!"

Russell scrabbled one hand through his hair and laughed. "There you are!" he repeated; "A man can smile and smile and be a villain. But now we know that he is a villain. Now we must quicken our rhythm. We must become evil ourselves, Vladimir, don't you see?"

"Like poor Hamlet," said Vladimir.

"Like poor old Hamlet. Just like poor old Hamlet."

"You'll finish up like poor old Hamlet if you do," said Jamesina, rising to her feet. "What about coming into the supper-room with me, Martin?"

"Absolutely ruthless, he said," returned Martin Russell, staring at his wife with blank eyes. "Absolutely ruthless. Now, I ask you, how could a man say that, looking at a harmless, pleasant evening party? How could he think of saying it if he hadn't an evil purpose?"

And so Martin Russell's uncertainties were resolved.

CHAPTER VII

Two of the Mission Staff — and ungraded Staff at that — were contradicting Mr Collins: Mabel Smith, Mr Bower's Secretary, and Mary Ballard, the Registrar. Even greater than Mr Collins's indignation was his surprise. What concern was it of theirs whether the cleaners had hot water or not?

"No woman can clean these waxed floors with cold water," Mabel was saying in her plangent contralto looking at the Deputy with gloomy reproach. "It simply can't be done, Mr Collins."

"Stuff and nonsense. Giving them hot water only makes them lazy. Let them scrub a little harder. We're not going to waste money on heating water for them every day."

"Very well, then, Mr Collins, they'll throw in their buckets and mops and quit," said the Registrar, briskly. "They asked us to tell you that. I doubt if you'll find cleaners in *this* country to take the job on with cold water."

Miss Ballard's delicate emphasis sufficiently conveyed the implication that Jamaica, which had reared Mr Collins, was still a den of tyrants and a dungeon of slaves.

The lines from the wings of Mr Collins's nose to the corners of his mouth deepened.

"What business is it of yours to encourage cleaners to come to you with complaints and threats?"

"They came to us of their own accord, Mr Collins," said Mabel Smith, "because we can speak Slavomanian."

"Perhaps they were encouraged by the fact that we treat them like human beings," added Mary Ballard.

Mr Collins frowned, pulled out his pipe and clenched his teeth fiercely on the stem, yet he was routed, and he knew it. A strike was out of the question. The cleaners would have to get their hot water.

But Mabel Smith and Mary Ballard were now ticketed in his mind as Open Mutineers. And not much later it became clear how right he was in affixing this label.

Mr and Mrs Collins had already noted that when they patronised the College Tea-Room they found themselves sitting cheek by jowl with Locally Appointed Staff. Mr Collins mentioned the matter to his Chief, knowing that Mr Bower was a sound man where the insubordination of subordinates was concerned, and the Chief agreed with him that it was highly embarrassing for senior officers of the Mission to find junior typists sitting perhaps at the very next table in the Tea-Room. Supposing a Distinguished Visitor were to arrive from Headquarters, pointed out Mr Collins, what must he think of it?

Mr Bower looked judicial. "There is the additional and not unimportant point that the food provided comes out of our rations," he said. "I know Victoria sends in a batch of cakes every week, and I believe she has provided flour for bread. The Tea-Room is for the use of College members, primarily, and, of course, for the Utopian Staff, but I do not see why Locally Appointed Staff should have the freedom of it."

"Besides, look at the time they waste," said Collins. "They come crowding in as soon as the Tea-Room opens at four o'clock, and I have actually seen them still lounging there at five. And my wife has sometimes tried to ring me up about tea-time and could get no answer because there was no one on duty at the telephone."

Mr Bower looked shocked and said: "H'm." Eyeing his Deputy with cold disapproval, he went on: "The administration of the office is your department, Collins. I shall be obliged if you deal with this matter. I should have thought you could see to it yourself that there is always someone on telephone duty."

Thus goaded, Mr Collins retired to his room and dictated his *ukase*,[1] which forbade the Local Staff, in the interests of discipline and efficiency, to appear at all in the Tea-Room.

He was not really surprised when the two mutineers sent in a request for an interview later in the day. He even rubbed his hands and instructed his Secretary in a more lordly tone than usual to take away a bundle of papers and attend to them.

"And see that I am not disturbed, Miss Finestone. When I want you, I shall ring."

Mr Collins sat up very straight as Miss Smith and Miss Ballard came in. He did not ask them to sit down and for a moment they stood before his desk rather uncertainly. Then Miss Ballard, in that composed manner of hers which seemed to Mr Collins almost insolent, said: "May we take these chairs, Mr Collins?" She had drawn up a chair and sat on it before he could give or withhold permissions, and Miss Smith followed her example, looking even gloomier than usual.

"We have asked to see you," announced Miss Ballard, "on behalf of the Local Staff, with reference to their being forbidden the use of the Tea-Room."

"Ha," said Mr Collins, "I thought as much. Interfering again in something that is no business of yours."

"Excuse me," said Miss Ballard, "I am in charge of the Typists' Pool, and it is certainly my business if the typists are in a state of resentful discouragement."

"The typists, like everyone else in this office, have to learn what discipline means," barked Mr Collins. "And it is not good discipline for you, Miss Ballard, to encourage your subordinates in making complaints. How did you know, may

---

[1] In Tsarist Russia, a decree with the force of law, often arbitrary or preremptory.

I ask, that they are feeling resentful?"

"I can see that kind of thing with half an eye," remarked Miss Ballard. "But, in point of fact, they told me."

"On your initiative? Who told you what?"

"I must decline to give you any names, Mr Collins."

"I suggest, Miss Ballard, that the grievance is entirely of your own concoction."

"Not at all, Mr Collins. I should be glad to know that no grievance existed," said Miss Ballard. "In the Army we were always led to believe that good discipline implied contented and willing personnel."

"Neither in the Army nor anywhere else does good discipline mean slackness and indulgence," retorted Mr Collins, who had not been in the Army and knew that Miss Ballard knew it.

"So you think that the Local Staff is slack?"

"The Local Staff charges into the Tea-Room at four o'clock, elbowing other visitors out of the way," declared Mr Collins, putting his own elbows on the desk. "I have myself seen some of them still there at five o'clock. And between four and five the telephone is quite unattended to, as I know from experience. Besides," — Mr Collins had just remembered the Chief's point — "the rations for the Tea-Room are provided by Mrs Bower." At this statement Miss Ballard and Miss Smith exchanged looks of surprise, which Mr Collins ignored. "Mrs Bower," he went on, "cannot be expected to feed the Local Staff out of her own rations. The Local Staff is appointed to do certain work, not to waste its time guzzling other people's rations in the Tea-Room."

"Then," said Miss Ballard, "the Utopian Staff . . ."

"Wait a minute, Mary," interposed Miss Smith. "Mr Collins. Ever since we came to this office, two years ago, Miss Ballard and I have made it our business to be on good terms with the Local Staff. They are paid a very small wage compared with ours, and they have much smaller rations than we have, and they might easily be made to feel inferior and of little account. We have done our best to establish a solidarity between the Local Staff and the Utopian Staff. And if the Local Staff are to be kept out of the Tea-Room, you will be undoing all our work. It won't be a good advertisement for the Mission if its Local Staff feel that they are being treated like dirt. Charity," said Miss Smith darkly, "begins at home."

"It is even less of an advertisement for the Mission if telephone calls are not answered," returned Mr Collins, pleased with his own smartness.

"Why don't you make a rota for the telephone?" countered Miss Ballard. "You can't expect one girl to stick to the telephone from half-past two till six without a break."

"In Slavomane offices that is exactly what telephone girls are expected to do."

"I thought we were supposed to be showing the Slavomanes that our way of life is rather better?"

"This is all irrelevant," said Mr Collins harshly. "I am determined to have discipline in this office. The Local Staff must learn its lesson. And you must learn to show more loyalty to the Mission than you have been showing, both of you."

"That is your last word, Mr Collins?"

"My last word, Miss Ballard. Mr Bower and I expect some self-sacrifice and loyalty from all employees of the Mission."

He rang his bell. Both his visitors stood up.

"Then, Mr Collins," said Miss Ballard, "in the name of the Utopian Staff of the Mission, I beg to inform you that we shall boycott the Tea-Room as long as the Local Staff are excluded from it."

"What?" said Mr Collins. "Do you know that this could be called mutiny?"

Miss Finestone appeared at the door, looking startled as she heard these words.

"Oh no, excuse me," said Miss Ballard. "It is only self-sacrifice."

Both ladies withdrew in good order, which, once they were outside, broke up into a series of indignation meetings, culminating in the library, which was a good strategic centre for unofficial conferences.

"And he practically said that the Local Staff were taking the food out of the Bowers' mouths!" said Mabel.

"Well, I know for a fact that Mrs Bower has been paid for everything," said Mary Ballard, who was on the Tea-Room Committee. "And she hasn't given nearly as much as Jamesina, who didn't ask for any payment and sent in kilos and kilos of flour. Mrs Bower enclosed a chit for the amount with every parcel."

"I've given more than I could spare in tea and coffee myself," said Mabel.

"And are you really going to boycott the Tea-Room?" asked Claude, his eyes popping.

"Of course we are. You're not a tea-hound, Claude, so we didn't bother about you, but all the others agreed to it beforehand."

"The Utopian Staff has behaved very well," conceded Mabel, in what sounded like lugubrious surprise. "Even Miss Finestone."

"We'll make coffee for ourselves upstairs on my coffee-machine," said Mary Ballard.

"Better not let Collins catch you wasting electric current," advised Claude.

Miss Ballard, who had for months been making illicit coffee for favoured members of Staff at eleven o'clock each morning, snorted and said: "Collins isn't the Gestapo, although he may think he is. Let him snoop."

The mutiny lasted for well over a week. Mr and Mrs Collins were content to have more privacy in the Tea-Room, as they said, but Mr Bower looked uneasy whenever he came into it. Sundry unusual visitors turned up in the Tea-Room, seeming much amused, and Mr Bower was sure that a knot of irreverent Press Correspondents, whom he knew to be friends of Miss Ballard's, sniggered at him when he passed by. The whole staff of the Embassy, also, seemed to have heard of the scandal.

Even the Ambassador twinkled an eye at Mr Bower one day and said: "What's all this storm in a tea-cup, Bower?"

Mr Bower, who was troubled by other matters during this week, began to suspect malevolence everywhere. He might have managed to remain on his own highest level, despite these and other pin-pricks, had he not received a letter from a friend of his at Headquarters. The cautious hints in that letter disturbed Mr Bower and kept him off his sleep. Some opposition, said his friend, was developing to Mr Bower at Headquarters, through the agency of His Excellency the Utopian Ambassador to Slavomania, who was reported to be trying to get rid of someone, perhaps Mr Bower, perhaps his Deputy, it was not certain which. Someone, certainly, was being objected to. It might well be the Deputy. "But," said the friend, "a word in season, you know."

A word in season can germinate fruitfully in receptive soil, and Mr Bower was receptive enough. His Master Plan had not yet been approved, for instance. He knew that Headquarters always took a long time to approve or reject suggestions, and he might have waited calmly on the event had it not been for this letter. But the mere hint of opposition on such exalted levels was enough to sap Mr Bower's confidence.

The Ambassador might very well object to Collins. He himself objected to Collins. He had had to stop letting

Collins represent him at official luncheons because of the tactless things the man said to Communist functionaries. But the Ambassador had shown no great approval of Archibald Bower, either. Perhaps it was merely Sir Edward's way. Perhaps he was accustomed to snub people and treat them brusquely. On the other hand, he seemed never to snub Martin Russell. And he was intimately friendly with Major Zelezny.

This was the point to which Mr Bower's thoughts kept returning. Ever since that evening in Prsht — but Mr Bower preferred not to think of the evening in Prsht, when Major Zelezny, purple with inexplicable rage, had rudely abandoned his Chief in the middle of a tour and returned to the office without him. What if he had gone straight back to the Ambassador with some cock-and-bull story? It was more than likely. More than likely. An enemy within the gates, said Mr Bower to himself, in the Biblical language of his pious youth.

Then there was the equally inexplicable rudeness of Doctor Dushki to consider. With Mr Bower's support — very able support, in Mr Bower's opinion — Doctor Dushki had dismissed Doctor Marsakova from her post as headmistress of the Utopian Grammar School and then he had appointed as her successor some Doctor Kudrski of whom Mr Bower knew nothing, not only without consulting Mr Bower but actually behind his back. Mr Bower had not been notified of the Committee meeting at which Doctor Kudrski was produced like a rabbit from Doctor Dushki's sleeve. And there was no satisfaction to be got from Doctor Dushki, who wrapped himself in evasions and parried the most persistent enquiries. Recently, in fact, he had refused to see Mr Bower at all. The excuses relayed through his secretary were childish; Doctor Dushki could not be perpetually in conference or called away on important business.

To trouble Mr Bower still nearer home, there was the uncertainty about the tenure of his house. His vindictive landlady and even more vindictive landlord who refused to recognise the legal contract on which Mr Bower took his stand, a contract leasing the house to the Cultural Mission for a period of five years, only two of which had elapsed. The landlady had been understandably vindictive because Rigg had cheated her out of the extravagant rent he had verbally promised to pay, but why the new landlord should be also vindictive was quite inexplicable. He had recently taken to sending Mr Bower personal letters hand-written in clotted, illegible Slavomanian, letters which Mr Bower shuffled out of sight, undeciphered, behind the Master Plan in his Locked Drawer.

All this arbitrary hostility charged the atmosphere around Mr Bower with menace, with apprehension. It was not surprising that he could not be brought to make a firm stand against the mutineers, as Collins demanded.

During a morning drive to the office he tried to confide in Martin Russell.

"Collins has no judgement, I fear, no judgement at all," he said. Doctor Russell made no answer. He, too, had become inexplicably uncooperative.

"I have, in fact, had to forbid him to attend public functions without me," went on Mr Bower.

"So I believe," said Doctor Russell.

Mr Bower threw everything to the winds, dignity and discretion alike.

"Martin," he said appealingly, "what do you think I should do?"

"Cancel the ban on the Tea-Room."

"H'm," said Mr Bower, out of habit. He drove in silence for a minute or two and then said, "But we have to maintain discipline."

"Look here, Bower," said Doctor Russell, "you don't seem to know the difference between a good golf-club and a broomstick."

"I don't quite follow you, Martin."

"Good discipline is supple, and bad discipline is stiff," said Doctor Russell.

"Yes, yes, I think I see your point, Martin."

"It isn't a *point*," muttered the irritable Doctor Russell.

"Well, what do you think I should do?"

"Why not consult Miss Ballard and Miss Smith on the best way of organising a tea-time break? I think you'll find that Miss Ballard knows how it should be done."

"You think I should call a conference?"

"I think you should consult Miss Ballard and Miss Smith."

"Would you attend the conference, Martin?"

"Oh, I suppose so, since it's the College Tea-Room," agreed Doctor Russell, somewhat sulkily.

Mr Bowers noted the irritability and the sulkiness. He turned down the corners of his mouth and said no more.

On that very morning, however, he called a conference. At first it was more like a trial than a conference, with Bower and Collins as prosecuting counsel and Russell as counsel for the defence. The prisoners at the bar were, naturally, Miss Ballard and Miss Smith. But in the course of the trial Mr Bower changed sides, which so disconcerted Mr Collins that prisoners at the bar found themselves acquitted.

After that, the Conference, having accepted, in principle, the necessity for a tea-time break, settled down to consider how that should be organised. Miss Ballard suggested that the Local Staff should attend the Tea-Room in shifts, each shift to be allowed fifteen minutes, the shifts to be so arranged that no department was left denuded of Staff. That would ensure someone being always on duty at the telephone. Mr Collins promptly countered this suggestion with another; that the two messengers be instructed to take cups of tea on trays to all the Local Staff at their desks. The Tea-Room would thus be kept free from contamination by junior staff.

The word "contamination" was not used by Mr Collins. It was produced by Doctor Russell, during the protracted argument that followed, in the course of which Miss Ballard confounded everyone by talking about psychology and quoting statistics of industrial efficiency in war-time, while Miss Smith insisted that exclusion from the Tea-Room was the source of all the trouble and that cups of tea on desks would not allay the Local Staff's resentment. Mr Bower at first was inclined to agree with his Deputy, but after Doctor Russell had said that no man had any right to administer people with whom he was out of sympathy, the Chief suddenly switched over and proposed a compromise. The Local Staff might use the Tea-Room, in shifts as suggested by Miss Ballard, for one month, on probation, to see how things worked out.

"A blasted waste of time," said Doctor Russell, as he left the conference room with Miss Ballard and Miss Smith.

"Come to my cubby-hole for some coffee and aspirin," said Miss Ballard. "I'm tottering on my feet."

"Two whole hours of being grilled," said Miss Smith. "I don't think the Gestapo could be much worse, Mary."

"A waste of spirit and an expense of shame,"[2] insisted Doctor Russell. "Thank you, Mary, I can do with some coffee. I must congratulate you both, by the way, on the stand you have made. People like Collins should never be allowed to administer anything."

[2] Adapting the first line of Shakespeare's Sonnet 129: "Th'expense of spirit in a waste of shame".

And so the Great Tea-Room Scandal came to an end. Doctor Russell's contention that it should never have happened, that its sole results were frayed tempers and wasted time, arose from prejudice and ignored many factors. It had various consequences, none of them negligible.

The first immediate consequence was that, over coffee, Mabel Smith confided to Doctor Russell her grounds for suspecting that Claude was the spy in the office. "He sucks up to Arch like anything when he thinks there's nobody else about," she said, inelegantly but lucidly enough. "I've caught him at it several times. I warned Mary about him before, and now I'm passing on the warning to you, Martin. You be careful what you say to Claude."

"Claude!" said Martin Russell, remembering irrelevantly, as it seemed, how he had seen Claude breezing in for a talk with Arch immediately after the last Staff Conference. "But Claude says as much against Arch as anyone."

"No, Martin, not now he doesn't. He leads other people on to say things. That's the difference."

"A blasted *agent provocateur*, do you mean to say?"

"I do mean to say it."

Mabel nodded several times, pursing her mouth. Doctor Russell's skin prickled lightly as he realised how much more ready he was now to accept insinuations of this kind, and that he was clearly promoted to be Leader of an Opposition which included the Mission as well as the College Staff.

The second immediate consequence was Mr Collins's feeling of resentment at his defeat. His Chief had Let Him Down.

The third, and perhaps most important consequence, was not yet known to anyone but Mr Bower. Small conferences, he decided, could be tactically useful. They looked well on paper. He would convene many small conferences.

Chapter VIII

Mr Collins was still smarting when he went back to his hotel for luncheon. He complained bitterly to Maisie, but the kind of sympathy she gave him was not at first soothing.

"I do think that we are not properly appreciated, Bob. The Chief doesn't give you enough scope. And look at me, stranded here in this hotel, with no chance of taking my proper share in entertaining. I do think you should put your foot down, Bob. It's high time we took our rightful place in this Mission."

Bob Collins took immediate action by striding about the room, jingling the keys in his trouser-pockets, while his lady wife drooped in her chair.

"And having to be so careful about money," she went on, "is really getting me down. I know we couldn't help giving up the sitting-room suite, now that we have to pay so much of the bill ourselves, but think what it means for me to be living in a bedroom all day! And such a nice house as Victoria Bower has!"

"But you agreed with me that none of the flats we have seen would do for the kind of entertaining we have in mind."

"Of course they wouldn't. The only one that was at all suitable was in a slummy quarter. And we *must* have a garden for Francis to play in. It's so bad for him to be cooped up all the time, or just to go walking in a park. I couldn't help thinking yesterday, when Victoria and I took the children to tea at the Owens', how much nicer their flat was than anything we have seen so far. In fact, I thought it was rather wasted on them."

Bob Collins stopped jingling and stood still. He saw a possibility of real instead of sham action.

"Owen's flat? Where is it?"

"Right in the middle of the diplomatic quarter," returned Maisie, plaintively. "And it has a garden. And a garage."

"I remember it has a garage, now that you mention it. The mauve elephant's parked there. You went to tea, did you?"

"Only to a kind of scratch children's tea party. The Owens have two little girls, you know; rather pretty little girls. Francis enjoyed it *so* much."

"Well, I happen to know," said her husband, deliberately unpocketing and lighting his pipe, "that the furniture in Owen's flat" — puff, puff — "was put in for him by the Mission. I came on the inventory among my files. And the Mission pays the rent, of course," — puff, puff — "so the flat is entirely at the disposal of the Mission."

Mrs Collins had been gradually sitting straighter, and now she clasped her hands and cried with animation:

"Oh Bob! Do you really think . . .?"

Mr Collins threw a match away with a masterful gesture.

"I may tell you in confidence," he said, "that Bower means to get rid of Owen. Then, of course, we could have his flat."

"Oh, Bob, that would be lovely! It's just right for us, that flat."

"Well, if we want it, I'm sure we can have it. But all this is in the strictest confidence, Maisie. Russell doesn't know anything about it, and I fancy Bower doesn't want him to be tipped off beforehand. So don't say a word about it to anyone."

"Russell would make trouble, I suppose, wouldn't he?"

"Of course he would. And Bower is so damned cautious." Bob and Maisie exchanged a glance which relegated Mr Bower to an inferior category of courage.

"Well," said Maisie, growing lively, "I couldn't help thinking that Grade Three had no *right* to be living in such a lovely flat while a Deputy and his family were homeless. Of course the Mission should reserve its best flats for the best people. Oh, Bob, I feel quite different already! And do you know, I thought I was going to have a nervous break-down. You *will* speak to Mr Bower at once, won't you? When is Owen likely to go?"

"As soon as Bower can manage it, I think. Oh yes, I shall speak to Bower. Most certainly I shall," said Collins. Once more he was beginning to feel that he resembled the daring buccaneers who had been his childhood's heroes. For weeks past, he was now aware, his Chief had been vacillating and temporising in a craven manner that would have brought him to walking the plank had he been the Captain of a pirate ship.

"I'fackins,"[1] he said to himself, and then, aloud: "Cheer up, my pretty sweeting. Francis Drake Collins shall yet have a garden to play in!"

So it was in a buccaneering style that Bob Collins set off to invade the Chief's sanctum that very afternoon, with a pirate cock to his hat and inaudible Yo-hos trailing behind him. Miss Smith, however, stopped him as he was striding through the antechamber.

"Mr Bower is engaged, Mr Collins."

"Oh . . . ah . . . but he can see *me*, I'm sure."

"Mr Bower is not to be disturbed by anyone, Mr Collins. The Bag[2] has just come in."

Mr Collins set his jaw and looked mulish. His Chief's propensity for shutting himself up with the newly arrived Bag before allowing it to be distributed had always annoyed him. It was high time that he Put his Foot Down. Besides, there was a malicious gleam in Miss Smith's eyes.

"Oh, that will be all right, Miss Smith," he said loftily and

---

[1] Archaic expression meaning in "in faith".
[2] The regular Dipomatic Bag containing documents from the Foreign Office in London.

thrust the door open.

"Well, is there anything for me in the Bag?" he roared across the Captain's cabin as he went in. Unfortunately for Miss Smith, the door shut again at that point, and although she could not help hearing the vibrant resonance of Collins's voice, she could not really make out what was being said.

Mr Bower looked up with a frown.

"What is the meaning of this, Collins? I thought I told Miss Smith . . ."

"Yes, yes," interrupted the reckless buccaneer, "Miss Smith did tell me you were engaged, but I thought . . ."

"I should be obliged, Collins, if you would come back in half an hour."

"But I want to ask you *now* about Owen's flat. You mean to get rid of Owen, don't you?"

It was a challenge. Mr Bower recognised it for a challenge. Collins had a nasty look in his eye which said unmistakably: "I know too much about your private schemes for you to brush me off like this."

"H'm," said Mr Bower. He glanced down at the document he had been studying, a communication from Headquarters marked "Confidential". Smoothing it with one hand, he went on:

"I intend to have Owen transferred, certainly. But let me warn you, Collins, that if you are not careful I shall have you removed as well."

"What do you mean?" said Collins, quite truculently, jingling his long-suffering keys.

"I have here a letter from Headquarters," said Mr Bower in his primmest voice, "which asks me whether I wish to retain you. Pressure has been brought to bear, through the Foreign Office, to have you removed. The Organisation is rightly unwilling to yield to pressure and asks me for my opinion. I may say that I am not surprised if the Ambassador is pressing for your removal. You have been, to say the least of it, tactless in your relations with prominent Slavomane officials."

"You know quite well," said Collins with heat, "that I was only carrying out your policy against the Communists. We've been over all this before."

"H'm," said Mr Bower. "My policy, if I may say so, is to remain on the best possible terms with the Government of Slavomania. You have been a Problem to me, Collins. You are still a Problem."

The Chief sounded cool and assured. The hesitations of the past few weeks had vanished. The lucid mind of the Master Plan was now in the ascendant.

"I don't mind if I *am* transferred," answered Collins, looking sulky. "I don't like this country. I don't have a house to live in. I have to spend more money than I can afford merely in settling hotel bills. My wife is likely to have a nervous break-down if this sort of thing goes on."

"It would not be a mere transfer, let me point out," said Mr Bower. "It would mean your removal under a cloud."

He paused to let the statement sink in. Collins chewed on his pipe, with a vague awareness in the back of his mind that it was he who was supposed to walk the plank.

"On the other hand," said the Chief, "it might take weeks to arrange your removal, and months to provide your successor. I am unwilling to have my plans so deranged, now that there is a possibility" — he caressed the document — "of seeing them realised. I am prepared to overlook much, Collins, and to retain you here, provided . . ."

He broke off and stared at Collins.

Collins said nothing. He was frowning heavily and biting strongly upon his pipe as if he needed tense muscles to keep his features from working loose.

The cold prim voice in which the Chief had relegated him

to impersonal anonymity, as a factor in deranging or futhering plans, had chilled the ardent buccaneering boy who still struggled to survive within Bob Collins.

"Provided," went on Mr Bower's level tones, "that I can count on your unswerving loyalty."

The tension in Collins's face relaxed when he heard that familiar word, so that he looked as if he might be going to cry.

"You know quite well that I have always been loyal to you," he muttered, looking like a nervous schoolboy. The word "sir", although unspoken, seemed to be hanging in the air.

"Not always," stated Mr Bower. "You have sometimes set your judgement against mine." He settled his spectacles more firmly on his nose. "I repeat, I shall expect unswerving loyalty from you in future."

He stared at Collins, his lenses glittering, until Collins bit his lips and looked away.

"Look here," said Collins, "I've always . . ."

Mr Bower raised a hand to check him.

"Unswerving loyalty," he said again, "and in return you can rest assured that I shall promote your interests as best I can."

Collins's pipe dropped from his mouth to the floor. He went down to grovel for it, and when he came up again he said: "Thank you very much. Er . . . er . . . I think you'll find that you won't regret it."

"I trust not," said Mr Bower, looking satisfied. "And now, what is this about Owen's flat?"

When Mr Collins, instead of being thrown out immediately, as Miss Smith had hoped, emerged from the Chief's room half an hour later with a purified, yet triumphant air, Miss Smith guessed that something of importance had been happening. This conjecture was confirmed when she went in to answer Mr Bower's bell and found him looking like pussy full of cream, as she told Mary Ballard later.

"Will you take the Bag to Miss Ballard?" said Mr Bower. "And ask Major Zelezny if he can come to see me this afternoon, as soon as possible."

This was an unusual summons, and Miss Smith's surprise was evident in her translation of it.

"You're wanted in the Lion's Den, Dick. Arch is licking his lips and waiting for you."

"For me?" said Dick, also surprised. "What does he want?"

"I haven't a clue. But you'd better be careful; he's looking very pleased with himself."

As if in obedience to this advice, Dick smoothed his face into expressionless wariness as he opened Mr Bower's door.

"Ah, Zelezny," said Mr Bower, rearranging some papers on his desk, "I want to consult you about something. Will you sit down?"

Dick sat down, gingerly.

"The Ambassador tells me," said Mr Bower in a far-away voice, "that our man in . . . er . . . Prsht has been collecting round him what H.E.[3] calls political undesirables. He sent me a communication on the subject a few days ago."

Dick nodded. He had himself inspired that communication.

"I . . . er . . . wished time for reflection before taking any action," said Mr Bower, still in the same far-away voice, "and it occurred to me today that perhaps I had better consult you. Who are these political undesirables?"

"Mostly ex-collaborators with the Occupying Power," said Dick, promptly. "Hungaro-manians, for the most part. Mr Wickens seems to be having an affair with a Hungaro-

[3] His Excellency, a title used for ambassadors.

manian Countess, and her friends are always about the place."

"Mr Wickens, of course, was a protégé of my predecessor Rigg," interposed Mr Bower.

"The members of the Utopian Society in Prsht naturally will have nothing to do with him," went on Dick, ignoring the interjection, "and the position is very unsatisfactory."

"Yes, yes," said Mr Bower. "The Regional Centre in Prsht, the Ambassador says, has very few Slavomane members. Would you agree with that? It is, of course, difficult for me to distinguish between Slavomane and Hungaro-manian names on a Members' Roll."

"I think that Slavomanes hardly ever enter the doorway. No real friends of Utopia among the Slavomanes will go near the Regional Centre in Prsht, which is of course a ridiculous state of things," said Dick, with some warmth.

"H'm. I may say that I still doubt the truth of the accusation that all these Hungaro-manians were collaborators with the enemy. None the less, the position is, as you say, unsatisfactory," said Mr Bower.

He smoothed some papers on his desk and went on, grasping the nettle firmly:

"You did not inform me sufficiently of the position before I... ah... visited Prsht. I was quite unaware of these... ah... complications."

Major Zelezny flushed a dark red.

"I am now, however, prepared to take action," Mr Bower announced. "I shall strengthen the Regional Centre by sending Mr Wickens an assistant who can speak Slavomanian. Do you agree with that policy?"

"Anyone who could speak Slavomanian and get in touch with Slavomanes would be a godsend," said Major Zelezny.

"I am glad you approve."

Mr Bower began to rustle the papers on his desk, and

Major Zelezny made a move to rise and go.

"Er . . . one moment, Zelezny," said Mr Bower. "There is something else here in which you could be of some assistance to me."

He produced a large, thin envelope of the usual lavish, Slavomanian type and held it out to Dick.

"This communication has been sent to me by my landlord. It is so illegible that I cannot understand it. Will you be so good as to look at it and see if you can . . . er . . . decipher what he says?"

Dick unfolded the letter in the envelope and began to read it.

"But this is very serious," he said, almost at once.

"What does he say?"

"He says," translated Dick, "that as you have sent no answer at all to his other letters and so insulted him . . . er . . . as the birth of the baby is now near at hand he insists that you leave the house, as he suggested, by the end of this month . . ."

"The baby? What baby?"

"Apparently his wife is going to have a baby, and he wants it to be born in his own house. But the end of the month is in a week's time, Mr Bower. He is very angry, very angry indeed," said Dick, re-reading the portion of the letter which he had not translated aloud. "You should really have answered the letters, Mr Bower."

Mr Bower rebutted this reproach without an instant's hesitation.

"I have received no other letters," he said, his face wooden.

"I don't understand it, then." Dick's tone was polite.

"I understand it even less," returned Mr Bower. "Of course I cannot vacate the house at a week's notice. In any case, we have a contract which has still three years to run."

"Oh yes. I remember the contract," said Dick, a little uncertainly.

"Do you think it is not legally valid?"

"It is quite valid in law, yes. But it might be obstructed. There is also, you see, a decree for the house which was granted personally to Mr Rigg, by the Foreign Office. If I may advise you, Mr Bower, I think it would be wiser to give up the contract and get the Foreign Office to grant you a new decree for another house."

"H'm. The decree is in Rigg's name, is it?"

"As far as I remember, yes. And if you insist on the contract, there will be much trouble. It might be simpler just to get another house."

"Thank you, Zelezny," said Mr Bower. "I am obliged to you. May I ask you, do you think, to write a latter for me in Slavomanian to my landlord explaining that I shall vacate the house as soon as I get another?"

"I can do that, of course, Mr Bower," said Dick, with perceptible surprise.

"I think you would do it more tactfully and with more knowledge of the circumstances than my secretary," said Mr Bower. "And I should be much obliged if you would say nothing about it to anyone, Zelezny. Nothing at all. Either inside or outside the office."

The word "outside" was sufficiently stressed, but Mr Bower reinforced it by a sharp look.

"I want no tittle-tattle," he added. "And I shall myself inform the Ambassador of the action I propose to take with reference to the situation in Prsht. You need not mention that either. Thank you, Zelezny."

Chapter IX

Mr Bower, feeling pleased, and rightly so, with his campaign, convened a Small Conference next morning. Doctor Russell and Major Zelezny were summoned to attend it, together with Mr Collins.

"I propose to inaugurate a series of small conferences, like this, on the highest level," began Mr Bower. "We shall discuss points of policy on which I should welcome your cooperation."

"A Small Conference of the Big Four," put in Mr Collins, rubbing his hands.

"To begin with," went on Mr Bower, "I have some excellent news to impart. Despite the financial stringency at home, Headquarters are willing to allow us a Music Officer, who should arrive soon, a Medical Officer, who has long been a felt want, and an Education Officer. No less than three specialists."

This news was acclaimed with voluble enthusiasm by Mr Collins, who announced that high levels of achievement would now be possible, and that the Mission was much indebted to its Chief for pressing points home and opening up vistas. Major Zelezny, when appealed to, conveyed a guarded approval. Doctor Russell, who was wondering why Collins had omitted to say that Arch had left no stone unturned, made no audible comment, because it had just occurred to him, so that he was titillated by his own vulgar naughtiness, that the Organisation must have been leaving no stone unturned when they found Arch crawling somewhere.

His eyes rested on Mr Bower and thus intercepted a shrewd glance at himself from behind the spectacles. It was a momentary flash; Mr Bower at once went on to state that the next item on the agenda concerned the Regional Centre in Prsht. An unfortunate situation had apparently developed in Prsht, which was a field so important that the Ambassador himself was interested. After a ponderous exposition of the circumstances, Mr Bower appealed again to Major Zelezny.

"You agree with me, Zelezny, that a man who can speak fluent Slavomanian should be sent to assist Mr Wickens?"

Because of the shrewd glance, Doctor Russell had been feeling a vague unease, a sense of alarm so faint that he was trying to dismiss it as merely another of the unfounded nervous apprehensions which were beginning to trouble him. But when Mr Bower went on to say: "H'm. We have now to consider whom we should send," Martin Russell knew instantaneously that Bob Owen was to be got rid of.

"I hope you are not thinking of sending Bob Owen," he remarked, as equably as he could.

Mr Bower was taken by surprise.

"Er . . . h'm . . . yes, Martin, I was just going to suggest that Owen is the very man we ought to send."

"Owen is the only man we can send," insisted Collins, in his harshest voice. "He speaks the language and he knows how to make himself popular. I think the Chief has shown excellent judgement in suggesting him. No one with the interests of the Mission at heart can think of raising any objection."

"I can think of many objections," said Doctor Russell. "He is my Senior Tutor, to begin with."

"Er — yes — I know that it might be regarded as a kind of demotion for Owen," said Mr Bower. "But we can give him a local title. He can be called the Deputy Regional Officer, if he likes. Yes, that sounds well: Deputy Regional Officer."

"And who is to be my Senior Tutor?"

The continued quietness of Russell's tone allayed Mr

Bower's slight queasiness: he had not been sure that Russell would refrain from giving trouble. So he looked both relieved and benignant as he reassured Doctor Russell:

"I have thought of that, Martin, of course: there seems to be no reason why the Education Officer should not also act as Senior Tutor in the College."

"As a part-time job?"

"Well, yes."

"It seems to me a full-time job. And the Education Officer may not be here for months. I gather that you want to send Owen away at once?"

"The sooner the better," affirmed Collins, "considering the grave emergency in Prsht."

"If you do that, you are going to have a grave emergency in the College," said Doctor Russell. He sat up straighter in his chair. "I should not have to remind you that I am responsible for the College, which has nearly fifteen hundred people on its books. In theory, I am supposed to have a Staff of seven lecturers. I have never had that staff. But for the devotion of the Staff whom I do have, the College could never have carried on its work. And if you take away Bob Owen, there will be only two lecturers left besides myself. An impossible situation. We should have to cut down our teaching classes to vanishing point. Not that I think them the most important part of the work: I don't; but they have some importance . . ."

"Excuse me, Martin," interrupted Mr Bower, "I may say that Headquarters take precisely your view about teaching classes: that they are not of major importance. We should have to cut them down in any case, because of the financial situation."

"Leave them out of account then. Leave out Owen's choir and the orchestra, assuming that the Music Officer may take them over. That still leaves open lectures and study groups and members' evenings, which a Staff of three simply cannot cope with."

"I appreciate your difficulty," returned Mr Bower, putting his finger-tips together to reinforce himself, "but may I say that you are forgetting to take into account the other specialist officers?"

"I distrust specialist officers," said Doctor Russell in a louder tone. "They may know all about their subjects, but what do they know about our audiences?"

Mr Bower decided that Doctor Russell was being willfully recalcitrant. He pressed the tips of his fingers harder together and said primly: "I am afraid you do not realise, Martin, that the College is not ... er ... not a personal concern. We cannot confine ourselves to a public based on personal relationships."

"Certainly not," cried the eager Collins. "Besides, Owen's under contract to go wherever he's sent. The Chief is entitled to send him to any part of this country, if he thinks fit. And we have just been told that a state of emergency exists in Prsht. It's Owen's duty to go there, his plain duty. I can't see why there should be any discussion."

"You will have all the specialist officers at your disposal," said Mr Bower. "I may say that their numbers are likely to be augmented. Mr Collins, too, has kindly consented to act as Science Officer, and I myself am prepared to lecture in the College at any time."

"You'll have plenty of spare parts, Russell, to keep the machine going," said Collins cheerily.

"I don't regard the College as a machine." Doctor Russell's tone was very dry. "That's one of the differences between us. And our members don't regard it as a machine, either. I know they'll be upset if Bob Owen is removed."

Russell now looked pale and unhappy. In his mind's eye he saw the faces of the choir, the orchestra, the rest of the

University students, on being told that they were to lose Bob Owen.

"There will be a storm of protest, I shouldn't wonder," he added.

"H'm," said Mr Bower. "Couldn't you tell them that this is a temporary emergency?"

"Do you mean that Owen will be coming back once the emergency is over?"

"Yes, yes, I think we might say so. A temporary appointment — say, for three months."

"So he would be back by Easter?"

"Yes, you can tell them that, Martin."

"Very well," said Doctor Russell. "The College will do its best to carry on."

"May I take it as the sense of the meeting, then," said Mr Bower, "that Mr Owen goes immediately to Prsht?"

◆

After this conference Doctor Russell, on going home as usual for luncheon, ate very little and talked even less during the meal, though what he did say was violent, startling his wife into silence.

Presently she supplied him with a pack of patience cards and sat watching as he laid them out in rows.

"How's Bob taking it?" she ventured to ask when the second game was under way.

"Badly. He sees it, of course, as the thin end of the wedge. Which it may be."

"But, you say, Dick assured you that there's a genuine emergency in Prsht?"

"He did. I had him in to tell Bob all about it. One can believe what Dick says."

"Meaning that you and Bob don't believe what Arch says?"

"Of course we don't."

"Aren't you being, well, rather perverse?" suggested Jamesina, trying to smile. "I think you're turning Arch into a bogey."

"We're not turning him into a bogey. He just is one, the little horror."

"Surely he isn't a bogey to Victoria, for instance?"

"Victoria is fundamentally a rather stupid woman."

"I must be a rather stupid woman, too, then, for I can't see Arch as a bogey."

Martin Russell did not smile, and Jamesina had the fleeting but painful impression that her husband considered her quite as stupid as Victoria.

"He's such a commonplace little man," she pleaded.

"A very commonplace little man."

"You say he's trying to get control of the College," went on Jamesina, "but how can he, while you're there?"

This genuinely puzzled Jamesina. Like many Mission wives she had no clear view of the Organisation behind the individual functionaries. She saw it only refracted, as by a lens, through her husband's temperament.

Martin Russell began to speak rapidly, as if the words had been running through his mind for hours until their sequence had become automatic.

"I haven't a car. I barely have a secretary. I have difficulty in getting necessary typing done for the College. I'm going to be without a Senior Tutor for three months, or longer, since I don't believe Bob will ever come back. The Education Officer will be straddled over on to the College, and Arch will have a finger in every pie there is."

Jamesina, who was wont to say that she could not see much farther than her nose, perceived clearly enough that her husband was cut off from her by an opaque wall of grievances past which she could not see; it was as if he were filled with darkness.

"But that's only machinery," she said. "Human beings are more important than machinery, surely. And all the Slavomanes in the College know you and like you, but they don't know Arch at all."

"They're going to," said Martin. "He's going to lecture to them. I shan't be able to prevent him. I shall probably have to take the chair for him."

"But won't that be rather comic?" persisted Jamesina. "Get him to give the lecture on the Tertiary Use of the Preposition that he gave at the University. I'd love to hear it myself. The students are still asking you what it meant, aren't they? I'm sure he'd be pleased to give it again. We might even find out what the tertiary use of the preposition *is*."

"Oh, Jamesina, it would be damned funny," said Martin Russell, becoming visible at last through the darkness, "if only the whole thing weren't such a tragedy."

Jamesina's voice was much lighter as she returned: "But is it a tragedy?"

"It is a tragedy. And it isn't only here that it's happening. It's happening everywhere."

Martin Russell brushed his cards aside and folded his hands together, sensitive hands with slim pointed fingers.

"You don't suppose that Arch lectures to the University students because he's interested in them, do you? That lecture of his was miles over their heads because he was out to show off, not to enlighten. Of course they didn't understand one word in ten. But Arch wanted to sound important, and he probably did. It will be the same in the College. He's not interested in our members, he only wants to impress them with his importance. And when you have man exercising power over people, for the sake of being important, for the sake of power, without any sympathy for the people themselves, you have an extension of the disease that I think is killing our civilisation."

"But, isn't that the kind of thing the Nazis did? You can't surely image that Arch . . ."

"I think that he follows the same pattern," insisted Russell. "And so does Collins. The hierarchy they're setting up is the negation of democracy, of what we're supposed to stand for, Jamesina. It was Dick who helped to clear my mind; he has a very lively sense of what democracy means. He told me about Arch at Prsht, for instance. You remember, we all rather wondered what had happened when Dick came back from Prsht without him."

"I always thought that Dick came back simply because he couldn't stand Arch for another minute."

"Quite right. Dick says his stomach suddenly turned. You know how Dick idealises Utopia; well, he had been telling his Society in Prsht all the usual things about Utopians at home — modest and friendly and helpful, willing to trust people, and so on. And then Arch came along, suspicious and non-committal as usual, being his pompous little self, cold-shouldering the decent people and fawning, Dick swears, on Hungaro-manian Counts and Countesses. You can image it, I understand very well why it was suddenly too much for Dick."

"And yet," said Jamesina reflectively, "Arch is a frightened little man. He's even a bit afraid of *you*, Martin."

"I shouldn't wonder," commented Russell. "No, I shouldn't wonder if that was in the pattern too. It probably takes a frightened little man to misuse our Organisation as he does."

"I wish the word *organisation* didn't make me feel so woolly-minded," complained Jamesina. "I don't really understand it. And I can't understand why our Organisation should choose Arch to be the Head of any Mission."

"I've come to the conclusion that they think of us all as

standard parts of a machine. And any spare part, of course, can be fitted into a machine, and one spare part must seem just as good as another."

"It sounds like a Robot world," said Jamesina, "something in a nightmare."

"It is a nightmare," returned Russell. "A nightmare spreading over most of the world, I think. Our office is well inside the nightmare by this time."

"Don't let the nightmare get right inside *you*, Martin," said Jamesina.

"Ask me something easier," said her husband, rising to his feet. "I've got to go back to it again."

"Well, come home all in one piece, will you? We have the Literary Group tonight, remember."

"So we do. Who has the floor?"

"Zmrzlik, I think; on Social Realism."

"Another variation of the nightmare," said Doctor Russell.

◆

A still more dreadful variation of the nightmare, thought Jamesina that evening, as she sat back, after pouring out coffee, and listened to Zmrzlik explaining that for Social Realists the individual had no importance except as a function of the social structure.

Like many Slavomanes, Zmrzlik was fond of abstract terms, and Jamesina's attention soon drifted away from him, turning back to the moment after luncheon when from his darkness her husband had looked at her as if she were a stupid stranger.

But Martin's voice brought her attention back to the present. "What you call the de-personalisation of Society," he was saying, "which you speak of as if it were a clean wind blowing away murky private emotions, seems to me a wind of death, that would kill literature and freeze our European civilisation in a new Ice Age. It's a wind that's beginning to blow, I grant you, in all modern States . . ."

He was interrupted. "Beginning," cried Havran, "beginning! It's already a blizzard . . ."

Havran, a small, dark, lively man, pointed out that in Slavomania, for instance, politics were already de-personalised.

"We are dominated by parties," he said, "by party tickets and names, rather than by known individuals. The average voter doesn't know the deputies on the list he votes for. They are just names to him, party labels. He doesn't even know them by sight. The other parties still do mention occasional names in their reports of Parliament, but the Communist papers only say that some anonymous member of such-and-such a party spoke in such-a-such a sense. Yet even the names that are mentioned are mere names to the masses of voters. We are governed not even by words, but by the impersonal ciphers that label the different parties. The party is all; the individual counts for nothing."

Doctor Russell had almost given up trying to head the Group off politics, which he was not supposed to discuss with them, yet he now made another effort.

"I don't see," he put in, "how social forces can ever find expression in literature, unless they are felt by an individual human being through his unique and individual conscious-ness. If there are to be no individuals, there will be no literature. You won't have any poets among your Social Realists."

"They mightn't be individuals in your sense of the word, Doctor Russell," returned Zmrzlik, "but in so far as they are functions of the social structure, surely they can record the impact of social forces?"

"If you write a play about a murder done for Nietzschean

motives," explained Havran, "you are a bourgeois individualist hyena, and your play is bad. But if the same murder is done in the same play for Marxian motives, you are a Social Realist, and your play is good."

Everyone laughed, even Zmrzlik, who, as they all knew, was the author of eleven rejected plays on symbolic abstract themes.

"Yet if you are only a function of social forces," insisted Russell, "you won't *want* to write a play. You may commit a Marxian murder, but why should you write about one?"

"You'll do what the Party tells you to do," said Havran. "If the Party wants a propaganda play to help on the agricultural collectives, for instance, it will send you to work on a collective farm for some years and then you will have to write a play about it or be thrown out of the Writers' Union."

"And why not?" asked Zmrzlik. "All the forces that impinge on the collective will have entered into your experience; you will be able to express them."

"You'll be allowed to express only the wishful thinking of the Party," retorted Havran. "The Party wouldn't trust you to express a personal point of view. The Party directive has always got to be right, and so it trusts nobody. I heard a lovely story the other day about the kind of thing the Russians are dreaming of. Someone has had the bright idea that all new blocks of flats should be built of glass; glass floors, glass walls; glass roofs; so that every comrade can see what every other comrade is doing. Think how delightful! You will perhaps get a special permit from the Party to hang up a curtain or lay a carpet at specified intervals for a specified purpose."

Jamesina joined in the laughter, but she said: "What a nightmare, if nobody can trust anyone else."

"We are already at that point, I think," remarked Havran

coolly. "In this country few people trust anyone else. Most people are too full of fear, a large part of it unconscious. Think how much unconscious fear lurks in the average man, an industrial worker, say, or a clerk, who feels that he is surrounded and governed by unknown forces. The small people work in large impersonal factories and live in large impersonal tenements. Somewhere unknown to them sit unknown forces directing their lives, causing employment or unemployment, wage cuts, shortages, wars. In sheer self-protection the small people are driven to join anything that looks big and powerful. They join a party as a kind of insurance. And the more they are afraid, the bigger and more blatant is the party they join. Hitler or the Communists, either will do."

That is the real Nightmare, thought Jamesina again: the darkness inside oneself, the fear and the hatred.

"And so your party does your fighting for you," went on Havran, "and draws off some of your fear. But there is always a residue of fear left in you. A totalitarian Party like the Communist Party, of course, governs you through that residue, indeed it enlarges your quota of fear, since it can discredit you utterly at any time. Social Realism simply means accepting that fact. A Social Realist knows he is hanging only on a party line. He can write only propaganda for his party; he must discredit opponents or be discredited himself . . . I am writing a novel about it," he continued, almost apologetically. "And Zmrzlik is writing another play to prove that I am quite wrong. Aren't you, Zmrzlik? A fine, modern play, all staged in a super-rocket that is being fired off into space. There are six volunteer types in it looking for a new world . . ."

"Eight," corrected Zmrzlik, imperturbably, "I have added two women."

CHAPTER X

Earlier that same evening Dick Zelezny was arrested by the Slavomanian Ministry of the Interior.

Dick and Eleanor had started their new married life in the simplest possible way, Dick having given up his furnished room and gone to live in Eleanor's little flat, which was within a stone's throw of the Utopian Mission, on the third floor of a modern building tucked into a medieval square of the Old Town. Ruzenka, Eleanor's faithful maidservant, needed little persuading that a man about the house was an asset. Dick's possessions were few; his books were pushed into the bookcase, room was made for his underwear in a chest of drawers and in the wardrobe for his suits, a card bearing his name was tacked to the front door, and the new household was established. The flat did not even look congested.

At exactly five o'clock on this afternoon the door-bell of the flat trilled its high note, and Eleanor, who happened to be passing through the hall, called out to Ruzenka in the kitchen: "I'll open the door, Ruzi."

An unknown young man in a great-coat stood there, smiling politely, and asked for Major Zelezny, with whom, he said, he had an appointment. Eleanor was not surprised that a strange young man should be wishful to see Dick, but she was a little surprised that an appointment should have been made at the flat for five o'clock, since in no circumstances did Dick ever leave his office until about six.

"I don't expect my husband home until six," she said, kindly. "Are you sure the appointment was for five?"

The young man said he had believed so.

"Well, of course," said Eleanor, "Dick may have thought he would get home earlier this evening. Would you like to come in and wait for him?"

The young man deprecated this offer; he wouldn't trouble her for the world; he must have been mistaken; he would go and get something to eat and come back at six o'clock.

Eleanor shut the door and went on through the hall, thinking no more about him. His business with Dick could not be urgent, or he would have gone to the office. Probably some private message had to be passed on verbally from one of Dick's ex-service legionaries.

At six o'clock precisely the door-bell trilled again, and Eleanor, certain that this must be the same young man, opened the door to him.

"I'm afraid my husband hasn't . . ." she began, but at that very moment the hoarser note of the street-door bell rang behind her, indicating, as usual, that Dick had passed the front door and was on his way up.

"Oh, that's my husband just on his way upstairs," she said, with relief. "If you go down now, you'll meet him."

If they had private business with each other, she had better leave them to it, she thought, and so shut the door again. But almost immediately came another trill at the flat door, and with a little amazement she opened it to see Dick, alone, wiping his feet on the door-mat.

"Dick, darling, didn't you meet the young man who came to see you?"

"What young man?" asked Dick, smiling as he always did whenever he saw Eleanor. Her lips opened to speak, but instead of saying anything she stood staring with wide eyes at something behind him. Dick turned round and saw a young man emerging from the stair-landing round the corner, accompanied by two policemen.

"Major Zelezny?" said the young man.

"That's my name," snapped Dick, with what seemed to

his wife surprising brusqueness.

"I have to tell you that you are under arrest and you must accompany us. May we come in first?"

He was advancing as he spoke; the other two closed in behind him; after a second's immobility Dick Zelezny retreated into the hall, and the third stranger shut the door with one hand while with the other he pointed a revolver at Dick, giving a small upward jerk with his chin which Dick seemed to understand, for his arms went up into the air. The second man began to search him expertly, turning out all his pockets.

The sight of Dick standing on the familiar floor with his hands up and his face darkening with rage while a stranger slapped at his pockets made Eleanor's throat close up, but she gasped: "Oh, *no*! This must be a mistake, a dreadful mistake."

"No mistake, madam, I'm afraid," said the first young man, still polite. "I regret we must now search the flat for papers and documents."

"It *must* be a mistake," insisted Eleanor. "There's nothing, absolutely nothing, to interest the police. Look, by all means, if you must, but I tell you that you will find nothing."

The young man was already opening drawers and turning over papers and clothes. The personal search being finished, the two uniformed policemen motioned Dick before them into the sitting-room.

"Is this your writing-desk, Major Zelezny?" asked the first young man. Dick, who was by now plum-coloured, said shortly: "No."

"That's my desk," interposed Eleanor, in as soothing a tone as she could manage. "These are all my household bills and correspondence. But of course you can look through them."

"Where are your private papers, then, Major Zelezny?"

"In my office," barked Dick.

"And where is your office?"

"In the Utopian Cultural Mission, as you know very well."

"Ah," said the young man. Dick glared at him and Eleanor put in quickly: "You are welcome to see all there is to see in this flat, but don't you think that my husband might drop his arms now?"

"Why, of course," said the polite young man. "Not only that, but he had better have his supper. We can wait. Only he must come with us afterwards. A mere formality, you understand."

"I'm sure it is," said Eleanor, laying a hand on Dick's arm. "Dick, darling," she went on, speaking now in her own language, "you and I know that this is just some ghastly mistake; they can't possibly have anything against you; they're bound to let you go again. Perhaps you'd better just have your supper first?"

Dick put up one hand and pressed her fingers, but he answered her in Slavomanian: "I couldn't eat; it would choke me." To the strangers he said, gruffly: "Let us go at once."

About three-quarters of an hour later, the telephone rang in the flat and Eleanor rushed to answer it.

"Dick!" she cried, eagerly. "Is that really you? Are you coming home?"

"I am allowed to tell you," said Dick's voice, very formally, "that I won't be coming back tonight. Don't expect me."

"Am I to tell people?" asked Eleanor, trying to rally her wits.

"Yes," said Dick.

"Am I to tell the Ambassador?"

"Yes," said Dick.

"Shall I . . .?"

There was a click. The connection was cut off.

Eleanor controlled her ridiculous impulse to go on calling: "Dick, Dick!" into the telephone. She replaced the receiver and leaned her head on her hand, trying to think. The Embassy, of course. Mr Bower, since he was Dick's Chief. Dick's brother-in-law, who would know what Slavomanes to get in touch with. She began to dial numbers.

The Utopian Embassy received her news with concerned surprise and put her through to the Ambassador himself. H.E. seemed upset and angry, yet he took pains to comfort her, saying: "I'll go to the Foreign Office myself, first thing tomorrow. We'll have him out in no time. Don't you worry too much. I'll keep in touch with you."

Feeling more in command of herself, Eleanor rang up Dick's brother-in-law, who said, very hastily: "Don't tell me any more over the telephone. I'm coming round at once." That was, on the whole, cheering, for she could not believe his implication about the telephone. There remained Mr Bower, who must, of course, be told; she reproached herself for being so unwilling to speak to him.

"Mr Bower? This is Eleanor Zelezny. I'm sorry to tell you that Dick has been arrested."

"What did you say?" came the familiar cold, prim accents.

"Dick, my husband, was arrested this evening by the secret police."

"What for?"

"I beg your pardon?"

"What did they arrest him for?"

"I have no idea. And neither has Dick, of course."

"H'm," said Mr Bower. "It must have been for something. Did they make no formal charge?"

"No," said Eleanor, carefully, "they merely said he was under arrest and must come with them."

"H'm," said Mr Bower again. "I suppose I'd better

inform the Ambassador."

"I have already done that."

"Did you speak to Sir Edward himself?"

"Yes, I did."

"Oh. What did he say?"

"He said he was going to the Foreign Office first thing tomorrow morning."

"I see. You have no idea whether the police have gone through your husband's office papers at the Mission?"

"No, Mr Bower. It was perhaps stupid of me not to think of that. But I have the impression that they came only to this flat. Do you think they might break into the Mission?"

"H'm. I don't know. You had better come to see me tomorrow morning sometime at the Mission."

"Very well, Mr Bower."

Eleanor hung up just in time to receive Dick's brother-in-law, a Social Democrat deputy called Honzik, who came rushing in with sweat on his forehead. "This is dreadful, dreadful!" he kept reiterating, so that involuntarily Eleanor found herself growing more composed.

"I always told Dick he was in a dangerous position working for a foreign power," insisted Honzik, mopping his brow.

"A delicate position, certainly," said Eleanor, "but surely not at all dangerous?"

"We'll have to get a good political lawyer," said Honzik, ignoring her demurrer. "Sova's the best man; he has the whole political set-up at his fingers' ends. I'll ring him up now, may I? What? Of course it's a political arrest. The Ministry of the Interior is trying to work up something against the West. My dear Eleanor, whether Dick is an innocent man or not is quite beside the point."

At that moment Mr Bower was saying to his wife: "Dick Zelezny has been getting himself into some kind of trouble.

Eleanor has just rung up to say that he's been arrested. I'd better go along to the office at once and go through his papers before the police get at them."

Mrs Bower was shocked and said: "Poor Eleanor!" Then she added, a little anxiously:

"Hadn't you better tell the Ambassador?"

"Eleanor Zelezny has already done that on her own responsibility," said Mr Bower. "Zelezny and the Ambassador have been hob-nobbing far too much with each other. I don't know what the Ambassador may have led him into doing."

"Oh, Arch! You don't mean that Dick may have been doing some *spying* for the Ambassador?"

"I just don't know what they may have been doing behind my back."

"But that would mean getting the Mission into trouble," cried Victoria. "It would be *most* unfair if the Ambassador has really — I can't believe it, Arch."

Mr Bower put on his wooden look. "People don't get arrested for nothing," he said. "And Zelezny has been constantly seeing the Ambassador without any reference to me. Most improper. Most improper. I cannot be responsible for things that are done without my knowledge."

"Of course you can't," cried Mrs Bower, even more anxiously. "I *do* hope there's nothing of that kind in it."

The expression on Mr Bower's face told her that he feared the worst.

"At any rate," said Victoria, "Eleanor can't know anything about it. Poor Eleanor. I think I should ring her up, Arch."

"H'm," said Mr Bower, already on the way out. "Better not, Victoria. Er . . . if the Ambassador should ring up, just say that I am out. Don't say anything about my going through Zelezny's papers."

"Which I am quite justified in doing, quite justified," he said to himself a moment later, as he unlocked the garage door.

There were lights in the palace, and movement, but as far as he could see, nothing out of the ordinary was happening. The College was staging a debate of some kind, he believed. With a spasm of indignation he remembered that he was never consulted beforehand about the College programmes; he must bring that up at the next Small Conference.

Dick Zelezny's office was quite in darkness, deserted. Stupid of the police, he thought, locking the door behind him.

◆

The police, at about that time, were settling to the work of grilling Dick Zelezny. A couple of interrogators were sitting at ease behind a desk, relieving each other, while Dick stood before them with powerful arc lights shining full on his face. There were still twenty minutes to go before the second relay of questioners came on duty; the reliefs had been organised so that the grilling could go on continuously all night and all next day, if necessary.

"You know quite well that the Utopian Mission is a spy organisation. Answer!"

"No," said Dick.

"Your agents in Skrs have already confessed, so it is quite useless to take up this attitude," said the second man, the bland one. "You may as well confess and have a cigarette and a drink."

"No," said Dick, "I have nothing to confess."

"The Utopian Mission is a spy organisation, isn't it? Answer!"

"No," said Dick.

◆

Mr Bower replaced the last file and sat back in the chair, sagging a little. He had found nothing. He had already searched through all the loose papers. There was not even one memorandum or draft of any report to the Ambassador. The carbon copies of Dick's letters were all correctly filed, and were mostly concerned with points of organisation and procedure in his various societies. There was not a reference anywhere to Mr A. E. Bower, except in a copy of a letter addressed to his landlord, which Mr Bower now detached with a frown and put in an inside pocket.

The complete innocence, the aggressive innocence, of Zelezny's papers was in itself suspicious. Genuine innocence, Mr Bower felt, would not have been so careful. Probably all the relevant papers were in the Embassy somewhere, safe enough from the police, of course, but inaccessible also to the Head of the Cultural Mission. Mr Bower began to frame an indictment in his mind, which would in a day or two become a Confidential Report to Headquarters.

CHAPTER XI

Doctor Russell heard about Dick's arrest when he climbed into Mr Bower's car next morning. Mr Bower threw cold water on his indignation and concern at the news, imparting in a far-away voice his own suspicions about Zelezny's sly and secret work for the Embassy and making it quite clear that the Cultural Mission must dissociate itself from such goings-on. Russell's asseverations that it was sheer nonsense to think of Dick as a spy Mr Bower treated with the disdain he knew they deserved.

But the Mission Staff had no desire to dissociate itself. Rumours and counter-rumours filled the office; by eleven o'clock it was generally known that Dick had been arrested on a charge of espionage for a Foreign Power. Doctor Russell, coming back at half-past eleven from the University, contributed the information that on the previous evening Professor Kodichek and the Librarian of the Utopian Department had both been taken to police Headquarters and abominably bullied because they were, respectively, President and Secretary of the Utopian Society in the capital. Still, after insults and questioning, they had then been allowed to go home. But sixty members of the Skrs Utopian Society, it was said, had been arrested and were still at police headquarters, being interrogated.

A little after midday Mr Bower, newly returned from the Embassy, summoned Mr Collins and Doctor Russell to his room and favoured them with the real facts. The Ambassador had called earlier at the Foreign Office and had been told that Major Zelezny was under arrest for military treason, and that according to the police the written evidence of his guilt was so damning that he had confessed it.

"This written evidence," said Mr Bower "was discovered,

I understand, in Skrs. Thirty-six members of the Skrs Utopian Society are also under arrest. The Embassy, of course, cannot intervene in a case of treason and military espionage. I need not stress the fact that the whole affair is no concern of ours, no concern of ours whatsoever. I shall be obliged, Collins, if you will restrain the evident desire of the Staff to indulge their taste for melodrama."

◆

The police officer shifted in his chair, cocked his right leg over one arm of it and lit another cigarette.

"You have been organising Utopian Societies as a cover for military espionage," he said and blew a smoke ring. "The Utopian Mission is a spy organisation, isn't it? Answer!"

"No," said Dick Zelezny.

His colour was mottled, the flesh on his cheeks hung in folds, he was sweating and trembling. But he was still on his feet. It was not until about four o'clock in the afternoon that he fainted. The interrogation was then broken off and he was carried to a cell.

◆

The Embassy could not formally intervene in a case of alleged treason, yet the Ambassador himself, a quick-moving highly-strung man, was determined to apply all the pressure he could.

According to Slavomanian law, the police could keep an arrested person *incommunicado* for forty-eight hours, but after that they should deliver their prisoner to the City Jail, and hand all available evidence to the examining judge, who was from that moment in charge of the case. His Excellency had made up his mind to prevent the police from evading this provision for too long, as it was rumoured they had done in previous cases, on the plea that the compilation of evidence was still incomplete.

At three o'clock he had a consultation with Sova, the political lawyer, and Honzik, the deputy. They both confirmed, what he had been told by others, that the examining judges were known to be honourable men, untouched as yet by the political corruption of the police, and that once Dick Zelezny was removed to the City Jail he could be sure of obtaining justice. To this end, then, all their efforts were to be directed.

Sova brought some fresh information. Through his connection with various subordinate officials in the Ministry of the Interior, he had been told, confidentially, that Major Zelezny's share in the suspected treason was negative rather than positive, that his case, so far, was clear.

"Clear!" said His Excellency. "I should just think so!"

And what the devil, he added to himself, had Doubky meant in the morning by handing out that guff about damning evidence? Doubky, of all people, couldn't have expected him to believe a word of it.

The sheer malignity of things, thought Sir Edward, had removed the Foreign Minister from the country on a diplomatic mission at this juncture, so that it was the Communist deputy Minister with whom one had to deal. But, of course, that might be why the Ministry of the Interior had chosen just this moment to strike at Dick; because Comrade Doubky was left in charge at the Foreign Office. Might be? Very probably. *Very* likely.

His Excellency's hawk-like face grew more hawk-like. Doubky needn't think he could have the Utopian Ambassador on toast. There had been a flicker in his eye that morning which suggested a desire to probe the Utopian Ambassador to the quick, to see him squirm.

These lies about damning evidence against Dick might have been produced merely to observe the reaction on himself, to see if he would give away anything. There was dirty work behind all this somewhere, damned dirty work.

◆

Doctor Vladimir Mladski, an inconspicuous onlooker at the interview between Doubky and the Utopian Ambassador, had also observed the flicker in Doubky's eye. Comrade Doubky evidently thought that he had spotted something, some sign of complicity in Sir Edward's face. Mladski shot one glance at Sir Edward and dropped his eyes again. Sir Edward was certainly feeling strongly in the matter, but you never could tell with Utopians; most probably he was moved by simple anger at the arrest of a man he liked. Doubky, being a comrade, was trained not to accept apparently simple reactions at their face value and so would be incapable of appreciating a frank human attitude. Sir Edward's complicity might be merely that of a man involved in personal feelings of outraged friendship, yet Doubky would read it as guilt.

If I only knew! thought Mladski to himself, while being careful to preserve his poker face. How he wished that he knew whether the Utopian Embassy had also stumbled on the Secret. Surely even the most stupid diplomat — and his friend Michael Grey was far from stupid — must have perceived by this time that the region beyond Skrs was a sensitive point for the comrades?

Yet why were they now drawing attention to it? Short-sighted of them, surely, to do that, even assuming that they were being pushed from Moscow. Sir Edward was angry and he would make a stink.

The ghost of a smile wavered on Mladski's lips as he thought of the stink Sir Edward would surely make. Moscow might be excused for not understanding Sir Edward's character, yet Doubky ought to have known better. Unless, of course, Doubky had no real power, like so many of their figure-heads.

But did Sir Edward know anything? Had Dick Zelezny inadvertently come upon something? Would it be safe to drop a hint to Michael at this juncture? Probably not. He must go warily; the premature twitching of a filament might mean not only his own disappearance, but the precipitation of disaster for his country. After all, he had only guessed at the Secret; he had as yet no precise information. But what did it portend, this hardihood of the Comrades in drawing attention to Skrs?

◆

Sir Edward was certainly determined to make a stink. His angry energy, like a high wind fanning embers into flame, drove Honzik and his fellow-deputies of the Social Democrat Party into action, roused the ex-service legionaries and harassed the lawyer, Sova, as well as the Slavomane Foreign Office, until the detention of Major Zelezny and thirty-six members of the Skrs Utopian Society was brought up in Parliament, made headlines in the newspapers and engaged the attention of the public.

Sova, indeed, was driven so hard, not only by the Utopian Ambassador but by Major Zelezny's Utopian wife that he began to wonder if all Utopians had a devil in them. He could not vent his irritation on Sir Thring, so he did his best to quell Eleanor, who was now worrying him about getting a change of linen to the prisoner. Clean linen, indeed!

"Don't you realise that your husband is a soldier and accustomed to roughing it?" he growled. "Besides, I haven't been allowed even to see him yet. He's still at Police Headquarters. And that's no sanatorium."

The tears stung Eleanor's eyes, but she replied:

"Will you see, then, that a parcel from me is conveyed to him just as soon as he is in the City Jail?"

Sova shrugged his shoulders.

"That will be a matter for the Chief Secretary of the jail."

"And who is the Chief Secretary?" persisted Eleanor.

Well, it can do no harm, thought Sova, eyeing Eleanor. She was a woman of natural elegance; all her movements, the turn of her wrist, the way she sat down, the way she walked, were graceful. Sova rubbed his chin, thinking again: it can do no harm to try.

"I'll find some way of getting you in to see the Chief Secretary," he promised.

"Oh, thank you, Mr Sova, thank you," said Eleanor. "You see, I'm sure that Dick will be feeling depressed; it would be a great help to him to know that we are thinking of him."

"Come, come, it's only four days since he was arrested."

"It seems like four years," said Eleanor.

She had slept very little since Dick's arrest and she had spent little time in the flat. As long as she was out seeing people, following up Sova's threads of information, interviewing deputies, legionaries, Embassy officials, she could feel that something was being done for Dick. What she could not bear was to sit at home doing nothing. Ruzi was nearly always in tears over her inability to eat or rest or sleep, but how could she help it while Dick was still kept *incommunicado* at Police Headquarters?

One minor consequence of Eleanor's restlessness was that none of her friends could reach her on the telephone. Jamesina Russell, for instance had to content herself with a tearful message from Ruzenka that Madam, before going out, had said she would get in touch with Mrs Russell just as soon as she had any news of the Major. Whenever Ruzenka mentioned the Major, her voice broke.

CHAPTER XII

On the evening of this day, the fourth since Dick's arrest, the Russells were due to attend officially the gala *première* of a Utopian film. Mr Bower had told Doctor Russell that he and Collins were going to appear properly dressed in dinner jackets and black ties, and that Doctor Russell would please be so good as to follow suit. To Doctor Russell, who was just on his way out to see Bob Owen off at the station — in the excitement caused by Dick's arrest, Bob Owen's departure went almost unnoticed — this instruction had seemed, perhaps unwarrantably, the last straw; he had been gloomy and pessimistic when he met his wife and the Owens at the station, and he was still gloomy when he arrived in the foyer of the cinema. A warm welcome from the junior of the two Utopian consuls did not lighten his mood, for the consul was wearing no black tie, no dinner jacket, only a comfortable lounge suit.

Doctor Russell put on his spectacles and cast harassed glances around the foyer. Jamesina, too, he noticed vaguely, was looking round her, but he assumed, without putting the thought into words, that she was moved by the same desire as himself, to catch sight of Mr and Mrs Bower or Mr and Mrs Collins in time to avoid them. More Slavomane acquaintances than usual were pressing forward to greet the Russells; they seemed almost to be making a point of it, thought Jamesina. Doctor Russell, anxious to get into his seat without meeting any colleagues, could well have dispensed with these attentions.

At last the Russells reached their seats, in a small side box on a level with the central balcony.

"I wonder if we're safe?" muttered Martin as they sat down.

Jamesina seemed to divine his meaning, for she said: "There are no other chairs in this box. Arch and Collins, anyway, would be sure to get themselves more important seats, much nearer the Ambassador."

Martin smiled a little and prepared to lean back at ease; his hand, carelessly holding a programme, lay on the ledge of the box in front of him. All at once Jamesina saw the programme flutter into the stalls below, while Martin's fingers clenched on the ledge. She turned in alarm towards him.

"What is it, Martin, do you feel ill?"

"Nothing," he said. "It's nothing."

He was pale and fagged-looking; there was a strained expression on his face. That was not unusual these days; but Jamesina thought that he also looked sick.

"Have you a pain?" she asked.

"Nothing at all," came the short reply.

Jamesina said no more. She was herself depressed and believed that she knew well enough what was troubling Martin. It seemed somehow dreadful to be sitting at a film *première* in full fig[1] while Dick was in prison.

The lights went down and Martin Russell was able to consider what had happened to him. It had come as a shock. Leaning back easily, all unwitting, he had suddenly felt a tentacle from some loathsome creature touch him in the region of the solar plexus, reaching him from a part of the house he knew he had not even looked at, obliquely to the right of him. The touch sickened him instantaneously and when he raised his eyes to identify the tentacled creature he saw Mr Bower.

He was still shaken and sickish; the very thought of the loathsome sensation made him shudder again. An invisible tentacle! Was he going out of his mind? Yet he knew

[1] In smart or formal clothes or dress uniform.

precisely where it had come from, and precisely at that spot, in the box next to the central balcony, sat the squat figure of Archibald Edgar Bower, with high lights glinting off his spectacle lenses and his stiff shirt front.

Do they call it extra-sensory perception? wondered Doctor Russell as he gazed at the screen. It was the kind of fantastic phenomenon that could very well be presented in a film. One would see a dark cloud emanate from the villain, thicken and shoot out a sudden nasty finger. The actors on the screen would think that they were moving free in full daylight, while this coiling evil, visible only to the audience or to some individual like himself, gradually spread alarm and despondency.

He sat without moving until the lights went up at the first interval, and then said to Jamesina: "Come outside for a cigarette, do."

Mr Bower did not smoke and was not likely to come on to the marble stairway where they leaned over a balustrade, exchanging greetings with passing acquaintances.

Jamesina, finally disentangling herself from a vivacious lady who hailed her as "Darlink!", turned to Martin and said in her low, soft voice: "It does seem rather dreadful, doesn't it, all this, while Dick's in jail?"

"Yes."

"I haven't caught sight of Vladimir yet," went on Jamesina, "but I think he's sure to be here. I'd like to ask him what he knows about Dick."

"He probably knows nothing."

"Do you really think that the right hand of this Government doesn't know what the left hand's doing?"

"I shouldn't wonder."

He spoke so tonelessly that Jamesina was again alarmed.

"Martin, don't you feel well?"

"Oh, well enough," said Martin rather irritably, but at

119

once made amends by adding, with a quick and charming smile, "as well as can be expected, that's to say."

"I know, I know," said Jamesina.

Her husband pulled himself together and tried to chat.

"A lot of nightmarish stuff in this film, don't you think? I never realised before how much nightmare there is in Dickens."

"I suppose we've become more aware of it," said Jamesina. She paused for a moment and then went on: "Europe has been full of nightmares. And now I'm beginning to feel nightmarish about this country too. Ever since Dick's arrest."

"Nightmare isn't a monopoly of the Slavomanes," said Martin.

Jamesina gave him a troubled look.

"Is it as bad as that?"

"As bad as it can be."

"Hello, hello," cried a gay voice behind them, and they turned round to see Vladimir Mladski, with his friend Michael Grey, a tall young Third Secretary from the Utopian Embassy.

"Good evening, Mrs Russell," said Grey. Vladimir, in excellent spirits, bowed with exaggerated deference.

"We don't often see you dressed in all your glory, Doctor Russell," he said.

"Blasted orders of my blasted Chief," growled Martin Russell and then looked embarrassed.

"I don't always see eye to eye with my Chief, you know," he added, apologetically, to Michael Grey.

"Who could?" returned Grey, with a smile.

This light remark so heartened Russell that he was able to start with zest a discussion on Dickens as the precursor of surrealism.

Presently Grey caught a lady's eye and excused himself.

Vladimir accepted a cigarette from Martin. Jamesina, single-minded as usual, said: "Vladimir, can you tell us anything about Dick Zelezny?"

Vladimir Mladski, the cigarette still in his fingers, turned his head quickly this way and that, put his left hand under Jamesina's elbow and steered her into a remote corner, saying loudly: "Come over here, where we're more out of the traffic."

"Oh, Vladimir," murmured Jamesina, "I'm so sorry. I didn't think."

"Fortunately, I don't suppose anyone heard you," said Vladimir, using his hand as cover while he lit the cigarette. "But, Jamesina, you *must* learn to be careful."

Jamesina looked stricken.

"It's a good thing you don't have a carrying voice," said Vladimir. "A wise provision of Nature. May I give you a light? Well, regarding that matter you mentioned . . ."

"Yes?"

"I can give no information," said Vladimir, severely, putting on his non-committal face, "about treason cases."

Jamesina looked at him incredulously.

"But, Vladimir, Dick isn't a traitor. He's a completely innocent man."

"Is he?"

"I know him very well, and he's quite incapable of being a traitor to his country. He loves it too much. And in any case he's not that kind of man. He's no more capable of being a spy and a traitor than you are yourself."

"My dear Jamesina."

Jamesina laid a hand on his arm.

"I understand that it must be dreadful for you, my dear to think that your countrymen could arrest an innocent man on a false charge. But I *know* Dick, I tell you. I *know* the kind of man he is."

Vladimir took her hand in his own, raised it to his lips and kissed it.

"If that is so — and you are probably right, Jamesina — you needn't worry. I can tell you this much; Sir Edward Thring, in my opinion, is going the best way about it to get him out of the hands of the police."

But the last word that evening was provided, as was only fitting, by Mr Bower. On their way out, moving slowly through the foyer, the Russells were caught up by the Bowers.

"Oh, there you are, Martin," said Mr Bower, seeming very pleased with life. He cast an appreciative glance at Russell's black tie. As if I were a blasted clothes horse, thought Doctor Russell. "We looked for you earlier but couldn't find you. A full house, wasn't it?"

"Yes," said Jamesina, "and people have gone out of their way to be nice to us."

"Precisely," said Mr Bower. "It was, I am convinced, in the nature of a demonstration. I have had that confirmed, too, from another source. I have been talking to the correspondent of the Utopian Times, and he assured me, positively assured me, Martin, that none of the Slavomanes believe that the Foreign Power mentioned in the charge against Zelezny can be Utopia!"

Mr Bower beamed at them all. So innocently did he strut and preen himself that for a moment Doctor Russell was regretfully aware how happily, in other circumstances, he might have appreciated Arch as a character.

Chapter XIII

Mr Bower's chief complaint about the house he had inherited from his predecessor was that it contained no sanctum for himself. Downstairs, three large rooms opening out of each other formed an impressive flight of *salons* for a reception but were not designed for privacy; upstairs, the bedrooms were nearly as large and therefore few, so that he had not even a separate dressing-room to shut himself into. An alcove in the second drawing-room was all he could command, and although he had partly blocked it by having the grand piano moved a couple of feet, it was still open to invasion. Mr Bower did not care to have any breach in his defences; even under the lee of the grand piano he never ceased to be aware that his front was exposed. He had laid upon his wife the charge of seeing that he should not be interrupted whenever he withdrew to the alcove, and she could be trusted to fend off children or housemaids or even official messengers, long before they reached the piano; yet there was no guarantee that Victoria herself would not interrupt.

In any case, he was now committed to having his privacy invaded twice a week during the luncheon break by a philologist, a Doctor Smetanka, who was to instruct him in the Slavomanian language. "Doctor Smetanka, it means Doctor Creamlet," this personage had said on being introduced, and Mr Bower had engaged him with some reserve. But the experiment was proving a success. On this occasion, his third lesson in the language, Mr Bower, with the grammar on the table and a block of writing-paper before him, faced Doctor Smetanka with happy eagerness. He had discovered that Slavomanian was a well-organised language, and he said so.

Doctor Smetanka received this tribute with a proper blend of gratitude and deprecation, pulling at his dusty-looking beard. He felt that in the previous lesson he had been a trifle overbearing when he had disparaged the Utopian language in extolling the beautiful economy of Slavomanian, which represented each sound always by the same letter. Mr Bower had admitted that Utopian spelling and pronunciation might be termed idiosyncratic, if not anarchic, yet he had made the admission reluctantly, and Doctor Smetanka was relieved to find that his pupil bore no grudge.

The grammar-book was opened, and Doctor Smetanka became aware that Mr Bower, far from bearing any grudge, genuinely appreciated the well-ordered paradigms set out in it. Not only was he prepared to learn, and equipped to master, the nouns with hard and the nouns with soft endings, he found pleasure in the differentiation between animate and inanimate neuters and approved the use of interesting case-forms such as the locative and instrumentative. Doctor Smetanka recognised a kindred intellect. He ceased to regret that Madam Bower had declined to join the lessons, on the ridiculous plea that she was picking up enough Slavomanian in the kitchen and in the shops and had not time to waste on grammar. This was a pupil after his own heart. Doctor Smetanka became benevolently authoritative. It was a successful lesson, a harmonious lesson, in the pursuit of pure knowledge. Teacher and pupil began to like each other well.

On these high levels where he loved to range, Mr Bower was little accustomed to the pleasures of untroubled companionship. Too many rivals infested his daily landscape, people with the desire to hurt and humiliate him. Doctor Smetanka's admiration and goodwill now flowed over him like soft water. Instead of his usual wry blank expression he had an open, absorbent look, the look of the Good Pupil, which any of the masters at his old school would have recognised.

Bursting into this intellectual paradise Victoria was too full of alarm and dismay to have room for regret at shattering her husband's rarely-won and blameless peace. Blameless in her eyes he was not; he was rather Nero fiddling while Rome burned.

"The house! The house!" she gasped, holding out a document. "Two men at the door — oh, good afternoon, Doctor Smetanka — two men who say we must give up the house in two days. Two days, Arch!"

"What did you say?"

The defensive phrase came automatically from Mr Bower's lips. It was only a momentary defence, yet it exacerbated Mrs Bower's dismay which curdled at once into anger.

"I *told* you to make sure about the house, and I don't suppose you've done a *thing*. Look at this paper, just look at it! A nice state of affairs if I'm to be turned out of this house at two days' notice, I must say. Is it usual in Slavomania, Doctor Smetanka, for people to be ordered out of their houses at two days' notice?"

"It is an execution, no?" said Doctor Smetanka, clinging a little helplessly to the back of his chair. "I am sorry, in our country executions happen sometimes with no warning. Official secret method, inherited from the old Empire. May I see the document?"

"I don't know whether it's what you call an execution or not," cried Mrs Bower, handing over the paper. "It's got a rubber stamp on it all right, from some Housing Office, and there's the date, see? In *two days'* time."

"Who is the man who is to have possession in two days?" asked the philologist.

"Our landlord, of course."

Mrs Bower turned on her husband again when she saw that Doctor Smetanka's scrutiny of the paper had yielded the same result as her own. "What are you going to do about it, Arch? The men are still in the hall. You *must* do something."

Mr Bower felt as if he were scrabbling for a foothold on a precipice; his levels had suddenly tilted perilously. With an effort he repressed this queasy feeling and composed himself by deliberately taking off his spectacles and polishing them. By the time he had replaced them his face had gone wooden and his voice had no tremor as he said:

"Let me see the paper, if you please."

"There's nothing in it but what I told you," retorted his wife.

Doctor Smetanka, with more fellow-feeling perhaps, passed over the paper wordlessly. Mr Bower perused it.

"This seems to be issued by a District Housing Office," he then said in his most formal tone, "not by the Central Housing Office. Is that not so, Doctor Smetanka?"

Doctor Smetanka was happy to agree; he craned over Mr Bower's shoulder and read out the name of the District, pointing at it with a forefinger.

"I shall, of course, go to the Foreign Office at once," said Mr Bower, still addressing Doctor Smetanka. "These men at the door can only be subordinates. We have nothing to do with them except to acknowledge receipt of this paper, I take it."

"They don't speak anything but Slavomanian," cried Mrs Bower, with perceptible venom.

"Perhaps, Doctor Smetanka, you would be so good as to interpret?"

The two men in the hall were wearing official-looking caps and showed a disposition to hector; each was the kind of man who thrusts a heavy foot into an opening door to keep it from closing again. Buttressed by Doctor Smetanka Mr Bower succeeded in maintaining his dignity, and even, on being assured that it committed him to nothing, signed the receipt form.

There is nothing more intimidating than officials, however subordinate, of a Foreign Power, brandishing documents in a language one does not comprehend. Had it not been for Doctor Smetanka Mr Bower might well have quailed, and he was grateful to his new friend. Their united masculine front, also, had efficiently excluded Mrs Bower from the interview. They shook hands with warmth once the door had closed on the intruders.

"I regret," said Mr Bower, "that I do not know whether our next lesson will take place in this house or not. I fear not. The Foreign Office may have to provide me with another house."

"For you I do not doubt the Foreign Office will perform wonders," said Doctor Smetanka, with a respectful little bow. "But you will let me know what happens."

What, indeed, was to happen? Sitting at the alcove table with her head in her hands Mrs Bower would have sobbed had she not been sustained by anger. Arch had again proved himself a broken reed. He was simply not to be depended on where his own family was concerned. Nothing counted with him but the office, the office.

Mr Bower returned from the hall to be, as he had expected, vehemently reproached. He polished his spectacles again.

"I must point out, Victoria, that it is my office which procured us this house, and will procure us another one. I am going to the Foreign Office immediately."

In her angriest moments Mrs Bower had never gone so far as to impugn her husband's reverence for impersonality; she respected it, even when she thought he went beyond bounds in his scrupulousness.

"You lean over backwards to keep from doing anything for your own family," she said, but her panic was already subsiding. She was beginning to feel that the impersonal workings of office might reach farther than merely personal claims. Yet she could not resist making a suggestion:

"Why don't you ask to see that nice young Doctor what's-his-name at the Foreign Office, instead of just dealing with the housing officials? Doctor Mladski that's it. I'm sure he could do something for us. And if we really have to leave this house in two days . . . ! Two days, Arch!"

The enormity of her plight overwhelmed her again. Mr Bower allowed compassion for his wife to break surface; he picked up the telephone and asked if Doctor Mladski could see him in ten minutes' time, on an urgent matter. Doctor Mladski, fortunately, was in the Foreign Office, and would be delighted to oblige Mr Bower.

Victoria Bower rallied at once.

"Oh, I'm sure he'll be able to do something for us!" she cried, starting to her feet. "He's such a nice, clever, young man! Will you ring me up as soon as you've seen him? Now, don't forget, Arch; do ring me up. I have to know whether I must start getting our things packed at once. You don't *know* what it means."

Even while assuring her husband that he did not know what packing meant, Mrs Bower, it must be admitted, was resolving that this time he should know. He needed a lesson.

◆

In the Foreign Office Mr Bower laid his case and the ejectment order before young Doctor Mladski, who listened courteously.

"Yes," he said at intervals, "yes, I see."

"And I am the Head of a Mission."

Doctor Mladski sat gazing at the surface of his desk for so long that Mr Bower feared he had not taken in the last statement.

"The Head of a Mission," he repeated.

Doctor Mladski looked up and gravely corrected him:

"The Head of a Western Mission."

"Is that important?"

"Very important. Yes."

Doctor Mladski sat in thought for a few more minutes and then roused himself:

"I think the best way to manage this affair, Mr Bower, is for me to go and see my Chief about it, at once, if you will excuse me. Will you help yourself to cigarettes? I'm sorry I can't offer you a drink, and I seem to have no Utopian newspapers, but I can't be away for more than ten minutes or so."

Ten minutes should do it, he said to himself, smiling a little after he had shut the door on Mr Bower. Comrade Doubky was already in a nervous state. The Foreign Secretary was due to come back in a couple of days and publicity about the Skrs affair was still exploding round Doubky's head. Not only that; there were signs that Moscow was getting restive about it. Doctor Mladski guessed that comrade Doubky had been ticked off.

Yes, Doctor Doubky was still chain-smoking and looking harassed.

"May I talk to you in private for about ten minutes? Something rather urgent," said Doctor Mladski, in his most soothing voice.

Doctor Doubky shrugged, but sent his secretary away.

"It's about Utopia," said Doctor Mladski, and paused for a moment.

"Sir Edward again?" came the quick, irritable query.

"Not yet . . . The Utopian Cultural Mission. The Head of

the Mission is being ejected from his house at the end of this month, in two days' time. Shall we provide him with another house, or do we . . .?"

Doctor Mladski again paused.

Doctor Doubky stubbed out his cigarette with unnecessary violence and lit another.

"Who's ejecting him?"

"Oh, not Doctor Pachek, of course . . . Merely a District Office. But I doubt if we could quash it."

"What have we got to do with it, then?" asked Doctor Doubky, scowling, as expected, at the mention of Doctor Pachek.

"We should, I think, find ourselves involved. You know Sir Edward . . . But perhaps you would like to divert Sir Edward's attention from the Skrs affair?"

Doctor Doubky stared hard at Doctor Mladski.

"We've had enough publicity of that kind," he said at length. "More than enough."

"We could make a gesture, then and provide a house. In fact, sooner or later we should be compelled to find a house. After all, he ranks as the Head of a Mission."

"But have we any houses?"

"Ah," said Doctor Mladski, permitting his features to relax. "I have come on something very interesting. There *is* a house, in the Diplomatic Quarter, belonging to some German Jew, present whereabouts unknown, which has been standing empty for a month or so and has most unaccountably been passed over by Doctor Pachek every time he has been asked to provide diplomatic accommodation."

Doctor Doubky's eyes began to twinkle.

"You think Pachek means to snaffle it for himself?"

"Either for himself or some friend of his."

Doctor Doubky laughed outright and laid down his

cigarette.

"Good," he said, "good! We'll hang him in his own rope."

"So I shall let Mr Bower have the house, shall I?"

"Bower, is it? Pompous little man, isn't he?"

"Very pompous."

"Oh, let him have it. See that Pachek does it himself and that everything is tied up tight."

"Doctor Pachek," said Doctor Mladski, at his most solemn, "cannot raise any objections to bestowing a house on the Head of a Western Mission. But, all the same, may I quote your authorisation, if necessary?"

"If Pachek makes any trouble, you send him in to me," said Doctor Doubky smiling.

"O.K.," said young Doctor Mladski.

◆

Mr Bower was standing by a tall window which dwarfed him so much that he looked a little forlorn, yet he turned a brave front when at last the door opened.

"Well," said Doctor Mladski, briskly, "we can give you a house at once, Mr Bower, in the Diplomatic Quarter."

Mr Bower raised his arms; he might have been indicating the size of some fish he had caught. His mouth opened, but for a second or two he stood dumb. Then he said:

"Are you sure? Are you quite sure?"

"Quite sure. Here are the keys, look."

Doctor Mladski rattled a bunch of keys as if he were amusing a child, and went on:

"That's why I've been so long, I went to get them from our Housing Department. We'll have to look over the house at once. I suppose you have your car here?"

"But this is extraordinary. I must say, I hardly expected — isn't there a housing shortage?"

"Oh yes, there's a housing shortage."

"Is the house vacant?"

"It's been standing empty for some time, but I'm told its in good order. A very suitable house, Mr Bower, but you must grab it quick. It's just after three now," said young Doctor Mladski looking at his watch and then reaching for his overcoat. "Come on!"

The corridors of the Foreign Office stretched for miles, it seemed to Mr Bower as he trotted a little breathlessly beside Doctor Mladski. The matter was urgent, yet still, he could not help thinking, even as he trotted, this haste was surely unseemly?

"Will you excuse me if I tell your chauffeur to call on the way at a certain address?"

Mr Bower, bemused, nodded assent.

"We have to take a locksmith with us," explained Doctor Mladski, climbing in.

"But you have the keys?"

"I have the keys," agreed the young man, looking mischievous. "But if you like the house and want it, we must get new locks fitted on at once and new keys cut."

"I don't quite follow."

"Aha, an old Slavomane tradition, Mr Bower".

By the time the locksmith was taken aboard with a bag of tools Mr Bower was regaining his composure. It occurred to him that another call might be paid.

"Would you mind, shouldn't we perhaps go round by my place and pick up my wife?" he suggested.

"Why, of course. An excellent idea. Mrs Bower ought to see the house. Besides, the new house is only a couple of streets away from your present one. Very convenient, you see."

Despite her voluble surprise and gratitude, Mrs Bower was still almost tearful.

"Oh, I can hardly believe it!" she cried. "I was quite sure

we shouldn't have anywhere to go. It's *very* good of you, Doctor Mladski. Isn't it *very* good of him, Arch?"

"We are much obliged to the Foreign Office," said Mr Bower.

"I don't believe the Foreign Office would have done it so quickly if it hadn't been for Doctor Mladski. Oh, are we there already?"

The house stood perched above the street, with a stone stairway at one side leading up to a loggia that opened on a square lawn.

"Oh, isn't it lovely!" cried Mrs Bower, gazing up. "Quite closed off from the street, and so safe for the children!"

It was a pretty house externally, and the interior pleased both the Bowers. There was a small room which could serve as a study, and all the rooms were light and airy, even the kitchen, as Mrs Bower remarked, yes, even on a winter afternoon.

"Will it do?" asked Doctor Mladski.

"Oh, it's delightful. And it doesn't feel at all damp. Look, there's an open fire-place in the drawing-room as well as central heating!"

"It seems a well-built and well-planned house," admitted Mr Bower.

"Fine," said Doctor Mladski. "Then the locksmith had better set to work at once, before it's too dark. You'll have the new keys in an hour or so, and one of your staff should sleep in the house tonight. You could get a bed in by this evening, couldn't you?"

"Why must we do that? Is there any doubt about our getting the house?" asked Mr Bower.

"The house is yours without question if you take it now. But somebody else might try to jump your claim, you know. I recommend you strongly to get some furniture in and a member of your staff sleeping in the premises tonight. Then you'll have no trouble."

"I'm sure Doctor Mladski knows what he's talking about, Arch," insisted Mrs Bower. "But didn't you say the house has been standing empty for some time, Doctor Mladski? Then why didn't the Foreign Office Housing Department put you on to it sooner, Arch? You *did* ask them about a house, didn't you?"

Mr Bower, in his embarrassment, looked as impervious as he could. Young Doctor Mladski intervened:

"Ah, there are wheels within wheels, even in the Foreign Office, Mrs Bower. Too many people clamouring for diplomatic housing. And my advice to you is to occupy this house at once. I'll see that you get the decree for it, properly drawn up, by tomorrow afternoon, but you should have somebody in possession tonight. Your chauffeur would do, or one of the maids."

"The chauffeur will do it if *I* ask him to," cried Mrs Bower.

"Then that's that. I'll just make sure that the locksmith understands his instructions, and then I must get back to my office."

"Oh, Arch will give you a lift back, Doctor Mladski. Won't you, Arch? And will you drop me at the other house first? I suppose it's safe for me to leave this one?"

"Not for too long, Mrs Bower. One moment, till I speak to the locksmith."

Whatever Doctor Mladski said to the locksmith, who was busily unscrewing locks, it made both of them chuckle.

"I think that's all right, Mrs Bower," said young Doctor Mladski, returning. "You'll have the keys by five o'clock, and I think you're safe till then. Better have someone here, all the same, in about fifteen minutes, to stay on guard while the locksmith goes off to cut the keys."

"This country seems to me sometimes rather too

exciting," said Mrs Bower, settling herself in the car. "But I am *very* much obliged to you, Doctor Mladski."

Such a nice young man! she was thinking.

"And is it usual, in this country, to turn people out of houses at two days' notice, Doctor Mladski? Two days! I can't get over it."

"It's unusual, certainly, but not unknown." Mr Bower's embarrassment had not escaped the young man, nor Mrs Bower's propensity to harp on unwelcome strings.

By this time Mr Bower had decided that Doctor Mladski was sympathetic, although perhaps too young, too airy, to be quite dependable. Certainly, a helpful young man. And so, as they were bowling along towards the Foreign Office, he brought out, after a few false starts, the casual question:

"I suppose you don't know how the Zelezny affair is going?"

"Not in my Department," said Doctor Mladski, promptly. After this disclaimer, he glanced at Mr Bower and added: "All the same, I shouldn't be surprised if it took a turn for the better soon."

"Indeed," said Mr Bower. "H'm."

Now why, said young Doctor Mladski to himself, as he got out of the car in the vast courtyard of the Foreign Office, why should Bower dislike the idea of Zelezny's affair taking a turn for the better?

CHAPTER XIV

The noise of Victoria Bower's removal to the new house echoed through the Mission for the next two days and lost nothing in the reverberation. Her husband's secretary, Miss Smith, was requisitioned for odd jobs such as taking the children out for the afternoon, and Mr Bower himself was made to fetch and carry.

Feeling in the office ran strongly in Mrs Bower's favour. "Two days' notice!" people said to each other. "It's really a bit thick."

Yet in private Miss Smith admitted to having suspicions of this story.

"Two days' notice my eye," she said. "I bet Arch was warned out of the house long ago and never mentioned it to Victoria."

"What makes you think that?" asked Miss Ballard.

"Something Dick let fall. Besides, I've seen letters, I'm sure they were from the landlord, shoved into the secret drawer."

"Oho. Victoria the Victim, you think, all unwitting of her doom?"

"Something like that, poor woman."

"Well, it's her own fault for marrying Arch."

To Miss Ballard's astonishment, Miss Smith refused to concur.

"She's a very kind woman," insisted Mabel. "And the children are little dears."

Mrs Bower herself was happy; activity suited her temperament, especially when she could see the result of it. Moving into the new house was the beginning of a new life freed from the fret of uncertain tenure caused by a hostile landlord. The deeper, vaguer fret caused by an uncertain political situation, blurred yet intensified by her husband's ambiguities, had also subsided, soothed into quiescence by Doctor Mladski's gaiety and helpfulness.

"We must ask that nice young Doctor Mladski to dinner," she said to her spouse. "I am *so* grateful to him."

This generous impulse rippled wider until the dinner became a house-warming party. But on the very day of the party Mrs Bower was again reminded that life in Slavomania could provide harsh surprises.

Having been assured by Doctor Mladski, by the Senior Consul's wife, and by the charming wife of the First Secretary of the Embassy, that Slavomanian electric fittings were always private property and that the pretty glass chandeliers in the old house must have been bought and installed by Mr Rigg, she had ceased to exclaim at the naked flex hanging from the ceilings of her new house and had ordered the chandeliers to be transferred. The workmen had done the job thoroughly, wrenching from the old ceilings even the hexagonal wooden plates into which the chandeliers were screwed. And now, on the day of her party, just before noon, after a morning's shopping, she came home to find her ex-landlord in the drawing-room shouting directions to a workman who was unscrewing a chandelier, while the cook and the parlour-maid stood by chattering like angry blackbirds.

Mrs Bower's voice was sharper than any as she demanded the meaning of this outrage. Her ex-landlord shook one fist in her face, displayed a hexagonal wooden plate in the other, and, as far as she could make out, called her a thief.

"That thing!" cried Mrs Bower, understanding at once that the dining-room chandelier had been already dismantled. "Is it only because of *that* wooden thing? Why, you can buy these anywhere."

The ex-landlord, the cook, the parlour-maid and the

workman were now all scolding at once. Mrs Bower sent the maids to the kitchen, ordered the workman to be careful with her glass-ware, and while the ex-landlord was choking with spite informed him that he had no right to force his way into her house. In another ten minutes the place was clear. Yet the wooden plates were gone and the chandeliers lay drunkenly on the carpets.

They were in place again, with new wooden plates, by the time the guests arrived, and provided a fresh element in Mrs Bower's conversation, thus helping to make the party go. "Two days' notice" had been re-iterated so often that Mr Bower was relieved to hear his wife saying instead: "Wooden things you can buy anywhere! And he was so *rude!*" The wife of the First Secretary (who was a baronet) enjoyed the story so much that Mrs Bower found her more charming than ever. And when Doctor Mladski, edged into a corner, assured Mrs Bower once more that the decree for the house was indubitably valid so long as the Bowers should remain in Slavomania, that it was non-transferable and that nothing short of Mr Bower's expulsion from the country could cancel it, Lady ffolliott, vaguely overhearing, confided later to Mrs Bower: "If you ever do want to transfer the house to anyone, don't tell the Foreign Office a thing about it but just quietly pass on the keys. We always do that in the Embassy."

These words: "We always do that in the Embassy," sang in Mrs Bower's mind. She could not resist quoting them to Mrs Collins, nor could she refrain from pointing out that Lady ffolliott had a little girl just the same age as her own elder boy, that Lady ffolliott was going to invite the children to tea, and that Lady ffolliott had asked for some advice in the procuring of a nurse-maid. Mrs Collins, who had not been the hostess of a successful house-warming party, told her husband that if Victoria mentioned Lady ffolliott again she would scream.

"And when are we going to get into *our* new flat, Bob?"

"As soon as Owen's transfer is confirmed from Headquarters, I think. Bower wants to do the thing properly and in due order."

"I don't see that it would be at all improper if we simply moved in now. Why shouldn't Mrs Owen take her turn of living in a hotel?"

"Well, you know Bower."

"I know that he needs prodding. You must keep at him, Bob."

◆

A couple of days later, on the way to the office, Mr Bower said to Doctor Russell:

"I'm afraid, Martin, the Foreign Office here might make trouble if they find that a flat of ours is not being occupied by the official to whom it was given, or by an official of our Organisation."

"You mean Owen's flat, I suppose?"

"As far as the Foreign Office are concerned, Owen's flat is now technically vacant, and I know they are short of diplomatic accommodation. We don't want to let the flat slip out of our hands."

"Bob Owen's coming back at Easter, isn't he? I can't see that his flat's vacant technically or untechnically."

"H'm," said Mr Bower.

Doctor Russell, who feared that Bob Owen was not meant to come back at Easter or at any time, reported this to his wife. Mrs Russell, therefore, was unpleasantly but not unduly surprised to hear in the afternoon from Mary Ballard, spending part of her half-day off in the Russells' flat, that the office suspected Proud Maisie of wanting to turn Iris Owen out.

"I heard her myself saying to Victoria that she wouldn't

mind letting Iris Owen have *one* room in the flat."

Mrs Russell's indignant exclamations were not echoed by Miss Ballard, not even when Mr Bower's hints about the Foreign Office were relayed to her. Miss Ballard became if anything more composed and finished embroidering a petal before she said:

"So that's the pattern, is it?"

"And Iris has been having trouble enough with little Rosemary."

"Yes, Mabel told me about that. Gone all peaky, hasn't she?"

"Eats no more than a sparrow, Iris says. You wouldn't think a little girl of three would take things so hard, would you? She misses Bob acutely. Oh Mary, it wouldn't be decent to turn Iris out."

"I suppose they'll say she can move to Prsht. But the housing shortage in Prsht is even worse than here. Bob's having to shake down in Wickens's place; he can't even get into the hotel. Some Ministry or other has reserved most of the rooms in the hotel, Iris says. Where could she go to, with her two little girls and one of them delicate?"

Miss Ballard went on stitching and Mrs Russell sat watching the small, busy needle.

"Where did you learn to do such exquisite work?" she asked. "One doesn't associate an Army Captain with fine sewing."

"I was at a Convent School."

"Were you really?"

"Besides, I like sewing. This handkerchief is for Mabel's birthday next week ... Do you know, she's gone all sentimental about the little Bowers?"

"Mabel should have had six children of her own, don't you think?"

"At least six. She'll have to go sentimental about the little

Owens soon, and then she'll find herself in a cleft stick," said Miss Ballard, spreading out the handkerchief.

"Isn't there anything we can do about it, Mary?"

"Well . . ."

Miss Ballard took some embroidery cotton and filled another needleful.

"It did just cross my mind," she said, "that if Iris were to take in Jane Lidgard there would be an official of the College occupying the flat."

"Oh, that would be an excellent move!" cried Mrs Russell. "What a good Captain you must have made, Mary."

"I wasn't so dusty," agreed Miss Ballard.

The more they examined the scheme, the better it seemed. Somebody had to protect Jane against herself, said Miss Ballard, and everyone knew how her present landlady exploited her. Besides, she would be doing a really Christian act in lodging with Iris to save her from expulsion.

"That's precisely the argument to convince Jane," said Mrs Russell. "The only kind of argument she would ever listen to."

◆

At a Small Conference, smaller than ever because of Dick Zelezny's absence, Mr Bower repeated his conjectures about the probable dismay at the Foreign Office should it become known that Owen's flat was not being occupied by any official of the Cultural Mission.

Doctor Russell then quietly dropped his bomb. Miss Lidgard, he said, was going to live with Mrs Owen, and, as acting Senior Tutor in the College, she could be regarded as Bob Owen's representative. In any case, she was an official of the Mission, so there was no need to fear Foreign Office intervention. Mr Collins, white with rage, nearly bit his pipe-stem in two.

"This is incredible impertinence!" he cried. "Has Miss Lidgard actually moved in?"

"Not yet. And I can't see that her moving in would be impertinent. Mrs Owen may well be lonely and may be glad of her company."

"Will she actually be paying rent to Mrs Owen, whose rent is already paid by the Mission?"

With one hand Mr Bower silenced his Deputy.

"I think this problem should be discussed and settled on the highest level," he said. "The position is this: the Foreign Office has granted us by decree the possession of three unfurnished apartments, the house I occupy, your flat, Martin, and Owen's flat. In view of the shortage of diplomatic accommodation we can hardly expect the Foreign Office to decree us another house while one flat of ours is technically vacant. In fact, I have been led to understand that the special effort made to provide my present house was all that we could expect from them. Now, when an Organisation has three official apartments it is a well-understood principle that these should be occupied by the three highest officials of the Organisation. You would agree to that, Martin?"

"I'm not sure that I should."

"You must remember that official apartments are granted for official purposes, for representative entertaining, not for private convenience. In principle, the more responsible officials, who have to do the most entertaining, should have the representational accommodation. I don't see why you hesitate to agree."

"You are putting a hypothetical case, which seems to be irrelevant."

Mr Collins crossed one leg over the other and began to jerk the upper leg impatiently. Mr Bower settled his spectacles more firmly and continued to speak with taut patience:

"If there were one available house and one official, you would agree that he should have the house?"

Doctor Russell, his lower lip curling, said: "Why not?"

"Well, if there were one house and two officials, the higher official should have prior claim to the house?"

"Ah," said Doctor Russell, "but if there were two houses and two officials, the question wouldn't arise, would it?"

"In this case," said Mr Bower stiffly, "we have three senior officials, myself, my Deputy and you, Martin, as the Director of the College. And we have three official apartments. It seems to me indubitable that Collins should have one of them."

"And for the sake of this hierarchical machinery you would turn Bob Owen out of his flat?"

"Bob Owen is not *in* his flat; that is the point."

"He will be, at Easter time. And his wife and children are there."

"I am surprised, painfully surprised, may I say, at your failure to grasp a matter of principle," said Mr Bower. "The principle holds good whether Owen returns or not. There are other flats in the city he could have. But this is a representational apartment."

"With one of the highest rents paid by the Mission in this country," interjected Mr Collins.

"You are mistaken in that assumption" said Russell, ignoring Mr Collins. "Bob found that flat for himself. And if there are other flats to be had in the city — which I don't doubt — why can't Collins find one for himself?"

The sudden petulance of his tone matched the expression of sick distaste on his face.

"I don't see why I should be dragged into this at all," he added, beginning to curl his lip again. "If there is nothing else to discuss . . .?"

He rose from his chair and made a formally courteous inclination. "Perhaps you will now excuse me? This is rather a busy day for me."

Mr Bower, looking angry, said: "Of course, Martin. We can resume this discussion at another time."

CHAPTER XV

Next day Mrs Collins saw her way clear to doing something positive at last. Little Francis was engaged with the Bower children and their nurse; she would not see him again till evening. Bob and the Chief were to attend some tiresome official function at the Ministry of Information. Her time was her own, therefore, until the Tea-Room Committee meeting at three o'clock; she could quite well walk down to the Mission and invite Jane Lidgard to a tête-à-tête luncheon at the hotel. It should not be difficult to make Jane Lidgard see reason, surely? Although a Graded official, a cut above Ungraded Staff like Secretaries and Registrars, Miss Lidgard belonged to the lowest grade of all; and she had her career to think of, surely?

The Mission was not more than five minutes away by the short cut through one of the interior courtyards that made a warren of the city. Mrs Collins disliked having to pick her steps along the crowded and slushy Square with its uneven mosaic paving that caught high heels so treacherously, but she enjoyed strolling through the courtyard passage, where there was a smooth pavement, merely a little damp underfoot, a glass roof overhead, and interesting shop windows showing expensive curios and underwear. She had put on her best ear-rings and her smartest hat and could not help noting that her slender reflection in the shop windows looked elegant by comparison with the Slavomane women in their clumping felt boots.

As one conferring a favour she advanced upon Jane Lidgard's desk and extended her invitation. Miss Lidgard accepted it with apparent meekness and began tidying papers into neat piles, on two of which a couple of huge, shining rosy apples were serving as paper-weights.

At that time in Slavomania fresh fruit was as rare as fine gold, and Mrs Collins could not keep her eyes from the apples.

"Where did you get these lovely apples from, Miss Lidgard, excuse me for asking?"

"I'm afraid they're bribes," said Jane Lidgard, her face lighting up with a delightful smile. "They were smuggled on to my desk this morning while I was out, but I think I know who left them and I shall hand them back firmly."

"Oh, wouldn't it be a pity to hand them back? It's *so* difficult to get fruit of any kind."

"But if I kept them I should be sunk. I've very nearly trained the Diploma Class not to bring me bribes, though original sin still sometimes crops up. But if I accepted these apples I should fall from grace. Just like Eve in the Garden of Eden," said Jane Lidgard, twinkling.

Mrs Collins became aware that there was an improper contrast between Miss Lidgard's style of conversation and her appearance. In that sober grey dress, with the neat muslin collar and cuffs, her honey-coloured hair plainly folded, Miss Lidgard looked like a governess and should have talked like one, surely? Mrs Collins resented, too, Miss Lidgard's intimidating forehead, and was relieved to see that when it was extinguished beneath a small hat the woman was reduced at once to dowdiness. Yet she began to have a premonition that this interview might conceivably prove more difficult than she had expected.

Noblesse, however, *oblige*, and it was with practised graciousness that Mrs Collins ushered Miss Lidgard up the steps leading from the hotel foyer to the enclave reserved for the privileged holders of diplomatic ration-tickets.

"There's so much marble in this hotel," commented Miss Lidgard, "that when I come into it I always feel like something on a fishmonger's slab."

"Oh, really?" Mrs Collin's eyebrows went up but she brought them down again and offered her guest the choice of sherry or a cocktail.

"May I have some tomato juice?"

"Not a cocktail?"

Mrs Collins ordered one for herself. An extravagance, yet in the circumstances, she felt, a pardonable extravagance. Would she be justified in offering Miss Lidgard some wine?

"But you will have a glass of wine with your lunch?" she asked, charmingly. "One can get good French wines here, of course."

"Their names are so attractive that I sometimes regret being a total abstainer," said the disconcerting Miss Lidgard. "Mineral water for me, please."

Mrs Collins raised her eyebrows again and ordered mineral water for two.

"The first time I saw wine it was such a disappointment to me," remarked Jane Lidgard. "I was brought up on the most romantic hymns, filled with the glamour of wine. We were always being urged not to sip poison from the sparkling cup and not to quaff the ruby drop from the tempting bowl, so that I expected wine to glow like jewels, or neon lights at least. Compared with my imaginings it looked commonplace when at last I saw a glass of wine. But the names of the vintages are still full of romance."

Mrs Collins did not share her guest's appreciation of romantic hymnology. The whole trend of Miss Lidgard's chatter struck her as ill-bred.

"I suppose that total abstinence seems peculiar to you," went on Miss Lidgard, "like high tea, and being a Baptist, and all the other things I was brought up to. But I prefer sticking to my family tradition."

"Surely you can't still take it seriously?"

"Oh yes, indeed I do."

There was a horrid, upstart independence about Miss Lidgard, and it seemed that she was prepared to prattle interminably. Mrs Collins began to feel impatient. There was no use in beating about the social bush with this creature, who was now actually beginning to describe Baptist immersion ceremonies.

"I really wanted to talk to you about the rumour that you are going to stay with Mrs Owen," she interrupted. "Is it true, by the way?"

"Yes," said Miss Lidgard a little surprised at the suddenness of the thrust. "Yes, it's quite true."

"Well, now, perhaps you are not aware that the Owens aren't entitled to keep that flat any longer?"

"No, I am not aware of that".

"I assure you that it's true. Mrs Owen has no longer any claim on the flat now that her husband is away in Prsht. Don't you think you would be making a grave mistake in taking up residence there?"

"In what way, Mrs Collins?"

"Surely you don't want to get on the wrong side of the Chief, do you?"

Miss Lidgard flushed and her blue eyes sparkled, but she folded her lips together and made no answer.

"You have your career to think of, surely? You are only at the beginning of it — you're in Grade Four, aren't you? — and you don't want to be known as a trouble-maker, do you?"

"My career!" said Miss Lidgard, her voice iced with scorn. Then she began to crumble bread, regretting her bad manners and perhaps hoping to crumble them away.

"Yes, your career. That's of some importance to you, isn't it?"

"My career, as you call it, Mrs Collins, is I hope, clear enough before me. In any case, it is my own concern. As I see my career, it consists in doing what is right and doing it as well as I can."

Mrs Collins could not help shrugging her shoulders a little. Then she put her head on one side and said: "You should, of course, always do what is right, Miss Lidgard. But surely in this case obedience to the Chief's wishes is right for you?"

"The Chief has expressed no wishes in this matter to me. And I doubt if he will."

"Really, Miss Lidgard! Of course he will. You don't understand the situation at all."

Mrs Collins was now on fortified ground, with the lines of her argument traced out and her points well driven in.

"When the basic furniture in a house is supplied by the Organisation and the rent is paid by the Organisation, the house is entirely at the disposal of the Organisation. And in this country that means: at the disposal of the Chief. I have been looking up the regulations, and I could show it to you in black and white."

"There's no need to go to such extremes, is there?" said Miss Lidgard, smiling a little. "You say I don't understand the situation, Mrs Collins. I understand very well that you and Mr Collins would like to have Mrs Owen's flat, but that's not the same thing as being entitled to have it, or do you think so?"

"You are quite, quite mistaken, Miss Lidgard." Mrs Collins's temper was beginning to fray. "Surely you realise that this is a *representational* flat? Surely you understand that the Organisation needs it for entertaining Distinguished Visitors?"

"I thought Mr Bower did all that."

"The Deputy Chief has to take his share," came Mrs Collins's tart retort. "I know that these are matters outside your province, but you can take it from me that that is how things are, Miss Lidgard. And this is a Mission flat, with Mission furniture, and must be available to the Mission."

"Well, if it comes to that, I am a Mission official. And Mrs Owen is the wife of a Mission official."

Mrs Collins tore a roll to pieces. Her ear-rings trembled.

"Very subordinate officials," she said.

"You mean insubordinate, I suppose," said Jane Lidgard, again smiling a little.

"I do mean insubordinate, Miss Lidgard. And if you persist in going to live in the Owens' flat, let me tell you that you'll be turned out of it when they are. The Chief has every right to turn them out and he's going to do it."

"There are perhaps other things to consider, Mrs Collins; human rights, for instance. You're forgetting, aren't you, that the young Owen girl is rather ill? She's a sensitive and delicate child . . ."

"My child is a sensitive and delicate child and he's had to live in a hotel all this time," interrupted Mrs Collins, throwing down the fragments of her roll. "Human rights, did you say? What about *my* rights, Miss Lidgard? Mrs Owen hasn't had to move once since she came here: *she's* never had to live in a hotel."

The stream of self-pity, once tapped, overflowed and bogged down all Mrs Collins's carefully fortified ground.

"Mrs Owen has been living in the utmost comfort at the Mission's expense for years, and it's high time she took her turn of the discomforts."

As soon as she saw her opportunity, Miss Lidgard, who had long before collected her gloves and handbag, rose to her feet.

"Excuse me, Mrs Collins, I must go now. Thank you very much for the luncheon."

◆

While Mrs Collins lay sobbing on the day-bed in her hotel room, Jane Lidgard went back to the Mission and took the bad taste out of her mouth by correcting a pile of exercises. Then she looked at her watch and went to call on Doctor Russell.

Her immediate reason for disturbing the Head of the College at his desk was the Interpreters' Course, which she had taken over from Bob Owen, and which was running into difficulties, although it had been started at the request of the Slavomane Ministry of Information.

"It's practically a new batch of people every time, Martin. There's no continuity at all".

"How many do you get?"

"Anything from twenty to forty. And I count myself lucky if there's half-a-dozen in the class that I've ever seen before. I have to keep harking back and harking back to the same elementary beginnings. They're all at sixes and sevens. You couldn't call it a *course*."

"You don't think someone in the Ministry is doing a spot of sabotage?"

Doctor Russell asked this question in a matter-of-fact tone, and Jane Lidgard showed no surprise.

"No-o," she said, trying to be fair, "No. I think it's only the usual improvised muddle. For instance, I never have the same room twice running, just as I never have the same students. They just push me into any room that's handy in the Ministry and send along anyone who happens to be about, it seems to me."

"I suppose we'd better send the Ministry some kind of protest, then. Let's call it a statement."

Between them Doctor Russell and his Acting Senior Tutor sketched out the Statement which was to suggest to the Ministry of Information that an Interpreters' Course needed some minimum of Ministerial organisation.

"Then there's the Students' Petition," said Jane. "Are we to do anything about that, Martin?"

"A petition? What for?"

"Haven't you heard? A petition praying to have Bob Owen back. I believe Kosina's responsible for it, and he says he has eighty signatures already. They're talking of sending it direct to Headquarters if Arch won't accept it."

"And it won't be the slightest blasted use," said Doctor Russell, throwing his pencil down with a clatter. "Headquarters will only refer it back to Arch."

"Oh, I suppose so."

"No I remember, Kosina did mention it to me, but I thought I had dissuaded him from it."

"I've been trying to discourage him too but he's dead set on it."

Doctor Russell scrabbled one hand through his hair.

"This affection that they have for Bob is quite wonderful, Jane, don't you think so? Long after they've forgotten anything we ever did for them, the students of this country will be remembering Bob with affection."

"They'll remember you too, Martin."

"Some of them here and there may perhaps remember you and me, but not with the warm enthusiasm they feel for Bob. And that, I suppose, is just why Arch had no use for him. Oh, blast and confound it!"

"Shall we let the petition go on, then?"

"I don't see why we should interfere," said Martin Russell. "Let them find out for themselves what Arch is like . . . A nasty attitude to take up, Jane, I know I'm turning nasty and dirty myself in this fetid underworld."

"Talking about nastiness," said Jane, smiling, "do let me tell you about my ordeal at luncheon."

She gave him a spirited account of the interview.

"And when Maisie said: surely you don't want to get on

the wrong side of the Chief, I nearly retorted: he's on the wrong side of me already. I practically bit my tongue in two, Martin. And then it was: you have your career to think of, surely! You don't want to be known as a trouble-maker. And so she went on threatening me until she actually threatened to show it to me in black and white."

In spite of Jane's chuckles Doctor Russell was not amused.

"I hate all this trouble," he said. "It seems so unnecessary, so trivial. I suppose, Jane, it's quite possible that Arch may report you to Headquarters as a trouble-maker, although, God knows, the trouble is none of your making. Perhaps you'd better keep out of it."

"Why should little Rosemary be turned out of her home?"

"Why indeed? But you must consider yourself occasionally, Jane."

"My career, I suppose, depends on my toadying Arch. I'd rather resign. I can always go back to my research work. But I'm not going to give way one inch," said Jane, looking like her native whinstone.

"But this posture of resistance makes one rigid, don't you find? It hardens the spiritual arteries. I sometimes feel as if I am petrifying, I'm growing so cramped and stupid with resistance."

"No," said Jane, "I can't say I feel like that." Her eyes and brow were quite clear as she spoke, unlike Doctor Russell's. "It's just like doing one's job. One tries to do the right thing. There always comes a moment when one has to hold fast to what is right, and when the moment comes, one holds fast. But in between these moments, Martin, I can't say that I think much about it."

"I envy you, Jane. I wish my forebears had been Baptist woollen manufacturers."

The door flew open and Jamesina came in impetuously, as if she were surging on top of a wave, crying: "Oh, Martin, darling! Jane, my dear! Do you know what's happened? Dick has been transferred to the City Jail! He's out of the police clutches! Eleanor rang me up half an hour ago. Isn't it wonderful?"

Even Martin Russell's face brightened.

"Eleanor's *so* happy. She's sure everything's going to be all right now. It's only a matter of time, she says. The whole world feels different, she says."

Jamesina's breathless little sentences urged them all towards certainty and joy.

"And it's quite true. Even for me, the streets *felt* different, when I was coming here. You know, just as if the sun had come out. Even when I was squashed on the tram, Jane, by a man carrying what I *think* were two lavatory pans, I didn't mind."

"Dick's not out of the wood yet," said Martin Russell, slowly.

"But he's out of the ogre's den, darling. And it's just a spindling little wood, now. Nightmares don't last for ever, Martin".

I wonder, said Martin Russell to himself.

◆

Jamesina sat down beside Lida Dunovska, a Slavomane member of the Tea-Room committee, and out of her radiant cloud beamed upon everyone, even on Mrs Collins whose thin face, she thought, looked more discontented than usual.

"You'll all be delighted to hear," she said without preamble, "that Dick Zelezny has been at last transferred to the City Jail. Eleanor has just rung me up . . ."

"Poor Eleanor," said Mrs Bower. "What makes her so sure that Major Zelezny will be set free? I should be very glad for her sake if it comes true."

Jamesina, explaining that Eleanor would be thankful for food coupons, should anyone be able to spare some from the Diplomatic rations which the Mission Staff enjoyed, barely noted a faint surprise at the back of her mind that Victoria Bower should be glad only for the sake of Eleanor.

"She will be able to send in meals to Dick, you see, now that he's away from Police Headquarters. They feed people in the City Jail very badly, she says, but their families are allowed to send in extra food. So if anyone can spare coupons, especially for meat and butter, Eleanor would be *very* grateful. I thought I would just tell you."

The flurry of pleased excitement round the table died away and Miss Ballard, Secretary of the committee, recalled the ladies to the business in hand. The Tea-Room funds showed a gratifying surplus, and some of this was to be used in running a social evening and dance for the members of the College.

Jamesina withdrew into her cloud. The questions now under discussion were quite beyond her grasp, since they involved much calculation and she had never been able to count successfully except on her fingers. She enjoyed her recovered serenity while voices wrangled around her about the tax payable for a dance band of three, four or six instruments. Slavomania had stopped being a sinister country; she could again like Slavomanes without feeling sorry for them.

Lida Dunovska stirred and looked round at her with a smile, which she returned.

"What do *you* think, Mrs Russell?"

"About what?"

"Should members be allowed to bring husbands or wives?"

"Why not?"

"But we haven't room for more than three hundred and fifty," cut in Mrs Bower. Figures again. Jamesina resumed her meditations.

Before Dick's arrest she had often forgotten to remember that she was an alien in a foreign land; now she could forget it again. Nightmares didn't last. They were only nightmares.

The words "Mrs Owen" suddenly caught her wandering attention. Victoria Bower was speaking.

"I think Mrs Owen might perhaps be feeling lonely, and would enjoy meeting people. Shouldn't she be asked to help in arranging the games?"

So there were going to be games? Jamesina came out of her cloud and accepted various duties proposed to her. Victoria, she thought, must have Iris Owen very much on her mind, for she kept bringing in her name. "Mrs Owen might be glad to do this," and "I'm sure Mrs Owen could do that." A kind woman, after all, decided Jamesina.

Miss Ballard undertook to get precise details of the various taxes to which the entertainment was liable and the necessary permits; the ladies then drifted into the Tea-Room.

Mrs Russell was not surprised to find herself sitting at the same table as Mrs Bower and Mrs Collins; if there had been any manoeuvring, she was unaware of it. It seemed quite natural, too, that Mary Ballard should slip into the seat beside her.

"These are lovely little doughnuts," said Victoria Bower. "Are they your contribution, Jamesina?"

"Yes, I brought them with me. My dear Annushka makes them very well, doesn't she?"

"*My* cook makes the most extravagant cakes if I don't keep an eye on her. She would think nothing of putting nine eggs into a single cake — nine eggs! I have to fight her for every egg I need to have boiled for the children . . . By the way, speaking of children, how is Mrs Owen's little girl, do you know?"

"She still looks a bit peaked, I think," said Jamesina, as yet unsuspicious.

"Is she having proper medical attention?"

"Oh yes. Iris has called in a children's specialist, a man I know, a very good man."

"Well, you know, Jamesina, if *I* were Iris Owen I should take these children back to Utopia. There's no place like Utopia for young children."

Mrs Russsell's vague personality came into focus instantaneously; her attention sharpened.

"I know *mine* were blooming when they came from Utopia," went on Mrs Bower, "and now they're going white and pasty. *All* the children here look white and pasty, don't you think?"

"Some Slavomane children do, perhaps," conceded Mrs Russell, "but may not that be from the kind of feeding they get? So many floury things stuffed into them while they're mere infants."

"I don't know," countered Mrs Bower, "*I* think it's the climate. After all, this city lies in a kind of basin and bad air never gets properly blown away. These low-lying river-shores are quite unhealthy, I'm sure."

"Do you know where the Owens live in Utopia?" put in Miss Ballard. "Because if it meant going back to an industrial city, the children would be better off here, wouldn't they?"

"Oh, I don't know; even in industrial regions," insisted Mrs Bower, "there's something about the Utopian climate — probably the damp sea-air — that makes it admirable for small children."

Mrs Collins now joined in the skirmish, on Mrs Bower's side. The devastating effects of foreign climates on Utopian children were exhaustively discussed, until Mrs Bower gave the finishing stroke: "Why doesn't Mrs Owen take little Rosemary back to Utopia for, say, three months? You should suggest it to her, Jamesina."

"But she'd have to take Anne too," objected Jamesina. "That would come very expensive for the Owens."

"Well, we *all* do it, Jamesina!"

"But, Victoria" — Mrs Russell faltered and grew embarrassed. "You forget that this isn't India; it's only Slavomania."

Now I've hurt Victoria's feelings, she thought, and immediately made matters worse by adding, in a voice which sounded to herself brightly false and snubbing: "I shouldn't *dream* of suggesting such a thing to Iris Owen."

In Martin Russell's room she confessed her guilt.

"I'm afraid I was rather horrid to Victoria."

"Perhaps she asked for it," said Martin.

"I don't really think the Owens could afford to send Iris back to Utopia with the children, do you?"

"Probably not. Bob wouldn't get any subsistence allowance for them if they left Slavomania."

"Is that really so?"

"I believe it is."

"The *cheek* of Victoria!" said Mrs Russell, with soft vehemence.

Chapter XVI

"That was Vladimir on the telephone," said Martin Russell later in the evening. "He seems to be down in the mouth for some reason or other, and wants to look in on us tonight."

"Some of that pleasant white wine would do him good, and us too," said his wife. "Such a day as we've had! I'll get it out."

When Vladimir Mladski was dejected he was literally down in the mouth; he turned down his lips and raised his shoulders a little in answer to any remark, as if repudiating a nauseous draught. The Russells probed gently to discover if it were mere frustration he was suffering from or deep despair. His eyes were so dead, his cheek-bones so sharp, that despair seemed the more likely.

He had been walking about. Just walking. Oh, for some hours.

I wish we had a fire-place, thought Mrs Russell, as Vladimir drooped more and more in his arm-chair after each silent shrug, letting his lean shoulders sag forward.

Even without the fire-place, in spite of the central heating, the room seemed like Utopia to young Dr Mladski. The authentic Utopian arm-chairs, into which one sank so comfortably, the few Utopian pictures on the walls, the books untidily piled on the floor beside Martin's chair, the absence of rubber plants and cactus-pots, created an illusion of Utopia around the figures of his Utopian friends, so long as he kept his back to the windows and refused to admit Slavomania.

And yet he shivered. Without a word Jamesina rose and went out to order a tray of food for the visitor. An omelette, perhaps. Obviously he had had no dinner.

As if the departure of Jamesina made it easier for him to

speak, Vladimir said abruptly: "There's no meaning in anything, Martin."

His mouth turned down in the grimace of nausea and he shrugged again:

"Things just happen, that's all."

"But . . ." said Martin Russell, and then checked himself in surprise that he had shaped the syllable.

"I've been nearly at that point myself," he said. "But I find that I still do believe . . ."

He said no more, for Jamesina came in again and he could not examine his beliefs dispassionately within Jamesina's ambience. She carried with her an assurance that the mystery of life was to be accepted without the irrelevancy of belief or disbelief.

"I suppose I'd better tell you," said Vladimir at last, un-hunching himself a little. "Well. I went to see my uncle to-day."

The Russells knew about Vladimir's uncle, the General, although they had never met him. Before the Occupation, the General had been for years the Chief of Slavomania's Secret Service, with such inscrutable secrecy that not even his family knew it. His wife was now dead; he had no children living; he had withdrawn into retirement somewhere outside the city, alone, although the Government had offered him his old job. From time to time Vladimir went to see him, but he visited no one, not even Vladimir's mother, his only surviving sister. A legendary and mysterious figure, the General, remotely wrapped in a cloak of unguessed-at knowledge.

"I went to see him, said Vladimir, "because I thought the time was ripe for — for something I know, which could be made use of. I suspected that the old man was still in touch with many of his agents, and I thought he could advise me what to do and how to do it."

He gulped some wine.

"Well. I found he knew all about my little secret, and more. Instead of my telling him things, he told me things. And he forbade me to do anything but wait. Wait, he said."

Again he made the grimace of nausea and repeated: "Wait".

"But what was it all *about*, Vladimir?" asked Jamesina.

"I can't tell you that. But I can tell you this much. The Russians could take over this country tomorrow, if they liked."

He looked up, a spark of anger kindling in his eyes so that they no longer looked dead, and said in a hard voice:

"I'm ashamed of my country."

The Russells protested simultaneously. Any statement of this kind rouses shame and guilt in listeners; they could not bear to hear it, least of all from Vladimir.

Little by little they drew from him, in spasmodic bursts of candour, his indictment of Slavomania, which amounted to the charge that Slavomania had lost its ideals and was now merely truckling to whatever looked powerful.

"We learned to do that kind of thing before we got our independence," he said. "We had a habit of submitting to authority and cheating it wherever we could. We accepted an alien Government as a peasant accepts bad weather, grumbling and thinking up ways of circumventing it. Then when we got our independence we had to learn to act like free men, and we were only beginning to do that when the Occupation came and knocked us farther back than ever. Cheating became a virtue again. Suspicion and mistrust grew rank. We were always inclined to be suspicious and mistrustful anyway."

"Not *you*, Vladimir," put in Jamesina.

"Of course me. Look here, Jamesina, when you meet someone for the first time, you look for his good points, don't you? Well, I'm a Slavomane, and I look at once for people's bad points. Saves me from disappointment later — I should have done that with my country, too."

Here he hunched himself again and brooded. Then he resumed:

"Well. The one thing we learned from the Occupation was the need to belong to a winning side. A big side. Our country wasn't strong enough to stand by itself. A big side, a winning side, was all we cared for. A powerful side. Nothing else mattered. No nonsense about truth or justice would help us. We had believed in them before, some of us, anyway . . ." He made a wry mouth and went on: "and they hadn't saved us from humiliation".

"Well. The two biggest sides in the world were Russia and America, so we had to choose between them. And America had left us in the Russian zone. The West either didn't want us or had had to give way to Russian pressure. And Russia is anyhow a Slav power and quite close: America is far away. Russia is a power on the up and up, successful and astute in policy, where you know who's boss and what kind of policy to count on. In America nobody knows who's going to be boss in seven years' time.

"That's how my countrymen have been thinking, Martin. America, they say, is a progressive country, but it's remote and unreliable, while the Russians are skilful progressives just round the corner. Why hesitate? The Russians may be alien to Europe, but so are the Americans. And what has Europe done for us, anyway? Why not be friends with Russia?"

Although the pause Vladimir made was merely rhetorical, Martin Russell could not resist interposing:

"This is a very distorted picture you're giving us, my dear boy. But you know that, don't you?"

"If there's a distortion, it's not in my mind but in the

minds of my countrymen, Martin. Too many of them, I tell you, have been thinking just like that. And not only the working-classes. The middle classes. Even some of the aristocrats.

"They've all been truckling to the Communist Party ever since the liberation, simply because the Communist Party looks powerful and has been behaving like a governing class. Our bourgeoisie have been collaborating with the Communists just as they collaborated with the Occupying Power, and from the same mean motives of expediency and with the same intention of cheating . . ."

Here the Russells again protested. They did not believe all these rumours of collaboration. Nearly everyone they had met, from the porter at their first hotel to the Rector of the University, had suffered terribly in the Occupation.

Vladimir shook his head impatiently. "You must have noticed in the first months you were here how many people began every conversation by assuring you that they never, never had collaborated. Well, then! . . . And how could they help collaborating if they owned factories or had a national museum, say, to be responsible for? They may have thought they were collaborating for the good of the country. And most of them were maybe prepared to risk their lives but not their livings . . ."

"I think you're simplifying everything far too much," persisted Martin. "Here, for instance, you're taking a fine and complex cobweb of motives and rolling it up into a few dirty shreds, just like a politician."

"Well, it's politicians I'm talking about," retorted Vladimir. "In that sense we're all politicians now-a-days. That's what I'm trying to tell you. We think only in terms of power systems. And the power system that looms biggest here is the Russian. Look, Martin, let me go on."

He was going on, thought Jamesina, much as Martin had

gone on about his grievances in the office. Reeling it off, length after length.

"Thanks to the Russian Army of liberation, the Communists were in a position to set up People's Courts, as they called them, to damn or absolve the whole population of this country. And it was the first thing they did. They were in a position to accuse anyone of treachery, collaboration or what-not, and they sentenced people so vindictively that nobody dared say a word. Justice didn't come into it at all. It was a naked demonstration of power. What middle-class man was going to stick his neck out even if he knew that the Communist presiding over this or that Court had been himself a collaborator and a spy? If you were a member of the Communist Party you were automatically a good patriot. If you weren't, you had to save your skin somehow. So you truckled."

"But did you go on truckling? I don't believe it, Vladimir. I've met, I suppose hundreds of Slavomanes — yes, literally hundreds; all the members of my College, to begin with, — and very few of them, even including our young idealists, have any use for Russian Communism."

"I remember," put in Jamesina, "how unhappy they all looked when we first came. It took them three months to learn how to smile again. But now they *are* smiling. The nightmare of the Occupation has gone and I do think that the nightmare of the Kremlin is lifting."

"I'm sorry to say it, Martin," returned Vladimir, "but in your College you're preaching to the converted. I mean, your members are looking to the West already, or they wouldn't have joined you."

"What about my students in the University?"

"They wouldn't be taking Utopian Literature as a subject if they weren't already looking to the West."

"Well," commented Martin, "I get quite a lot of light on

politics reflected from my students. I agree that they're all too much obsessed by politics and too fond of repeating that this is a small country. And some of them are hag-ridden by the atom bomb. But on the whole they seem to me a hopeful crowd. I get no impression of a general truckling to Communism. And it's just nonsense to say that they wouldn't be in my class unless they were already looking to the West, for I have one of two Communists and a good few near-Communists in my seminars. I do think that you're distorting the picture, Vladimir. This country would never put up with a police state."

"My dear Martin, I don't say that we want Communism. What I'm saying is that we are now demoralised to the level of putting up no resistance to anything that seems as strong as Russian Communism. Look at the record of Parliament in these years since the liberation. When has any man ever stood up and said that the other parties also had good ideas and that the Communists were on the wrong track? Yes, of course, we want that too, is what the so-called democrats have all been saying; oh yes, we want that programme just as much as you do; we know it's what the People want; only go more slowly, please, only not just quite yet . . ."

Here Annushka came in with the tray. Jamesina set it across the arms of Vladimir's chair, saying:

"Ham omelette, cheese, bread and butter. And here's a napkin. Open another bottle of wine, Martin, will you?"

She stood beside the chair until Vladimir began to eat. In between mouthfuls he went on talking.

"The other parties have been grumbling subordinates of the Community Party, that's all. The Communist Party has been the big boss, I tell you. In Parliament the Communists even accuse the other parties of holding up laws by intentional delay. Intentional delay! That's their pretty description of democratic debate.

"And not one of the democrats in this country has ever accused the Communists of behaving like autocrats, which they are doing. How? Look, Martin, this is how."

Vladimir's beginning to feel better, said Jamesina to herself. He has stopped making these dreadful faces.

"An autocrat's not dependant on the favour of his subjects. He rules because he's master, and he lives at his subjects' expense. That's his privilege, whether he's a King or an aristocrat or a Communist leader. The Communist leaders are our feudal barons today, our governing oligarchs. Who pays for all their processions and public shows? Their subjects, the public. A feudal prince reserves for himself and his friends the privilege of carrying arms. Outside the Army, who carries arms in this country? The Communist police and the Works' Militia, which is a Communist private army. Even in the professional Army only Communists get promotion to the top posts. And in all the organisations of resistance fighters and the armies of exile, the Fighters for Freedom, it's the same story; you've got to be a Communist to get a top post in any of these . . ."

"That's not true of Dick Zelezny's Legionaries," interrupted Martin Russell.

"These Legionaries of Zelezny's are now being disbanded as an independent body. You don't imagine that if he gets out of jail he's going to be able to pick up things where he left them, do you?"

"But he *will* get out of jail," said Jamesina.

"That's quite likely," agreed Vladimir. "The judges are still more or less independent. But the ideas's beginning to spread that police and judges should exist only to destroy opposition to the governing class. Sooner or later the independent judges will be wiped out. If they set Zelezny free it'll be about the last thing they'll get the chance of doing. Any subject of Communist rulers is powerless and without rights, I tell you."

"I haven't been following affairs in Parliament," said Martin, "but I do know that Parliament helped to bring Dick's arrest into the open. I think you're under-estimating the democratic forces in this country."

"The democratic forces in this country are getting rattled," said Vladimir. "But it's too late. They've let their position go by default. They've been truckling so long to the Communists that now they're getting scared, but they're too blind to see that they can't cheat and intrigue their way round the Kremlin any longer. They still think they can get the Communists out of the Government by democratic means, and that they're sure to do it if they can only string along until the elections. Convince a Communist that he has nothing to fear from you, and he'll gratefully turn into a democrat and a patriot, that's what they think. Even the President thinks that. Not one of them understands that the sovereign power in the country has already shifted from Parliament to the Communist Party."

"But that's just what I don't see," said Martin Russell. His face was blurred and troubled; creases of perplexity lined his forehead and netted his eyes. "I hear that the Communists are likely to lose a lot of votes in the elections, for instance."

Vladimir bit into a piece of cheese until he had nibbled it away, although, from his expression, one could have assumed that each mouthful tasted worse than the other. "And that's just it," he said, flicking crumbs on to his tray. "If free elections mean that the Communists are going to lose, they won't let us have the free elections."

"Won't *let* you!" said Jamesina, shocked.

"We've got to become a Communist State one way or the other. So or so," said Vladimir with another shrug and grimace. "Either we go quietly, as you Utopians say, and make the best we can of a bad bargain, or we are violently kicked into it. That's what my uncle believes."

"But *why?*" cried Jamesina.

"The Russians daren't let us . . ." Vladimir checked himself and set his tray on the floor. He had agreed to say no word, for the present, about the secret mining concession beyond Skrs, where the Russians were unearthing so much uranium. "As soon as they think that cat's out of the bag, they'll fore-close on the mortgage they hold on our country," his uncle had said.

"The Russians daren't let us be independent," he went on. "We have too many things that they need. Heavy industry, for example."

His voice sounded flat and unconvincing, even to his own ears. He did not look at Martin or Jamesina.

"You're not quite sure in your own mind, are you?" said Martin.

"Do you think I'm trying to convince myself as well as you?"

"Something of the sort."

Martin smiled as he said this, yet the harassed look blurred his face again as he went on:

"You've succeeded in communicating your fears to me, my dear boy, but you haven't convinced me. Your fears I can easily understand. But apprehensions usually prevent a man from really apprehending any situation, and I think that holds true for you now. You should make quite sure that you're not jumping to the wrong conclusion. I suspect that your conclusion may be wrong, and that you're colouring your picture to match it. For instance, some of the working classes may be impressed, as you say, by the power of Communism. I grant you even some of the middle classes. But, in my experience, very few of them. And not the aristocrats, surely? As for the Parliamentarians . . ."

"Let me tell you what I heard just the other day,"

interrupted Vladimir. He named a prince whose domains had been largely confiscated since the liberation. "You wouldn't expect *him* to flirt with Russia, would you? But he was arguing that Stalin was too sly an old bandit to make the mistake which has always brought down tyrants, the mistake of being tyrannical. After all, he said, Augustus Caesar began as a murderous party chief and became a model Emperor. The Russians could do with a little civilizing, and why shouldn't Slavomania enter the Russian Alliance and help on a Slav Empire? The Americans despised nobles as relics of feudalism, but the Russians, he thought, would know how to make them valuable partners. Now, he may just have been saying all that to shock someone, but there you have it. These ideas are in the air."

"All kinds of ideas are always in the air," said Martin. "The prince is a delightful man, and I think he must have been thoroughly enjoying himself. But of course you can't take irresponsible jokes as relevant evidence, Vladimir; you've made too many of them yourself."

Instead of smiling, Vladimir leaned forward in his chair, clasped his hands tightly together and stared at them.

"This mountain of mine is no mole-hill, Martin," he said.

A new heaviness filled the room, an atmospheric sense of menace.

Like a cloud, thought Martin Russell. And one could not refute a cloud point by point, as if it were a line of argument. He could not find a word to say to Vladimir at the moment.

To Jamesina it seemed as if Vladimir were imagining fetters on his clasped hands. Her eyelids began to prickle.

"It's your uncle that's taken the heart out of you," she said. "How can anyone be so sure about what's going to happen? I think he's a wicked uncle."

Vladimir shook his head.

"He's a religious man, my uncle. Unless ..." He fell

silent. Had his uncle, he wondered, possibly been got at by the Kremlin? Whether or no, the old man's information was precise and presumably accurate. Not only the region beyond Skrs, he had said; the whole of the north-western frontier was already surveyed and mapped for uranium deposits. All done by ostensibly convalescent Russian officers, recuperating at the hot springs. And then there was the matter of the last new rifle issue, which had been diverted from the Army to the Works Militia . . . No, no, the old man was to be trusted.

"My uncle believes that it's the will of God that we should have an evil Government coming to us. He thinks we deserve it. He even thinks we need it, as a cure. And there he may be right — about the cure, I mean. We'll certainly have a belly-full of the big stick for the next fifty years, if we're not all blown to atoms."

"I still think he's a wicked uncle," insisted Jamesina.

"The biggest stick of all being wielded most violently from Heaven," said Martin, curling his lip. "Has your uncle been reading Pascal?"

"You don't believe me, Martin?" asked Vladimir, without looking up.

"I don't know." Martin Russell ran his fingers through his hair. "I'm so bedevilled by the same kind of thing in my office — on a much smaller scale, of course — that I'm an easy prey to apprehension. I know how helpless a man feels before an encroaching power-system. But I know also what it means to let oneself down into the underworld of resistance. That's why I ask you, my dear boy, to be very sure in your own mind before you commit yourself to this — this catastrophic belief."

He lowered his voice, and said:

"To fight power you must streamline yourself into lines of power; to fight violence you must become violent; to fight injustice you must become unjust. Even to resist without fighting cramps you in a rigid posture; the free play of the human spirit becomes impossible . . ."

He broke off, and then added:

"I am already committed to that kind of resistance, and it's like being in prison."

Vladimir glanced at his friend, sideways, and sat up.

"My dear Martin," he said, beginning now to smile, "don't, please, worry about me. I'm not like you. I'm a Slavomane, with an inherited talent for closing a door between the front rooms and the back rooms of myself. An old Slavomane tradition, I assure you. I can follow it without harming myself at all."

Then he glanced at Jamesina's troubled face, briskly slapped his hands on the arms of his chair and said in a firm voice: "Well. It's a relief to be certain at last . . . Yes, I am certain. We're only a piece in the Kremlin's game of chess, a piece that can be taken and must be taken. I am sure of that, Martin. As far as I am concerned, the Communist State in Slavomania is a *fait accompli*. And in this game I can at least see a few moves ahead; I have that advantage."

Turning round he looked deliberately out of the window for a moment or two. The curtains, as usual — how like the Russells, he thought — were undrawn, and he could see across the glimmering white garden as far as the wrought-iron gate piercing the wall, beyond which a large street lamp illuminated from below the branches of a tree. A lime tree, he remembered. There was an avenue of lime trees all along this street. Its black branches were outlined in white as if some artist had iced them with a palette knife, carving the icing smoothly into sharp ridges, so that the tree seemed spellbound by a glittering twin of frosted snow.

"What are you thinking of doing?" cried Jamesina in alarm. "You're not going to disappear, are you?"

173

Vladimir turned towards the room again. "I'm only going to close a door in myself," he said, still smiling. A glint of mischief lighted his eyes. "But the back rooms will be what you would consider very murky, Jamesina."

No one, he went on to point out, would notice any difference in him, except perhaps the Russells, and they were not to worry about him. Only, they must not let fall a word, or even a hint, of what he had told them, for his life might someday depend on their discretion.

"I should not have dared to say as much to one of my own countrymen," he said, looking from one to the other with affection. Then he lifted his glass:

"This is perhaps the last occasion on which I shall be quite open with you, my dear friends. Let's drink a toast to it."

"So you do believe in something, after all," said Martin Russell.

"My dear Martin! I don't believe *in* anything. I believe only that there are some things I can try to do . . . I went to school for the first time exactly when Slavomania got its independence. I grew up with my poor country, and I suppose I must do what I can to help it."

"Yes," said Martin Russell, absently, "yes. As long as there are things one can do . . ."

Chapter XVII

A disquieting letter from Bob Owen in Prsht brought his wife to see Mrs Russell.

"Bob says he's had an awful letter from Arch, and even if he comes back at Easter we'll have to give up our flat, since Arch and Collins and Martin have agreed that the three tops should have the three Foreign Office houses."

"I'm sure Martin never agreed to any such thing," said Jamesina Russell.

"I didn't think so either, but Bob's quite definite about it. Arch and Collins *and Martin*, he says. That's what Arch told him. He's very upset, as you can imagine."

Mrs Owen was prepared to believe that the Chief was lying; she did not accuse Doctor Russell of double-dealing, nor did she reproach Mrs Russell; yet there was a hard edge to her voice, a sharpness in her look, a readiness to show fight that put Mrs Russell on the defensive.

When Jamesina Russell was on the defensive, her nebulous personality condensed and changed its shape, shrinking until it focussed upon the immediate situation. At these moments one felt force and weight in her persuasions. Unaware of this transformation, she was conscious only of a need to do something practical and helpful, as now; she did not realise how powerful could be the influence she exerted, or that she might be blamed for it afterwards.

"Here you are," she said, spreading out on the table the Russells' Foreign Office decree. "It says: *granted to Martin Russell and non-transferable to any other person whatever.* Your decree must have the same formula in it. No pronouncement by Arch can alter the fact that your flat is in Bob's name and cannot be transferred to Collins."

Iris Owen worried each Slavomanian word in the

document like a dog worrying bones, but the interpretation stood fast.

"I'll tell you what," said Jamesina, with an air of clinching the matter, "take your decree up to the Foreign Office and see Vladimir Mladski about it. Didn't you say that Arch is threatening Bob with eviction by the Foreign Office if he doesn't give up the flat? That *must* be a bluff. Vladimir Mladski will be able to tell you just how you stand officially."

The uncertainty, the lack of confidence, underlying Mrs Owen's show of fight now became obvious. Like a forlorn little girl she looked appealingly at Mrs Russell and said: "I couldn't. The Foreign Office scares me. It's so enormous. I should never be able to find him."

"Wait a minute," said Mrs Russell and went out to the telephone in the hallway. She smiled as she lifted the receiver, for the thought had occurred to her that if she were married to Bob she might well think that all men were elusive and hard to pin down.

When she returned to the sitting-room she announced that there would be no difficulty at all. The porter at the main entrance of the Foreign Office was to have a messenger waiting to take Mrs Owen to Doctor Mladski's room at any time between three and half-past three.

"Run home for your decree and take it along," she said, like a mother. "I'm sure Vladimir will be helpful."

◆

Doctor Mladski was indeed helpful. Mrs Owen had brought with her not only the decree but also Bob Owen's alarming letter, relevant portions of which she read aloud. Here was a piece of trickery which it would be a pleasure to unravel, Doctor Mladski promised himself, as he recalled what Jamesina had confided to him on the telephone.

"This is interesting," he said. "I think I can assure you,

Mrs Owen, that we have no intention of cancelling your decree or turning you out of your flat. We are short of housing accommodation, yes, but not so short as all that. You might read me that last paragraph again."

Mrs Owen read it out:

"Another argument is that the Polish Military Attaché is living in one small room, the Swedish Ambassador has had to go home for lack of accommodation, a First French Secretary is having to live in a hotel with his wife and children, and, that being so, it is unethical of me to think of keeping a whole flat for simple domestic purposes, since the Foreign Office is so short of necessary representational accommodation."

"Very interesting," said Doctor Mladski. "For your information, Mrs Owen, I shall now betray some State secrets. There is no Polish Military Attaché here at present. The Swedish Ambassador has gone home, yes, but he was going home anyhow; his departure has nothing to do with his accommodation. A Second French Secretary is certainly living in a hotel, but he is a single man with no family."

Young Doctor Mladski and Mrs Owen looked at each other for a second, then one of them grinned and the other tittered.

"I think this information should be conveyed to your husband, Mrs Owen. I hope he hasn't answered the letter already."

A shade crossed Iris Owen's face.

"No, I'm pretty sure he won't have answered it yet."

"Ah. Then you might put it to him. Perhaps we had better make some notes."

Doctor Mladski took up his pen.

"First, Mrs Owen, how many are in your family?"

A family of four, it appeared, was the correct number by Slavomanian law for the flat of four rooms, excluding the unit comprising kitchen, bathroom and maid's room, which did not count.

"This confirms, you see," said Doctor Mladski, "that your flat is not supposed to be representational. We have granted you a decree because you are foreigners, but we have not given you diplomatic or representational accommodation. That is given to Heads of Missions and senior diplomats, and contains more rooms than the size of the family warrants. Yours is not a representational flat, and you cannot be turned out of it unless your husband leaves the country. That would be the official ruling."

"Would you be prepared to put that in writing?"

"Perhaps your husband should write me a letter first," suggested Doctor Mladski, "asking me what his position is. Then I can send him an official reply."

This suggestion was accepted with relief by Mrs Owen.

"I'll write to Bob at once," she said, gathering up her papers.

"And meanwhile please stop worrying," added young Doctor Mladski.

◆

The conferences about the Owens' flat, which Doctor Russell had done his best to keep inconclusive, seemed at last to be hardening to a point.

"Headquarters are insisting on my setting a term for Owen's occupation of this flat," said Mr Bower one morning, after he had invited Doctor Russell to his room for a private talk. "If I am to keep myself right with Headquarters, I must set a term now."

"What term were you thinking of?" asked Doctor Russell.

"I was thinking the end of this month."

"But that's in little more than a fortnight. How could Bob find himself a house in that short space of time?"

"H'm," said Mr Bower. "I could extend the term if necessary, I suppose . . . Perhaps you would be so good as to tell Owen that, Martin? You could tell him privately that of course I shall extend the term if he finds it needful, but that to put myself right with Headquarters I *must* set a term."

At that moment Mr Bower felt himself a martyr, a well-intentioned, conscientious official striving against enormous difficulties to do the best for everyone, with the minimum of co-operation. Surely even Doctor Russell must be touched by this appeal?

Doctor Russell, being by this time unable to see his Chief as a fellow human-being, let alone as the Chief saw himself, merely thought that Arch, the double-dealing villain, had suggested to Headquarters that a term should be set and was now using Headquarters as cover.

"No," he said. "I won't have anything to do with it. This is something you must do on your own responsibility, if you do it at all."

Mr Bower primmed his mouth, resenting Doctor Russell's tone and implications, and then said: "I fail to see why you are so unco-operative in this matter."

"Well, I've told you often enough. I simply don't see why Bob Owen should be forced to hand over his flat to Collins."

And if you can't understand plain language, I can wrap it up in verbiage for you, Doctor Russell thought to himself, and added: "You're moving as fast as you can towards a pre-determined conclusion which I cannot approve."

"What you do not see is that I am acting in the best interests of the Organisation to which we both belong."

"No, I don't see that," agreed Doctor Russell. "I think that you're ignoring far too many elements in the situation. You're not looking at it in the round. You're following a single line of action which may not even produce the results you want. You have no guarantee, for instance, that the

Foreign Office will let Collins have the flat."

"Oh, they will allow Collins the flat all right."

The comfortable certainty in Mr Bower's voice set Doctor Russell wondering if Bob had not yet written to the Chief as Vladimir had suggested. He had had plenty of time to do it, confound him.

"If I were you, I shouldn't take that for granted. And there's another thing which might affect our prestige: if it became known that Mrs Owen and two small children were being turned out to let Collins in, there might be a public scandal."

Mr Bower seemed taken aback.

"Oh, do you really think so?"

"Considering how gossip flies in this city, I think it's likely."

Mr Bower's glasses glinted balefully as he said: "Surely Owen would be discreet. In his own interests he would be discreet."

"His washerwoman mightn't be discrete, or his many Slavomane friends," said Doctor Russell, with a shrug.

"H'm . . . Perhaps it would be a good idea, Martin, do you think, if Collins were to go himself to Prsht and have a frank talk with Owen?"

A recollection instantaneously flashed into Doctor Russell's mind of something Jamesina had told him the day before; some message had come from Vladimir about the Chief's having said that he was sending Collins to Prsht to interview Bob. This, then, was no spontaneous suggestion.

"Is Collins to tell Bob that a term is to be set? Because, if so, the talk will hardly be frank and free."

"No," said Mr Bower. "He is not empowered to do that. I am the only one who can do that."

Doctor Russell was perhaps hasty in assuming that the setting of a term was thus temporarily shelved, that it would not be mentioned to Bob until after the frank talk; yet his relief made his voice perceptibly warmer as he said: "I should go slow in this matter, if I were you. It's humanly and technically difficult. There can be no harm in Owen's having what you call a frank talk with Collins. But it looks to me as if Collins is refusing other suitable flats simply because he has made up his mind to have this one."

Mr Bower's response to the faint sign of sympathy was immediate. He took off his spectacles and polished them, with a sigh, letting it be seen that he was oppressed by cares. "I may say," he confided, "that I do not at all like Collins's method of pursuing this flat."

◆

"I can't go on stalling indefinitely about Bob's flat," complained Doctor Russell when he went home to luncheon. "It's too tiresome and sordid. But it looks as if Bob will have to take a hand himself; Arch is sending Collins to Prsht to have what he calls a frank talk with him. Didn't you tell me something about that yesterday, Jamesina? What exactly did Vladimir say?"

"I don't know that I can remember *exactly*, but it was more or less like this. Arch rang up Vladimir and said that the Mission was thinking of having the flat transferred to Collins, now that Bob was in Prsht, and he supposed the Foreign Office would raise no objections. Vladimir told him that, as far as the Foreign Office was concerned, the flat was Bob's, and if Bob chose to turn in his decree, that was his own affair. Collins, if he wanted the flat, must stick to the procedure and apply for a new decree. Then after some humming and hawing Arch said Collins had better go to Prsht and see Bob personally about the arrangements."

"They're hoping to get Bob by the short hairs," said Doctor Russell.

"Vladimir thought that Arch must have rung him up because he had got Bob's letter and wanted to discover if he was behind it. But as Arch didn't mention it, he didn't either; and he said he was pretty sure that Arch would learn nothing from the tone of his voice."

"I don't believe that Arch has had any letter yet from Bob. There's no sign of it."

"You think Vladimir was being too subtle? Well, perhaps. He enjoys that kind of thing, you know. He's really looking forward to putting a quiet spoke in Collins's wheel if he should apply for a decree. Government by obstruction is a Slavomane speciality, according to Vladimir, and he's prepared to obstruct Collins till the cows come home — or till the Communists come home, I suppose. Now, all *I* care is to keep Iris and the children from being turned out."

"Well, I'm afraid they will be turned out. I can see it coming."

"Oh dear, oh dear," cried Jamesina, in double distress.

"It's no use refusing to see things," said Doctor Russell.

Jamesina, avoiding argument, tried raillery.

"Why must it always be disagreeable things that you and Vladimir can see coming?" she asked. "I won't believe either of you . . . Our Annushka, by the way, is just as bad as Vladimir, Martin. She's convinced that the Communists are planning something."

"Annushka? Who's been putting the wind up her?"

"The daughter, my dear, and the son-in-law. Do you remember when she wept on my shoulder about the Gouch?"

Martin Russell began to smile, as his wife had hoped he would. The word 'gouch', the Slavomanian version of the Western 'couch', amused him nearly as much as the story about the Gouch.

"I was puzzled, you remember," went on Jamesina,

"about the passion of woe she poured out about that Gouch; it seemed excessive. Well, it wasn't just Slavomanian temperament, Martin, nor was it just because her daughter thinks her an old stick-in-the-mud. I got it all out of her today. Her son-in-law is some kind of Communist official. He's in charge of that Russian book-shop in the square . . ."

"The devil he is!"

". . . and he's persuaded his wife that Annushka is so polluted by horrible bourgeois ideas that she's a bad influence in their household, particularly on the child. And you know how Annushka idolises her granddaughter, poor woman. It's an ingenious variation on the mother-in-law theme, isn't it? Well, now he wants to forbid Annushka the house if she persists in working for us, which he calls 'having treacherous connections with the West'."

"She's not going to leave us, is she?"

"The daughter is pressing her to leave us, but so far she hasn't given in. For one thing, she has nowhere to go. She's sold nearly all her furniture to get them the money for their new flat, where there's no room for her, and so her little house in the country is just an empty shell. For another thing, she likes being here. But now they're pressing her harder and hinting that time is short. Annushka is sure that something's in the wind. She's very upset."

"What did you say to her?"

"I comforted her as well as I could and told her how much we liked her. She's such a dear; it *is* a shame. That son-in-law must be a nasty type. You don't think, Martin, that the Communists are actually planning something?"

"I shouldn't wonder," said Doctor Russell, suddenly listless under the weight of his wife's volubility.

"Do you *really* think so?"

"I don't suppose they'll bring it off. They ignore far too many elements in the situation."

Here Doctor Russell paused and listened to a disturbing echo.

"I'm beginning to repeat myself," he said, with wry surprise. "I used the very same words to Arch this morning."

CHAPTER XVIII

A softer air now began to blow, delusively promising spring, and by the next Saturday morning the moist blankness of the winter landscape outside the city was already dimpling into life. Rings of bare earth showed around tree-boles; snow slid from burdened branches; the stems of leafless shrubs glowed as if they had been varnished amber or burgundy red. Even the sullen blanket of the sky wore thin in places.

It was a day to foster hopes, to give the lie to fears. In the capital city many and various hopes, invisible vapours, streamed steadily upwards, some of them coalescing with each other and mushrooming into ambitious political dreams. A few National Party Ministers were inspired to believe that the Communists' intransigence over the police might well be used as a lever to jerk them right out of the Coalition before the April elections; while Communist leaders began to wonder whether the time might not be ripe to offer the Trade Union Combine a direct share in the Government, since Parliament, to their way of thinking, was now discredited and no longer deserved the Government's confidence.

Hopes of lesser moment, though not so wide-spreading, rose just as high above the morning mists. A student sauntered in a park meditating a poem. Shop-keepers in the square resolved to dress their windows spectacularly. Young women went to have their hair permanently waved and exchanged tentative chaff with young men at neighbouring wash-basins, who were indulging in vibro-massage. The house-porter in the Russells' block of flats convinced himself easily that he could sell another load of furnace coke from the boiler-room to friends on the black market without being called to account. And Dick Zelezny, sitting on a backless bench in the City Jail, also palpitated with hope on this Saturday morning. The case against him had been quashed; he had reason to believe that he would be a free man by noon. Having put on a clean shirt and his good shoes he listened to the squealing of the street-trams outside, while his cell-mate, Odpustil, a gaunt wraith of a man, stalked up and down nursing a handful of withered chrysanthemums, he, too, buoyed by fresh hopes of yet overcoming his enemies.

◆

At the Utopian Mission Mr Collins took out what was still known as the College car and headed it towards Prsht. He had no doubts about his coming off victor in the encounter with Mr Bob Owen. Even without the letter from the Chief which he carried tucked into an inner pocket, he should be more than a match for that disobedient and disloyal servant of the Mission. He put on a burst of speed, as if his engine were running on moral indignation instead of petrol, and passed a car in front of him, with a sense of personal triumph.

In the Prsht Regional Centre of the Mission Mr Bob Owen was not only hopeful but elated, although his nervous elation, to an impartial observer, might have looked like fear. Yesterday morning he had finally re-drafted and posted his letter to the Chief, a letter which, he believed, contained all the answers to any argument that Collins might advance, and yet he could not assume that Collins's arrival, announced by telephone, had any reference to it. There had not been time for the letter to have reached Arch before Collins's journey was decided on. Something else must be in the wind. Arch must have done the dirty on him somehow at Headquarters and was sending Collins to tell him so. And yet, with the authority of the Foreign Office behind him and the decree for the flat in his possession, he was in a strong position; short of being given the sack, he could not be turned out of his flat.

Collins should arrive at any moment now. Bob Owen strolled downstairs to the front door, twitching his fingers a little but smiling his pleasant, crooked smile as he thought to himself that anyhow he was going to have a good luncheon at the Mission's expense.

Bob Collins's first question, after he emerged from his car with a curt greeting, was put in a harsh, suspicious tone that acted on Bob Owen's nerves like a bracer.

"Have you booked a table for lunch in the Star Hotel as you were instructed?"

"Certainly I have. It's only a step away; you can leave the car here, by the Centre. We always park here."

"I thought we might be more private in the hotel. I don't want to see Wickens".

"Mr Wickens isn't here, anyhow. He's off to the mountains for the weekend."

Bob Collins sneered silently as he locked the car and pocketed the key, then he said: "You're lucky, aren't you, having the mountains so close at hand. *We* don't find it so easy in the capital."

"It's not so easy here either. Round this corner, Mr Collins. There's nasty trouble brewing in the mountains — bandits and ex-partisans."

"Really? But not, I suppose, in the tourist resorts where you and Wickens go to enjoy yourselves?"

"Mr Wickens happens to be away lecturing, Mr Collins."

Bob Owen's light tenor was not even indignant; it sounded almost airily polite. With the same easy politeness he showed Collins into the hotel dining-room where a table had been reserved for them in a deep window recess. The alacrity, the welcoming smiles of the waiters, who beamed upon Bob Owen and exchanged with him what sounded like badinage in rapid Slavomanian, re-inforced Collins's suspicions that Wickens and Owen, behind the Chief's back, did themselves extravagantly well.

"Some soup?" suggested Owen.

"I don't think I'll have any soup, thank you," said Collins, in a tone that turned his formal gratitude into a snub.

"Well, they do a very good clear soup with liver dumplings; I'm going to have that."

The waiter presented the wine-list to Owen as if wine were a matter of course, thought Collins.

"I can't recommend the local red wines," Owen was saying, "but the white wines are delightful, as you may know. What are you eating, by the way, if you won't take soup?"

"A little fish, I think."

"Trout?" said Owen. "Some nice fresh-water trout here."

"May I see the menu?"

"Oh, you understand restaurant Slavomanian, do you?"

"More or less," said Collins, gazing with concealed dismay at a long list of comestibles written in a spidery cramped hand in purple ink.

"Yes, I think I'll have the trout," he said. "Nothing else, thank you, but a salad."

Only just in time he stopped himself from adding: "I am on a diet." He was not going to be drawn into making confidences, however insidious Owen might be. He frowned and felt in his pocket for the Chief's letter, which he skimmed across the table as Owen's soup was set down.

"A communication from the Chief, which you had perhaps better read."

Bob Owen swallowed two or three mouthfuls of soup before laying down his spoon and tearing open the envelope with a long, tobacco-stained finger.

The letter was short. He read it twice.

"I suppose you know what's in this letter?"

"I presume that it refers to Headquarters' instructions that a term is to be set for your occupation of that flat."

"It says that I'm to quit my flat in a fortnight's time."

Owen threw the letter down on the table-cloth and drank off a glassful of white wine.

"An ultimatum, that's what it is," he said, and began to savage one of the liver dumplings.

"I'm sorry, but I can't do the impossible, you know. And this is the impossible."

"The Chief has empowered me to say that he will extend the term for a week or longer, if you find it needful."

But out of that flat you must go, said Collins's hard eyes.

"If I can find a flat or a villa in Prsht, I'm perfectly willing to move my family into it, but until then I simply refuse to quit."

Collins's eyes did not soften at this declaration of perfect willingness to compromise.

"You've had more than a month already," he said, "to find accommodation for your family in Prsht — six weeks, in fact — and . . ."

"There's no accommodation to be had in Prsht, I tell you."

"Oh, I think it could be found if you were seriously trying to find it."

"Look here, Mr Collins, I resent that."

A small red flush rose to Owen's cheek-bones.

"I resent your whole way of trying to bully me out of my flat. For I suppose I'm to clear out just to let you into it. And you don't even know that the Foreign Office would let you have it."

"Oh, nonsense; of course they will."

"That's all you know," returned Bob Owen, aligning his spoon exactly in the middle of his empty plate. "I have the

Foreign Office's word for it, in writing, that mine is a private flat, not a representational flat. It's a private flat, just the right size for my family by Slavomanian law. It needs a family of four or more to occupy it. And your family is one short of the number it needs. You would never be allowed to have it."

This unexpected argument staggered Collins, so that he felt a momentary pain under his breast-bone. He put both elbows on the table and, apparently at random, fished a small paper-wrapped tablet from a vest-pocket, which, under cover of his joined hands, he slipped into his mouth.

The waiter brought Owen a vast platter of roast goose.

"I sent a letter to the Chief yesterday, in which I made the whole position clear," went on Owen, helping himself lavishly to goose and trimmings. "It seems a pity that you're not aware of it."

"Did you actually write to the Foreign Office without the Chief's permission?"

"I wrote to the Foreign Office asking what my position was," came the heated reply, "as any householder is entitled to do. And I have a ruling from them, in writing, that my flat is not representational but private."

"For the Slavomane Foreign Office it may not be representational," retorted Collins, "but for the Mission it is, because it has Mission furniture in it. That's the ruling in *our* Organisation."

"I'm perfectly willing to let you remove the Mission furniture. You can take it away whenever you like. It's only in two of the rooms, anyhow, except for one or two oddments. We can quite well get along without it. Take the furniture away, by all means."

And you know where you can put it, said Bob Owen to himself, reaching for another glass of wine.

In this *impasse*, Collins remembered, too late, that he had been warned by the Chief to go slow and to make sure of getting the decree out of Owen. That decree seemed to stick in the Chief's throat.

"Why don't you take a flat or a villa for your family somewhere in the country between Prsht and the capital?" he suggested, in what he thought was a conciliatory tone. "There can't be the same difficulty in finding country accommodation."

"And what advantage would that be to me?"

"I see your point," said the Deputy, putting his finger-tips together in imitation of the Chief. "Yes, I can see your point. But it would be for the good of the Mission in general if you were to do that, since the Mission needs your flat for entertaining Distinguished Visitors. A certain loyalty shown by you to the interests of the Mission would be appreciated in the proper quarters."

"A certain loyalty shown by the Mission to me would be more than appreciated. I'm doing two men's work for the Mission in this town; surely my family and I are entitled to reasonable treatment. And what is to happen when I go back to the capital?"

"Er — that's why I suggested taking a house midway between the two. But, as a matter of fact . . ." Collins cleared his throat. "A house nearer Prsht would probably prove more convenient, since, as a matter of fact, you are doing such good work here that the Chief is thinking of transferring you permanently to Prsht."

"I *thought* that was coming!"

The insubordinate disgust in Owen's voice and face excused Collins, in his own opinion, from further attempts at appeasement. He was brimming with virtuous contempt and he welcomed the chance of spilling it.

"The Chief, as you ought to know, has full powers to transfer anyone in his area without reference to

Headquarters. But he has consulted Headquarters about your transfer and is only waiting for their approval before notifying you. There can be no doubt that they will confirm it. The fact that you may be of some use in Prsht, considering the circumstances here, is your last and only hope, I may tell you, of being re-instated in the good opinion of the Organisation."

Bob Owen's fingers twitched on the stem of the wine-glass.

"And what do you mean by that?" he demanded.

"I mean that you are known to be a disloyal and unsatisfactory and extravagant servant of the Mission."

"That may be the Chief's personal opinion, but it simply doesn't correspond to the facts."

"You would have been sacked by Headquarters two months ago had the Chief not put in a word for you," said Collins, looking smug. "Headquarters are well aware that you are unsystematic and unreliable as well as extravagant. And now your behaviour about the flat has been the last straw."

Bob Owen's face whitened. Collins seemed to be coming straight at him, rasping and whirring like a lethal machine showing all its teeth. He shut his eyes for a moment till the whirring stopped. Yet he felt as if the machine were bound to hunt him down, however he doubled and ran.

The machine's whirring had stopped because a salad had arrived to feed the man. Bob Owen drank off another glass of wine while his own order, a nut and chocolate confection, was set before him.

"I have said that I am perfectly willing to give up my flat as soon as my wife and children have somewhere to go. That seems to me entirely reasonable."

This appeal to reason merely whetted Collins's appetite for logic.

"You were instructed by the Chief that the three senior officials of the Mission were to have the three Foreign Office houses. And instead of accepting these instructions, which it was your duty to do, you then wrote, most improperly, to the Foreign Office without consulting the Chief. That was unreasonable and disloyal. And I fail to see how you can possibly claim that the flat is your personal flat, since the rent of it is paid by the Mission and the furniture in it belongs to the Mission . . ."

"I have told you that I don't want to keep the furniture. And I'm willing to pay my own rent as long as my family needs the flat."

"If you mean to pay your own rent, which is, I may say, one of the highest in the country, by the device of collecting it from Miss Lidgard who collects it in turn from the Mission, that seems to me dishonest as well as impertinent."

"And my wife and children are to be turned out into the streets, are they? That's what all your threats and abuse amount to."

"The Chief has said that he is willing to extend the term until you find accommodation for them. But accommodation of some kind you must and will find as soon as possible. If you are as popular among Slavomanes as you like to think you are, you could easily persuade someone to take in your family, I should think."

Because it was quite unjustified, this sneer steadied Bob Owen. He spoke with dignity, gesturing only a little with his expressive hands.

"Look here, Mr Collins, you have called me dishonest and implied that I am a scoundrel and a sham. I am none of these things. I'm not even disobliging. I don't like disobliging other people; I never did. If you had come to me when I was leaving for Prsht and said, as man to man, that you would like to take over my flat, since there was little chance of my returning to the capital, and asked if we couldn't come to some arrangement about it, I should have agreed at once and all this unpleasantness would never have arisen. I'm only too willing to agree to anything that's put to me in a friendly manner. What I can't stomach is the *way* you're doing this."

"The Chief and I deliberately wanted to avoid making it a personal matter," declared Mr Collins. "We wanted it to be objectively established, as a matter of principle."

◆

Dick Zelezny sat listening to the trams with a growing sense of participation in their comings and goings. He knew exactly at what point, turning into the square on which the prison fronted, their wheels began to screech and squeal on the rails; he knew the stops at which they drew up; he knew the number of the tram that would take him home and every curve and twist of its devious route downhill to the Old Town.

Again and again in the past few days he had played the tram game, catching his tram just as it started, swinging himself up on to the end platform and asking for a ticket like any other passenger. It was part of the game not to fore-shorten the route, to recall every foot of the way, if possible, even to linger it out, until the last incredible moment when he pushed the button of the street-door bell and set his foot on the first step of the stair.

On this Saturday morning he needed more than ever to linger out the journey, since he had handed in his last book from the prison library and hope of imminent freedom made him restless. Surely by noon he would be discharged? On Saturdays the prison closed down at one o'clock; no visitors were allowed and no supper was given to the prisoners, who had to wait for their next meal until Sunday morning. It would be too much, it would be unbearable, if he had to endure another blank Saturday in his cell.

Tears rose into his eyes; a hot flush of resentment followed them so suddenly that he was disconcerted and ashamed. He had endured so much already; surely he could endure another Saturday?

The impatient movement he made started Odpustil off again.

"The President," he said, in a high, gabbling crow, "understands nothing about the soul, about the poetry of life. He is a mean, litigious haggler. The cage in which his soul cowers is barred on all sides by clichés. He cannot hear the songs the flowers sing."

He crooned over his chrysanthemums, nursing them at his bosom, until a spasm of dry coughing shook two of them on to the floor. With a cry of compassion he gathered them up again and comforted them.

It might be possible to do something for Odpustil, poor creature, thought Dick Zelezny. What if he *had* broadcast plays for the Occupying Power? It was pointless to keep him here, crazy, forgotten and starving on prison rations. There was so much that the Ministry of Justice must be ignorant of, including the starvation prison fare. For the Minister was a good man, a Social Democrat, and if he were only informed about the senseless cruelty of the system practised here, he would surely intervene.

Leaning forward, his hands clasped between his knees, Dick Zelezny pondered at length the arguments, buttressed by facts, that he would lay before the Minister. Incredible as it might seem, the routine established by the Occupying Power was still carrying on automatically in the City Jail; it had not been changed in a single particular. All inspections by the Ministry were announced well beforehand, so that the system could, and did, defend itself by producing for inspection only those prisoners whose friends sent in extra food for them from the restaurant outside or from their own stores. And the restaurant outside, of course, charged famine prices. For poor wretches like Odpustil, with neither money nor friends, prison rations meant slow starvation.

Zelezny felt in his pocket and then remembered that any money he had was laid by for him in the Commandant's office. It couldn't be much, but whatever the amount, he would leave it behind for Odpustil's benefit.

At last he allowed himself to look at his watch. The time was a little after ten. He would give them till half-past eleven. Of course there was a lot of paper work to be done. The examining judge would have to write out a full report, listing all the evidence and describing the procedure leading up to the verdict, and then he would have to collect various signatures from the Ministry of Justice before he could discharge his prisoner. Collecting the signatures alone would take time.

At half-past eleven Odpustil and Zelezny had finished their dinner but there was still no sound of important footsteps coming along the corridor. Suddenly dejected, Dick Zelezny hid his face in his hands. Odupstil sat down, or rather drifted on to the bench beside him, fidgeted and sighed loudly, then without a word tried to push one of his chrysanthemums into his fellow-prisoner's locked hands. At that the tears trickled through Dick Zelezny's fingers, and he let them flow.

The thought of Eleanor came as the first lightening of his misery. He had cause to be thankful there, deeply thankful. He rested for a while in the thought of Eleanor and then began to remind himself that few men were as blessed as he. What other woman would or could have done so much as Eleanor had done for him? It was like magic, what she had done. His good friend the Utopian Ambassador and his brother-in-law Honzik had wrought marvels too; but for them he would still be in police headquarters; yet Eleanor, alone, had made prison doors fly open before her. Never before in the history of the City Jail, he was sure, had the Chief Secretary connived at such doings. Zelezny could not help smiling a little, through his tears, to think of it.

"You have fought the good fight, my darling," Eleanor had said to him at that last interview in the Commandant's office. So he had. So he had.

The Utopian Mission would be grateful to him. He had stood out, he had not given in, he had not been browbeaten into providing any handle for use against the Utopian Mission. What did it matter that he was now in a tremulous state and that the merest trifle could move him to tears? It did not matter at all. Not at all.

His misery, he decided was mostly make-believe. Like the tram game. For of course he would not go home by tram. Eleanor would be waiting for him, whenever he was released, with a taxi, or perhaps even with a car from the Utopian Embassy or the Mission.

As twelve o'clock rang from the church tower in the square he dried his eyes and got up to take off his clean shirt and his good shoes. He folded the shirt and laid it on top of his bundle on the floor; slowly he shook out and donned the dirty shirt. In his old slippers he then turned to Odpustil and said in cheerful, belligerent tones: "The President is a Statesman of the first rank . . ."

Odpustil scuttled into a corner, backed against the wall and began to gabble. Zelezny walked round and round in the middle of the cell. Every now and then Odpustil darted past him into another corner, where he began a fresh tirade.

When the Commandant himself hastened along the corridor at a quarter to one and with a rattling of keys flung the door open, both Zelezny and Odpustil were taken by surprise.

◆

The soft wind was still blowing from the south as the afternoon darkened. "It almost smells of pussy-willows," said Mrs Russell to her husband when she bolted the verandah door for the night. At that moment the telephone rang and Dick Zelezny's voice spoke from it, saying: "Yes, this is me, myself. I'm home!"

Mr Collins was boasting to his wife how he had got the better of Mr Bob Owen, who was committed to handing over the keys of the flat, and the decree, as soon as lodgings had been found for his family. "And I'll see that lodgings *are* found, by next week, if possible," added Mr Collins, jingling the loose change in his pockets.

No less than five of the National Party Ministers had subscribed to the plan for eliminating the Communist Ministers from the Government, and were eagerly reminding each other that the Catholics and the Agrarians could certainly be drawn in too, and what about the Social Democrats?

And two leading executives of the Trade Union Combine — one of them the General Secretary — were privately agreeing to work in close co-operation with the Communists in return for direct representation in the Government.

All in all, an eventful day.

Chapter XIX

By Monday morning the wind was blowing from the east again and the temperature had dropped well below freezing-point. Mr Bower's car did nearly a half-turn on the glassy ice of the road-surface when he braked it to a stop outside Doctor Russell's gate. The stranger sitting on the front seat beside him cowered into his great-coat, looking miserable.

"This is Arthur Merrion, our new Music Officer," said Mr Bower. "Doctor Russell, Arthur."

Martin Russell took a back seat. As always, the atmosphere in the car blurred his mind with a chill fog of suspicion. When Bower and Collins sat together in front he usually felt that they had only just stopped aspersing him; to-day the new man, he was sure, had only just stopped listening to aspersions.

"When did you arrive?" he asked, trying to sound amiable.

"Saturday," said the stranger.

Well indoctrinated by this time, thought Doctor Russell. "Is your hotel comfortable?" he said aloud.

"Merrion is staying with me for the present," said Mr Bower.

Instinctively seeking to warm up his mind and rid it of suspicion, Doctor Russell said. "Isn't this grand news about Dick Zelezny?"

"Oh, you've heard about it, have you?"

"Why, of course. Dick rang us up on Saturday."

"H'm," said Mr Bower. "I confess I should feel happier if I had a letter from the Ministry of Justice to say that he is clear."

"You can't have any doubts about it, surely?" said Doctor Russell. "The case against him has been officially quashed.

Not that there ever *was* a case against him."

"I'm not at all sure that they may not be playing a cat and mouse game."

"What on earth should give you that idea?"

Mr Bower made no reply. Doctor Russell went on to say: "They're not likely to try trumping up another charge against Dick Zelezny after utterly failing to make this one good."

"I am inclined to fear, I must say, that this may be only the beginning and that we can expect worse things later," said Mr Bower in his primmest voice.

"I simply don't understand you."

Mr Bower drove the car cautiously round a corner and then explained that he was responsible for the Mission and that in his opinion the Mission incurred a grave risk, a grave risk, so long as it harboured Major Zelezny.

"Risk? What risk?" demanded Doctor Russell.

"The risk of his doing things without my authorisation," said Mr Bower. "He shouldn't send reports out anywhere without my seeing them, for instance. He shouldn't go to the Embassy without me. I cannot safely feel responsible for him while he indulges in unauthorised activities."

"You know as well as I do that both Dick and the Mission have done no spying of any kind. Now is the time, I should think, to write that innocence large. Now, if ever, you must stand by Dick Zelezny in a bold and generous manner," exclaimed Doctor Russell.

The new Music Officer gave a dry little cough. It was like a tap on the shoulder recalling Russell to suspicion and self-consciousness, so that he heard his own voice echoing too loudly. He said nothing more about Zelezny.

When the car stopped in the *porte-cochère*[1] of the Mission Palace, Russell glanced at the new man as they got out together, and was surprised to see a twinkle in his eye.

[1] carriage entrance

"I *have* got a cold, you know," said Merrion, smiling. "Just come from Cairo, and the difference in the temperature is rather trying."

Russell's answering smile transformed his face. "I'll be seeing you later, I suppose?" he said, and with a quick flirt of one ankle ran lightly up the steps.

"That was a cough of sheer amusement," he was thinking, "and no wonder!"

He waved a gay hand to Claude in the library, said to Mary Ballard: "Isn't it grand news about Dick?" and, still light-hearted, went into his room, where Jane Lidgard arrived a moment later.

"The new Music Officer's here," he confided to her. "I came up in the car with him. Do you know, Jane, I think he's going to be a man and a brother. An artist, of course, a musician; not a blasted official, thank God."

Half-way through the morning, when Doctor Russell was dictating letters, a tap came on his door and Dick Zelezny looked in.

"My dear Dick!" Martin Russell sprang to his feet and seized the visitor by both hands. "I never expected to see you here today — That'll do for just now, Jarmila — Come in, Dick, come in, and let me see how you are."

Dick Zelezny was thinner, almost haggard; his eyes were too large and too bright, thought Russell.

"It's good to see you again," said Dick.

"But what are you doing here, anyhow? Shouldn't you be taking it easy?"

Dick shrugged, laughed and sat down in the proffered arm-chair.

"Take it easy? I am to see the Minister of Justice this afternoon and the Foreign Minister this evening, and, more important still, I am commanded to the Chief's presence in about five minutes."

"Going to see Arch, are you?" said Doctor Russell, with a sudden sinking of the heart.

"He rang Eleanor up yesterday afternoon and made the appointment while I was asleep," said Dick, smiling. "Eleanor thinks he wants to hand me a bouquet or two. I suppose, if he does, I shall accept them with a good grace and ask for a week's leave of absence."

"Well, God knows you deserve bouquets," said Russell, looking anxious, "but, all the same . . ."

A fusillade of thumps on the door interrupted him and a medley of people entered the room, headed by Mary Ballard carrying two large and brimming cups of coffee.

"My spies told me you were here, Dick, and I felt that I must present you with a cup of my famous coffee to mark the joyful occasion."

"Oh, of course, special elevenses, isn't it, Mary? Thank you very much," said Dick.

"Oh, Dick, I *am* glad to see you," said Jane Lidgard.

"Turned up again, haven't you, like a bad penny?" said Mabel Smith, pump-handling him vigorously.

"Hello, old boy! They don't seem to have pulled out any of your teeth," said Claude.

Martin Russell managed to say, in an urgent voice. "Come and see me, do, when Arch is finished with you," before Dick, flushed and distracted, finally escaped to keep his appointment.

It was over half-an-hour before he came back. Hearing irregular footsteps in the passage outside Martin Russell opened his door quietly and quickly, so that Dick almost tumbled in. Moving like a blind man he groped his way to the arm-chair, propped his elbows on the desk and burst into tears.

Russell stood behind him, nervously patting him on the shoulder, and when the sobs were dying down put a handkerchief into his fingers.

"It is nothing, it will pass," said Dick, wiping his eyes. "I am a child at present; anything makes me weep."

"Blast and confound Arch," said Martin Russell. "What has he been doing to you?"

"I think he's trying to force me to resign."

"You haven't resigned, I hope?"

"No."

"Well, don't."

"Thank you, Martin."

"Have a cigarette."

"I am glad that I didn't weep until I came in here," said Dick. "I was very formal with Mr Bower, because he was very formal with me."

"What did he say?" asked Martin, knowing in advance the kind of thing he would hear. Dick recapitulated the conversation. Then he added: "So, you see, Martin, I am a liability to the Mission, not an asset. I am not to be trusted. Bower is convinced that I am guilty of something, only he does not know what. The Mission, in short, would be better without me. He suggested, I forgot to tell you, that I should leave the country until after the elections are over".

"Bloody nonsense," said Russell.

One should never be surprised at Bower's doing the mean thing, the timid thing, he was thinking; yet he had been surprised that morning in the car and he was still more surprised now.

"I suppose it's just because you're so vulnerable at the moment that Arch has been putting pressure on you," he said. "How like Arch!"

"He has always been jealous of my friendship with Sir Edward."

"That's it, of course! You've put your finger on it."

"I did not tell him that Eleanor and I are lunching at the

Embassy today, for I think he would have tried to forbid it."

"You're quite able to face the luncheon, are you?"

"I am always able to face what I want to do, Martin."

"And will you want to dine with us tomorrow night, as you said you would?"

"My dear Martin, Eleanor and I are looking forward to that dinner, very much."

"I promise you, we'll make it a celebration. And now, I think, I'll just see you home and go home early myself by tram . . ."

Flushing a little, Dick Zelezny protested that he was quite able to walk home without an escort, but Russell said:

"Do you think I want to stay here and possibly run into Arch after all this? I couldn't bear to meet him again this morning. The mere thought of him turns my stomach."

◆

Dick Zelezny's story, told at the dinner-table, made his hosts forget their duties.

It was best to begin at the beginning, said Dick, and so he told them simply how he was first interrogated at Police Headquarters, continuously, from seven o'clock in the evening until four o'clock next afternoon.

"My feet swelled up and hurt me," he said, "and in the end I couldn't help fainting. They kept asking me the same question, over and over again, like a constant drip of water on one spot: whether the Utopian Mission wasn't a spy organization. It's a technique the Russians have perfected, but I don't think our police are quite up to it yet, or they wouldn't have let me pass out. Fainting is an escape, you see. They should keep you just short of fainting until you would say anything to be let off from your misery. They told me between times that my accomplices had confessed and that there was written evidence of my guilt . . ."

"Oh yes," interrupted Martin Russell, "we heard next day about that written evidence."

"The only evidence they had, or could have, as I well knew, was the file of my correspondence with the Skrs Utopian Society. I didn't know, of course, what they might have forged; but it all came out at the hearing before the examining judge, and actually they had nothing at all except the Skrs file, which they had confiscated when they raided the Society. Eleanor and Sova, my lawyer, got hold of the corresponding file in my office, with the carbon copies of my letters, and put it in evidence before the judge to show how innocent it all was. My file and the Skrs file tallied exactly; the letters merely discussed the Society's charter and constitution, and the suitability of the secretary, Spalek . . . As for Spalek, when I was confronted with him and the other witnesses, Spalek simply broke down and withdrew all the charges, saying that the police had tied him to a radiator and beaten him until he could not help agreeing to what they asked. The whole case collapsed like a puff-ball. It was just a deliberate frame-up."

"And all this bullying and threatening and lying," said Jamesina Russell, "was deliberately done to incriminate an innocent man! Not to mention the thirty-six members of the Skrs Society — they were kept locked up too, weren't they?"

"Yes, they were. And I may tell you, if it hadn't been for Sir Edward and my brother-in-law, and other friends of mine who pushed the matter in Parliament, we should still all have been under lock and key in Police Headquarters."

"But Dick kept on saying: No," said Eleanor Zelezny.

"If they had been a little more subtle," said Dick, "if they had said to me: can you deny that the Utopian Mission is a spy organization, I should probably have said: No, for I had got set into saying: No. Most of the time I was past thinking or understanding anything: I only knew that I had to go on saying: No."

"It was very steadfast of you, Dick," said Jamesina.

"Dick came through it magnificently," said Eleanor.

Dick made a deprecating gesture and said: "One can never tell before-hand whether one can stand up to an ordeal. I couldn't have told. And I don't think I could do it again."

"You will never have to do it again," said Eleanor.

"I remember feeling sorry for Spalek, when he broke down before the judge," said Dick. "It might have been me, I thought."

He went on to tell them about his cell-mate Odpustil. His arguments with Odpustil, he said, roused him from apathy and strengthened his spirit. They were the craziest arguments, too, for Odpustil was quite mad, poor creature. He had been nearly three years in jail with no chance of coming to trial, and still insisted that he was going to triumph over the President. He carried some withered flowers about with him like icons, said Dick, and he was more a walking skeleton than a man, for prison fare simply meant slow starvation.

"Oh, Dick, slow starvation is what you're having here," said Jamesina. "Some more of this stuffed veal? Carve him another bit, Martin. And you haven't anything to drink, either."

"Dick left three hundred crowns in the Commandant's office for Odpustil," said Eleanor, "to buy him extra food. We're going to hand in some more and a bunch of fresh flowers."

"I'm very grateful to Odpustil," said Dick.

"What *did* they give you to eat in prison?" asked Jamesina.

Dick smiled and ticked off the meals on his fingers: "Breakfast, at six-thirty: one bowl of watery soup and one thick slice of black bread. Dinner, at eleven: one potato, good; one potato, bad; some sauce. Twice a week a small bit of meat. Supper, at three: one bowl of watery soup, no bread. That was all. On Saturdays we got no supper."

"But Dick has told the Minister of Justice all about it," said Eleanor. "Would you believe it, the Minister didn't know!"

"There was much the Minister didn't know," said Dick. "The discipline of the jail, for instance, is exactly what it was in the occupation. There was a commandant at that time who thought it a good joke to make the prisoners say: "Good morning the Commandant and the Commandant's lady", and the prisoners still have to stand at attention every morning and say that. Then there's an outer circle in the yard for exercise, and a small inner circle for invalids. But you join the inner circle only on a medical certificate, and the doctor issues these only in the mornings, so that if you're jailed of an afternoon with a broken leg you *must* hobble round the outer circle. And if you have money, or your friends have money, you can get food sent in. Prisoners who have these extra rations are the only ones shown to the jail inspectors, so that the Ministry has the impression that prisoners are fed well enough."

"But the Slavomanes who know about this," said Eleanor, "are going to bring it all up in Parliament. The Minister, too."

"The Minister is a good man," said Dick. "He was horrified at what I told him."

"So it may be all to the good that you were arrested?" said Jamesina, doubtingly.

Gossip ran like wildfire through the prison, Dick told them. The outer and the inner circle talked from the corners of their mouths as they passed each other.

"On my very first day every man in the outer circle said: Cheers for the West! And even the examining judge whispered to me: 'I'm for the West too.' He was a great comfort to me, that judge. He said one day: 'It won't take long.' And another day, when I asked for a fresh book to read, he said: 'How quickly you read your books! I'll get you one, certainly, but I don't think you'll have time to finish it.' That was when I began to allow myself to hope. And then . . ."

Dick looked at Martin, at Jamesina, at Eleanor. He picked up Eleanor's hand and kissed it.

"And then — my dear Eleanor came to see me in the Commandant's office. Such a thing had never happened before, I think, in the whole history of the City Jail. I could hardly believe my eyes when I was sent for to the office and saw her there."

"The Chief Secretary of the jail was *very* good to me," said Eleanor. "He did all that he could for me. He sent in my parcels of clean clothes and food to Dick, which was kind of him, but the greatest kindness of all was his letting me see Dick. He let me see Dick twice. I couldn't tell anyone, of course, because it had to be a secret, a close, close secret. Wasn't it wonderful?"

"I think we should drink a toast to that Chief Secretary," said Martin Russell, going round with the wine.

"The last time was just a week ago today darling," said Eleanor.

"Only a week ago?" said Dick. "It seems in a different dimension of time altogether."

"But, please," said Eleanor, setting down her glass after the toast had been drunk, "don't tell anyone else. I wasn't going to tell even you. My pet of a Chief Secretary mustn't get into trouble on my account."

"I'm very glad Dick did tell us," said Jamesina. "In the middle of so much dreadfulness it's a help to know that there are kind people in the world."

"Most people *are* kind," said Eleanor. "That's one thing I've discovered. Sir Edward and Lady Thring, for instance, have been kindness itself. Do you know, Sir Edward lent me one of the Embassy's cars? I had to keep rushing about to see the lawyer and all the other people, and I don't know how I could have managed without the car. And then, of course, I was able to take Dick home in it."

"Triumphantly," said Jamesina.

"Triumphantly indeed. And when we got upstairs, there was Ruzi laughing and crying at once, and we didn't know ourselves which to do."

CHAPTER XX

The Mission's usual activities were being disrupted, as sometimes happened, by an inconsequence of Distinguished Visitors. These luminaries, political, scientific or literary, had their courses plotted for them at Headquarters, courses which they followed across Europe more or less erratically. Several of them had now fetched up in Mr Bower's place, like clots in a blood-stream, and needed transit visas, train and hotel accommodation, extra travelling allowances or merely interviews with Slavomane notables and audiences for lectures. Senior officers of the Mission had to drop whatever they were doing and organise luncheons, improvise Press conferences, or sit through formal dinners arranged by Mr Collins in order of official precedence.

Doctor Russell was happier on this occasion than usual, since one of the visitors, a writer called Sandford, was a personal friend who had consented, after persuasion, to spend an evening at the College giving an informal talk and answering questions. It was like breathing a larger, freer air for a while. In this foreign service, Russell explained, one missed one's own background. At home, after a day in the office, there would be a circle of one's own to take refuge in, but Utopian officials here were thrown willy-nilly upon each other for company, if they wanted relief from the foreign atmosphere, and so, in a sense, they never got away from the office.

"I feel I'm turning into a blasted official myself," he said, to Sandford's amusement. "Seeing you is like an oasis in the wilderness."

"Is it because this is a Slavomane wilderness?" asked the visitor. "You wouldn't feel like that in France or in Italy, would you?"

"There might be less of a foreign feeling about France or Italy," said Russell, "but I'm in no condition to judge. The wilderness I mean is an official wilderness. I like the Slavomanes, especially my University students, and I like my work, but I hate the blasted officials I have to work with. There's a stifling, pettifogging atmosphere . . . Oh well," he broke off, "perhaps any other office would be as bad."

The new Music Officer seemed to belong to the oasis rather than the wilderness. Collins's table arrangements usually placed Russell and Merrion together, at a far remove from the Distinguished Visitors; they chatted to each other about new books, music and schools of French painting, which Merrion had some knowledge of, in an easy manner, without insistence or the obtrusion of private vanities. Merrion was a bit of a cynic, Russell decided; he had a way of touching his moustache, saying something derogatory, tossing off a glass of wine and shrugging his shoulders that was positively raffish. Russell enjoyed this raffish nonchalance and followed his colleague's example in drinking a good deal of wine.

An evening reception in the great ball-room was staged for the visitors after the last formal dinner on Thursday, so that the ladies of the Mission, who had been excluded from the dinner on a plea of economy, might grace the occasion adequately, though inexpensively. To save the cost of waiters Mrs Collins, who was in charge of arrangements, had instructed Miss Lidgard, Miss Smith, Miss Finestone and Miss Ballard to put on their best frocks, carry round trays and make themselves generally helpful. Mrs Owen was also invited, at the suggestion of Mrs Bower, who wished to have a few words with her in private.

"So you'll head the Receiving Line, Victoria," said Mrs Collins. "I stand second, Mrs Russell third, and do you really think Mrs Owen fourth?"

"Yes, I think that would be fairer than asking her just to carry round refreshments."

"Well, it does make the Receiving Line longer."

Mrs Collins had been shocked to see that there was no Receiving Line at the College Social Evening. Doctor and Mrs Russell had stood about near the door welcoming people in a casual manner, obviously unaware that the Bowers and the Collinses should have been given precedence and made known to the many College members who had not met them. This time, things were to be done properly.

On the way to the palace Mrs Bower called for Iris Owen, and, once the door of the car was shut upon her, began scolding. It was *most* inconsiderate of the Owens, she said, to insist on sticking to their flat when the Mission needed it so badly. She had expected better things of Iris.

"And your husband has written a *very* rude letter to Arch. I was astounded when I saw what was in it."

"Did you see the letter *your* husband wrote to him first?"

"But my husband is the Head of the Mission! It's really too much if Arch is to meet with impertinence from his staff, I must say. He's being dreadfully overworked; he's had to do all Major Zelezny's work as well as his own; he hasn't had nearly enough sleep; and now he has all these visitors on his hands; it's more than any man can bear to be met with rudeness from subordinates, on top of everything else.

"What business had your husband, for instance, to write to the Foreign Office? And what business had you to take Miss Lidgard into the flat, when you knew very well that you were supposed to leave it?"

Mrs Owen shrank wordlessly into her corner. But when Mrs Bower for the third time used the expression: "representational flat," she plucked up courage to say: "It isn't a representational flat at all; it never was; it's just our private flat."

"Well, Doctor Russell has always told my husband that he got these flats as representational flats, and, if yours isn't representational, he had no business to say so. In any case, how can it be your private flat if the Mission bought the furniture and pays the rent?"

"The Mission only bought some of the furniture." Mrs Bower made the sound usually transcribed as: Pshaw!

"If you had any consideration at all for other people, you would stop quibbling about your decree and simply hand it over with the keys. They always do that in the Embassy," she concluded, as the car drew up at the palace.

"Karnet," she said to the chauffeur, sharply, for her conscience told her that she should have picked up Mrs Russell as well as Mrs Owen, "fetch Mrs Russell now, as fast as you can, and then go onto the restaurant to help bring the gentlemen here."

◆

Mrs Russell had been surprised by an unexpected visit from her neighbours, Mrs Rychlik of the second-floor flat and Mrs Steiner of the top floor. Mrs Steiner, who could speak some Utopian and liked to air it, made herself the spokeswoman.

"Can we talk a moment, Mrs Russell?"

"Of course, of course. Do come in."

Knowing what was expected of her, Mrs Russell brought out plum brandy and liqueur glasses, asking:

"And how is your baby, Mrs Steiner?"

"Thank you, thank you, already five kilo," said the smiling mother. Yet her business was so urgent that not even her baby could side-track it, and not even the thought of her baby could keep the smile on her face. Mr Rychlik, she explained, had had occasion that afternoon to go down to the basement to rebuke the porter and had made the appalling discovery that the supply of furnace coke for the building was nearly finished. There was only enough left for less than a week's heating. And the allowance had been ample, thanks to the Russells' diplomatic ration of coke; it should have lasted until the end of March, or even the middle of April. What was to be done? That thief of a porter must have stolen it and sold it on the black market. It could never be re-covered. Doubtless he was a Communist and trusted that the Party would protect him if he were accused, but even if he were to be convicted, the coke was gone. "We shall all freeze to death, Mrs Russell," wailed Mrs Steiner. "We shall get no more from the Fuel Ministry. Unless you can claim extra from the Foreign Office, we shall all freeze to death."

Mrs Russell promised to see what could be done. A privileged foreigner, she felt it her duty to come to the rescue. Surely the Foreign Office, she said, would manage to get her some coke from the intractable Fuel Ministry. As for the unspeakable porter —!

Mrs Steiner's knowledge of Utopian broke down here under the vehemence of her wrath against the porter, and the three ladies relieved their feelings in rich Slavomanian invective against the porter, who, like all house-porters appointed by National Committees after the Liberation, was a Communist spy.

His only known qualification for the job, pointed out Mrs Rychlik.

"He'll freeze to death, too, if that's any comfort," said Mrs Russell, as she showed her visitors out.

This incursion delayed her, so that Karnet had to wait nearly ten minutes before she was ready; when she reached the palace the gentlemen were already beginning to arrive from the dinner, and the Receiving Line was hard at work.

She shook hands with Victoria Bower, muttering: "Sorry I'm late," slipped into place between Maisie Collins and Iris Owen, and began herself to how-d'ye-do the file of guests, who were passed along from one right hand to the next as in some truncated version of a country dance.

When a lull came, she turned to Iris, meaning to whisper: "Doesn't this make you feel a fool?" and found herself saying: "Iris, my dear, don't you feel well?"

"I have a dreadful headache," said Iris, whose face was grey.

Mrs Russell took her by the arm, saying: "Let's sneak out. Most of the guests have come, anyway."

She piloted the younger woman across the ball-room to the far end of the buffet, where Jane Lidgard provided a cup of strong black coffee and a chair.

"I have some aspirin in my bag," said Jane.

Iris Owen's teeth chattered on the rim of the cup, but she swallowed two tablets and drank up the coffee.

"I'll be all right," she said. "It's only — it's only . . ."

"Don't bother about it just now, whatever it is."

"Victoria simply attacked me in the car. About the f-f-flat. It's only nerves."

She blew her nose and dabbed powder on her face, shivering as she sat; unhappiness seeped from her and spread, so that her two companions instinctively drew together.

"I'll look after Iris," said Jane. "Hadn't you better go back to the line, Jamesina? You know what they'll say if you don't."

Mrs Russell hovered uncertainly.

"Go on," said Jane Lidgard. "As soon as is decent, I'll get Karnet to take us both home; he won't be needed by the high-ups for ages yet. I don't enjoy these parties and I'll be glad to get away."

"Plain Jane and no nonsense, yes, I know," said Jamesina, cocking an eye at Jane's high-necked grey frock.

"This is my elegant demi," retorted Jane, "and I've even put on my gold chain and cross. What more could Maisie expect?"

"Iris, my dear, will you go home with Jane in a little?"

"As long as I don't have to wait for Victoria, I d-don't care what I do."

Unwillingly Mrs Russell returned to duty. But the Receiving Line was already breaking up into clusters around Mrs Bower and Mrs Collins. Near them stood a solitary stranger who looked as if he had just been passed through the mill and was uncertain what to do next, a man with a keen, pleasant face. To Mrs Russell he seemed an easy altar on which to make her sacrifice.

"Are you one of the visitors from Utopia?" she asked.

"Yes, I am."

"Well, have you tried Slavomanian plum brandy yet?"

"No, I don't think I have."

"Sometimes it's crude, but when it's good it's very good, and I believe we have some of the export brand here to-night."

"Do you recommend it?"

Mrs Russell edged him away from the others towards the buffet, which was set out this evening on the long, high desk, much decorated in front with swags of ormolu, that shut off the dais at one end of the ball-room.

"A charming room," said the stranger.

"Yes, we live in gorgeous splendour, don't we?"

"How long have you been here?"

"About two and a half years."

"Then you could tell me quite a lot about Slavomania, couldn't you? Do you speak the language?"

"I do speak it," admitted Mrs Russell, picking up a tall

square-shouldered bottle and pouring into a glass what looked like clear white gin.

She stood watching Iris Owen at the far end of the buffet as she said: "How do you like the plum brandy?"

"It's much better than I expected. But aren't you going to have some yourself?"

Mrs Russell's attention came back as if a string had been tugged; her eyes met the stranger's with a shock of appraisal that told him how little she had previously been aware of him. Her obvious penitence made him smile.

"You will tell me something about Slavomania, I hope?"

"It's a distracting place," she said, smiling back. "But if it's trade statistics you want, or the inner workings of the educational system, I'm afraid I can't help you. I never know these things."

"I can get all that in blue-books," said the stranger. "I'd rather hear what you do know."

He spoke confidently, as if he had sensed that in using the word "help" she had committed herself.

"What I know is only what I happen to see and hear," said Mrs Russell, making up her mind that she liked this man. "But I can tell you something about that. Well, for instance, when we first came to this country, my husband and I, we found . . ."

In describing the effects on the populace of the Occupation and the Liberation, Mrs Russell, led on by suggestions from the stranger, surprised herself by drawing general conclusions from the particulars she related.

"When you are governed by an enemy who regards you as an inferior helot, you must develop a kind of double vision, I suppose; you see yourself with your own eyes and with his eyes too. For young people just growing up that's very bad, don't you think? . . . They were living in a general climate of humiliation. They had no experience of living on equal terms in a friendly world. And so we found it difficult at first to get the young Slavomanes to treat us as friends, to understand that we didn't expect them to look *up* to us, and had no intention of looking *down* on them, but wanted us all to look *across* at each other . . . The very way I tell you this betrays, doesn't it, how much we had to emphasise the free and equal attitude? And that was a bad thing too. Even now I sometimes hear myself overdoing it. But they are beginning to trust us, although I don't know how deep their confidence goes.

"These evils can't be cured in a couple of years, can they? Whenever I go into the great park at the end of our street, I still can't help remembering that Slavomanes weren't allowed to sit or walk in it during the Occupation. And if you are told, day in and day out, that your race has no higher intelligence, no literature beyond the folk-lore level, no independent history, no language fit for civilised uses, how can you grow a healthy self-respect? So a good few Slavomanes today are a bit unbalanced, a bit too intense . . . It comes out in odd ways, you know, some of them rather endearing. Once they start a party, for instance, or a sing-song, they never want to stop; they will go on and on and on, long after we are all worn out."

"That may be just a difference in temperament."

"Well, perhaps . . . I think Slavomanes do have more vitality than we have. But they work with mad intensity, too. And the same lack of balance comes out in their films, especially in the historical films, which are vehemently heroic and much too full of violence and loud bangs and shoutings."

"I suppose the Occupation has left a good deal of frustrated aggressiveness in them?"

"I shouldn't have thought of putting it like that, but yes, I suppose so."

"Delinquency must be a problem, then?"

"Now, that's the kind of thing I don't know. One meets it, of course, in particular instances. Our own house-porter has been stealing our coke. And there's a lot of petty knavery in the shops. A friend of mine bought a pretty umbrella, for example, and, when she put it up, first the handle fell off and then the cover shrank and crawled right up the ribs, so that it was only fit to be thrown away. But there are smart alecks of the get-rich-quick kind in every capital city, I should think . . . No, the disquieting thing is this: if you want to be violent, you have only to join the Communist Party and get into the police."

The stranger looked startled.

Mrs Russell told him about Dick Zelezny's experiences and added: "I have been thinking back over our time here, and I can see that some interested party has always been trying to stir up mud and malice. I am pretty sure now that it must have been the Communist Party. Not so very long ago I saw a crowd standing before the windows of the Party newspaper in the Square and I stopped to look. There was an enlarged photograph stuck up, labelled: Utopian atrocities in Greece. It was a mounted soldier in battle-dress with what looked like a severed head swinging at his saddle-bow. The soldier's head had been blacked out. I looked very closely at it, and the head at the saddle-bow, I could swear, was a plaster head, with the agonised expression you might see on a baroque statue, or representing Tragedy in a theatre, and it had been smeared with paint to look like blood, — or it may have been real blood. To my eyes, a palpable fake, even if I hadn't known that our soldiers don't display heads at their saddle-bows, far less pose for photographs of that kind. And the soldier's face was blacked out, so that his Utopian battle-dress didn't really mean a thing. Yet the Communists had deliberately prepared and stuck up that photograph to suggest that Utopians go in for atrocities. A deliberate incitement to hatred and anger. Well, that gave me a nightmare feeling. Since then, I usually stop at that window to see the latest exhibits and I notice that all their cartoons and photographs incite people to violence and hatred. At the moment, it's factory owners and merchants that are being reviled."

"How do the populace react, do you know?"

"They just stare and look expressionless; it's difficult to tell. But I think that they don't believe all they see or half of what they're told, even although the Communists are stirring up mud so frantically. After all, the vitality and strength of the Slavomanes come from the farms and villages; the layer of town life seems to me comparatively thin. And the farms and villages have old traditions — very old. Even today, at village fairs in the south, they show puppet plays about wicked Turkish pashas; their traditions go right back to the Turkish invasion of Europe."

Mrs Russell was now seeking to allay any alarm she might have communicated.

"I admit," she said, "that I did have a nightmare feeling for a while, and it's difficult not to spread one's personal nightmare over everything. But, after all, Dick Zelezny was acquitted.

"And in spite of the Communists we are popular here. Why, if you want to see a Utopian film you have to book a seat weeks ahead, while the Russian film shows are always more than half empty; you can walk straight in, I'm told."

They stood companionably together, leaning against the buffet, half turned away from the room, absorbed in talk. Mr Collins caught sight of them and at once began to radiate eagerness, like a terrier catching sight of a rabbit. Hastily he explained something to Mrs Collins and began to push his way towards the buffet.

"What makes you say that the layer of town life seems comparatively thin? The Slavomanes make a success of their heavy industries, don't they?"

"I can't tell you where the heavy industries come in. It has only struck me sometimes that farm ways and farm habits come right into Slavomane town kitchens, even in the capital. I have to buy traditional farm-style cooking-pots for my kitchen because I can't get any others, heavy industry or no. Pots that burn your fingers dreadfully; they have only small ears to lift them by, no handles, and the ears aren't even insulated. I have seen farm-house taps in modern flats here, with small splash-bowls under them and no sink, so that dishes have to be washed in a separate tin basin on a separate dresser. Then nearly all the Slavomane women I know spend hours on their feet giving themselves varicose veins, grinding and pulverising and triturating food and flavourings as if modern machinery didn't exist. And you should see the farm-house helpings they set before their men! Slavomanes even in the capital eat as if they had just come in from the harvest-field . . ."

"Hello, hello, there you are!" cried Mr Collins. "I've been looking for you all evening. You must have got into the wrong car. My wife is very anxious to meet you, my dear fellow."

Mr Collins, at his most matey, put a hand under the stranger's elbow and began to urge him away. The stranger freed his arm and said:

"I didn't come by car at all; I walked. It wasn't very far. And I've been having a most interesting talk . . ."

"I'm afraid I've rather monopolised you," interposed Mrs Russell, holding out her hand. "We'd better say good-night to each other."

"I have very much enjoyed meeting you," said the stranger.

"And I you," said Mrs Russell.

She watched him being introduced to Maisie, who fluttered in a way that advertised his social importance.

"Who's that man talking to the Collinses?" she asked her husband a few minutes later.

"That chap? Oh, a pleasant chap; he walked here from the restaurant with Sandford and me. I believe he's a law lord, but I don't remember his name."

"He *is* a pleasant man," said Jamesina. "The kind of man one can talk to. What a relief it is to meet people from outside, once in a while."

"Just what I feel about Sandford. And yet he told me that he would give his eyes to change places with me. I think he's fallen in love with all the neon lights in the streets."

"How little visitors know about what's really going on," said Jamesina, unaware of any irony in her words.

Mr Collins suddenly clapped his hands and called out in his penetrating voice: "Ladies and Gentlemen, the Chief has an announcement to make."

Standing near the piano Mr Bower said; "We are now to have the pleasure of listening to a sonata composed by Arthur Merrion and played by the composer himself." He looked round the room and added weightily: "This will be the first performance of the sonata in Slavomania."

With exaggerated nonchalance Arthur Merrion slouched rather than walked to the instrument, a cigarette in one corner of his mouth, twiddled the piano-stool, sat down and very carefully laid his cigarette on the rim of the piano-frame, the lit end well away from the wood. The agile Collins leaped forward and set a glass tray beneath the cigarette. Merrion, scowling at him, said: "Take that thing away; it'll rattle." "Oh, sorry," said Collins, and with great presence of mind removed both ash-tray and cigarette.

Merrion shrugged his shoulders, poised his hands and

almost contemptuously it seemed, brought them down on the keys but his touch was crisp, his playing brilliant. Crystalline arabesques of sound soared up and around him; patterns of harmony, patterns of discord, formed and re-formed, even, passionless, mathematical.

Martin Russell, on a small gilt chair beside his wife, looked puzzled for a while and then began to fidget. Between the first and second movements he whispered to Jamesina: "Frost-flowers, that's all." By the end of the sonata he was bored as well as restless. "Fancy skating on ice," he said, under cover of the hand-clapping. "Brilliant figure skating on ice; but ice, ice, ice."

"Is this the winter of your discontent?" said Jamesina.

"I fear so. I did have hopes of Merrion, but I don't like this at all."

CHAPTER XXI

Doctor Russell got up earlier than usual next morning to give his friend Sandford a hospitable send-off, but as he made his way back to the office, he kept suspecting, with some perversity, that his early rising had been prompted less by friendship than by a wish to evade the later journey with Arch in the Black Maria. The thought of the Small Conference which Arch had called for eleven o'clock depressed him and by the time he reached the conference room he was well below par. Too much junketing, he said to himself, looking with a peevish eye at the Chief, who seemed indecently perky. Merrion, on the other hand, attending a Small Conference for the first time, was clearly suffering from a hangover.

Dick Zelezny was not present. Mr Bower explained that Major Zelezny was being given a week's leave of absence to recuperate; indeed, a fortnight's leave of absence, or even longer, might prove desirable. Mr Merrion, however, was a welcome recruit to their numbers, and, he ventured to say, at no distant date other recruits would be forthcoming on the same high level.

"I have been summoned to Headquarters," said Mr Bower, "and I shall be leaving by air this afternoon. I shall be away until the middle of next week, and I am assured by Headquarters that when I return I shall bring back with me the new Education Officer and the new Medical Officer. We shall then be able to organise this Centre as it should be organised."

Collins was yes-yessing as usual, thought Russell, but wasn't Merrion yes-yessing too? Arch was looking complacent, beaming first upon Merrion, the momentary favourite, then upon Collins. Merrion was scowling rather than beaming, but he was nodding his head, so that one could assume he was saying "Yep" and not "Nope" whenever he opened and shut his lips.

"But now that we have our Music Officer," said Mr Bower, "I suggest that we should plan a series of really good concerts. What do you think, Arthur?"

This was an unexceptionable proposal; even Doctor Russell was yes-yessing now. It was Merrion who showed some recalcitrance when the Chief, in his enthusiasm, suggested that the first concert might come off by the end of next week, say Friday.

"I should need more time than that," he growled. "I don't know yet what resources there are."

"We have *you*," said Mr Bower, turning to him with affectionate indulgence. "And we all know by this time what a brilliant performer you are, Arthur. I confess I am eager to let the best musical circles in the city hear what you can do. You could carry the whole concert yourself."

Merrion muttered about "time to practice."

"We could lighten the programme for Merrion," put in Collins, "by inviting a Slavomane quartet to play a few items."

"A very good idea," said Russell, "a joint programme of Utopian and Slavomanian music would please everyone."

This surprising harmony of opinion did not reassure Doctor Russell, since he was groping in his mind for some explanation of the Chief's sudden trip to Headquarters, but it reassured and soothed Mr Bower, who was unable to differentiate between sympathy for his proposals and sympathy for himself. With sympathy flowing towards him, he could best unfold his powers and channel the flow in the right direction for any constructional engineering he had in mind. On this occasion he told himself that his Master Plan looked like being carried easily into effect, after all.

With a shrug, Merrion yielded to pressure and admitted that a concert next Friday evening might be possible, could a Slavomane quarter be procured at such short notice.

"Oh, there are so many of them," said Mr Bower, who was not in the mood to foresee difficulties, "that I feel sure we can get a good one. And you could get out the list of invitations by Monday or Tuesday, Collins, I think? We shouldn't invite too many people; quality, not quantity, is what we must aim at."

He and Collins began to rehearse the names of functionaries and notabilities who should be invited.

"The Professor of Music in the University," said Mr Bower.

"The Director of the National Theatre," said Mr Collins.

"The conductor of the Slavomane Philharmonic."

"Count and Countess Polishensky" —

"I suppose we'll have to change the College programme for that Friday night, then," said Doctor Russell.

"Oh, do you have something on?" asked Collins.

"We have something on every Friday. Tonight, for instance, we have a Symposium on Winter. And next Friday we have a Brains Trust down on the syllabus. But we could put that off for a week, of course, and let our members attend the concert instead."

A silence fell. The milk of human kindness, which had been flowing so freely, seemed to have curdled all at once. Before a word was spoken Doctor Russell was aware of the curdling.

He was in a perverse mood, as he knew, despising himself and suspecting others, but he knew also that he was not mistaken in sensing hostility to the College, even although he had been deliberately probing for it. There it was.

Mr Collins was the first to give tongue. It was quite out of the question, he said, to sacrifice quality to quantity in an audience; the Chief was perfectly right. One could not send out invitations to distinguished people and then let then be swamped by every Tom, Dick and Harry.

"You talk as if I were proposing to let loose a rabble of sans-culottes on a royal garden-party," said Doctor Russell. "May I point out that many distinguished people are members of the College?"

"I am afraid, Martin, that it is a question of numbers," said Mr Bower. "This is to be a series of small and select concerts on a high level, for the musical élite of the city, a series to be sponsored by the Mission, not by the College."

"The people who join the College pay a substantial yearly fee for the privilege," persisted Doctor Russell, "and they may feel slighted if they are to be excluded from these concerts."

"Is there any reason why they should know about the concerts at all?" said Mr Bower with quiet smoothness. "We can take it, I think, that your regular Friday night programmes should not be interfered with for the present, and that we can postpone our first Concert until Saturday, say, or Sunday evening. But there is no doubt that the audience should be small and select; you agree with me, Arthur, don't you?"

Arthur Merrion did agree, and Doctor Russell was left in a minority of one.

This was not what made him look sick, although the others thought so. What sickened him was his conviction that Arch's hostility to the College had now hardened in a set pattern which could not be unmade. He was certain that Arch saw the College and the Mission fronting each other like two incompatible powers.

So he was not surprised when Mr Bower, almost casually, just as the conference was breaking up, remarked: "Oh, by the way, Martin, I have just heard from Headquarters that

Owen is to be regarded as permanently transferred to Prsht. Headquarters think that his services in Prsht are too valuable to be dispensed with. It looks as if our little scheme of utilising the Education Officer as Senior Tutor in the College will now have to come into operation."

Quite mechanically Doctor Russell said: "And Bob Owen will have to give up his flat, I suppose?"

"Owen will return his flat to the Mission, of course," said Mr Bower, with some stiffness.

Doctor Russell, as he left the conference room, told himself, using a favourite expression of Bob Owen's, that Arch was going to Headquarters not merely to do the dirty on Dick Zelezny, as he had been suspecting, but also to do the dirty on the College.

◆

Mrs Russell, too, was feeling out of sorts that morning. As usually after an evening function, she had found it difficult to fall asleep and had spent too many of the small hours in going over, with dissatisfaction, what she had said and done at the reception. In especial she was dissatisfied with what she had said to the pleasant stranger about Slavomania. How could one generalise about a whole country? Any impression one had, of a foreign country in particular, was likely to be blurred and biased, far from accurate. And then to generalise from details like cooking-pots and wash-taps! She had been heavily sententious, she felt, and full of false information.

Yet what she had said about Dick and the police was true enough. And all that story about the fake plaster head was true and relevant. In the cold lucidity of these restless small hours her mind invalidated everything she had been formulating on the previous evening except these rather disquieting, rather sinister facts, the nightmare elements which she had been at such pains to play down. They were left hanging like a menacing back-cloth behind the stage of her day-time activities.

With more decision than usual, therefore, she belittled the alarmist gossip which Annushka brought back from the milk-shop and the news-agent's, where the cooks and housewives of the neighbourhood foregathered for the morning milk and newspapers. Today the rumours concerned Austria. Austria was on the point of going Communist, which would inevitably cause the Western Powers to intervene with atomic bombs.

"What *nonsense*, Annushka!"

"True, someone did say that the bombs would not drop until Italy went Communist too," admitted Annushka.

"Don't you believe a word of it. I wish I knew who starts all these silly rumours."

For her own sake and Annushka's Mrs Russell began to weave again that tissue of reassurances which, like Penelope, she had unwoven by night. She was therefore unwilling to accept the prognostications of disaster to the College which her husband brought home with him at luncheon time.

"We have passed the point of no return, as somebody or other said," lamented Martin Russell. "The situation has stopped being fluid."

Mrs Russell, who disliked fatalism, was mildly sarcastic.

"The eggs, I suppose, have begun to scramble and can't be unscrambled."

"Oh, any metaphor you like," said Martin Russell irritably. "But Arch will go on now until he has swallowed up the College. He's bringing his new Cabinet Ministers back with him on Wednesday."

He stared at his wife with a distraught look.

"He'll play them off against each other until he has them all yes-yessing around him like Merrion and Collins."

"I think you should go to bed for the afternoon. We have

the Winter Symposium tonight."

"Oh, damn! There's a final rehearsal this afternoon, and I forgot to tell you."

"What time?"

"Three o'clock."

"Nearly an hour and a half yet. And we can take a taxi." Mrs Russell was solicitous now instead of sarcastic. "Do lie down for an hour, darling. You may have caught a chill this morning going out so early; it was bitterly cold."

And that reminds me, she said to herself, after she had coaxed her husband into lying down, I haven't been able to get hold of Vladimir yet, about the coke. And Dick's away in the country.

She looked out her script for the Symposium, a programme of prose and poetry pieces about winter in Utopia, selected and fitted with a narrative framework by Martin Russell, who was himself to be the Narrator. A diversification of lyrics and children's rhymes, which a volunteer choir of three voices from the Mission staff had agreed to sing, had been inserted to give the Readers a respite. A nice programme, thought Mrs Russell, running her eye over it, but it'll be the better for a final rehearsal. I hope Martin isn't sickening for influenza. — No, no, of course he isn't; he's only tired.

Yet the anxiety in the background of her mind kept on projecting unbidden fears, for when she rang up the Foreign Office later, only to be told again that Doctor Mladski was not in the building, her first thought was that he might be ill, her second that he might have been arrested.

She dismissed these apprehensions, too, yet they only returned to base, as it were, and skulked there, ready to spring out in another form. When she finally picked up the telephone receiver to order a taxi, a discouraging line from a poem she had once read came into her mind: *vaguely life leaks away;*[1] while at the same time she felt that if she did not manage to get a taxi, it would be an omen.

A harsh voice from the taxi-rank replied, the taxi came, and so the Russells' departure was not ominous. Huddled in the small taxi, jolting through busy, indifferent streets that looked the same as usual, both the Russells were shaken out of their preoccupations. Then the stimulus of immediate tasks, the need to be open and friendly with one person after another, to join in reading a script, to control the timing of three unpractised voices belonging to Miss Finestone, Miss Ballard and the Mission Accountant, acted upon them both as the point of a needle acts on the reluctant cog-wheels of an old watch, pushing them round until the mechanism ticks over of itself.

After rehearsing, the cast adjourned to the Tea-Room, where there was a buzz of general cheerfulness. Mr Merrion looked in, seemed shrinkingly surprised at the light-hearted gaiety of the atmosphere, ventured across the threshold, got himself a cup of tea from the buffet and sat down beside Doctor Russell. If Merrion had been told that there was a rift between Mission and College, thought Russell, he must now be feeling perplexed by the good-humoured comradeship between Mission and College Staff at the small tables. The split certainly did not originate from below; it was made from above, and did not extend far down.

Merrion kept looking round the Tea-Room, saying only a few words now and then to Doctor Russell, and little by little abandoned his defensive; he had a second cup of tea; he ate a sandwich.

"You seem very gay in here," he remarked at last.

"Gayer than usual, I think," said Russell, "and I really don't know why. Unless it's because we've just had a good rehearsal and will probably give a good show tonight."

[1] From "As I walked out one evening" by W. H Auden.

"Your shows are always good, Martin," put in Miss Ballard. "That isn't why we've all gone gay. I could easily tell you why, but you should be able to think it out for yourself."

Doctor Russell looked blank for a moment and then said, smiling: "Oh. The mice are playing, are they?"

"We've got till Wednesday, anyhow," remarked Miss Ballard to Miss Smith, as they moved off.

"There's still Collins," said Mabel, in her gloomy voice.

"And who cares about Collins?" said Mary Ballard.

◆

"Come and talk to me in my office for a moment, will you?" said Russell to Merrion.

Merrion, who had not previously seen Russell's handsome room, surveyed it with appreciation. "You've got a nice view over the courtyard," he said, "and you're beautifully quiet. My room's at the front, and it's infernally noisy."

"I chose it just because it's quiet and well away from everything. I was able to have first choice, you see, because this palace was originally given to the College; the Mission only moved into it later. Cigarette?"

Merrion accepted a cigarette without comment.

"It's about the College that I want to talk to you, Merrion. We've had a good choir and a potentially good orchestra . . ."

Russell described Bob Owen's work with the choir and the orchestra, and ended with the direct question: "Would you be willing to carry them on?"

"No," said Merrion. "I won't have anything to do with them."

He slewed round in his chair and swung one leg over an arm of it.

Doctor Russell looked at him in silence.

"I haven't got your missionary zeal," said Merrion, "and I can't stand amateur performances."

"That seems a pity."

"I didn't come out here to run a youth club for boy scouts and girl guides."

Doctor Russell, recognising the phraseology, thought it best to say nothing.

"I'm going to have enough to do listing the stuff that's lying about before I can even begin to build up a Music Library. And the Organisation's going to unload a lot of new records on me, which I'll have to lend out to the other Centres and keep track of. I've told Bower that I'll need a full-time secretary if I'm to cope with that besides arranging concerts. Not that I mind the concerts. Bower wants them to be good and I'll see that they're good. The concerts are O.K. by me. But I'm not going to be pestered by potty amateur activities into the bargain."

"I see. I'm sorry you feel that it would be pestering; I don't want to pester you. I only hoped that you would be willing to help the College."

"Well, the College is hardly my job."

"Oh, I don't know. The College provides live audiences willing to absorb the Utopian way of life, which includes music, doesn't it?"

"Music is an international art." Merrion unhooked his leg from the arm of the chair and shifted restlessly on the seat.

"Music can find an audience anywhere. You literary blokes may need special audiences, but I don't need any College to provide listeners for me. In fact, the less I know about the people listening to me, the better."

"Would you just as soon play to a roomful of blasted officials as to real people?"

"Just as soon," affirmed Merrion, lighting another cigarette from the stub of his old one. "I tell you I haven't any of your missionary zeal. I don't much like people, come to that. And I've been sent here to be a blasted official myself."

He laughed a little and threw the dead stub on the floor. "All I care about is to keep my job, because it keeps me, and to get my own work done. I'm not going to be drawn into any potty little intrigues, and *also*," he said, with jerky emphasis, "I'm not going to waste any time going agin the Government. I warn you."

Russell leaned back and said slowly: "You mean that as a tip for me, don't you?"

"Take it as you like."

"Well, thank you for it," said Russell, recognising an impulse of queerly distorted good-will. "You've told me nothing I don't know — if that makes you feel better. I had already guessed that I'm supposed to be agin the Government. But thank you all the same. And I'll give you a tip in return. This Government you're going to serve isn't the kind to let you keep your independence. It's a one-man power-system. You'll have to be a satellite. You won't be able to call your soul your own."

"I can always go and get drunk, can't I?" said Merrion.

CHAPTER XXII

Mr Collins, left in charge of the Mission, felt instinctively that he should not merely sit back and wait for Mrs Owen's surrender. He had better intimidate her as well, to make it certain that she would give up not only the flat but the decree, which he had learned from Bob Owen was in her keeping.

Before departing, the Chief had explained why he attached importance to securing the decree. Some hostile influence, he suspected, was working against the Mission in the Foreign Office; it might, perhaps, be Communist-inspired. Doctor Mladski had suggested that Collins had better apply for a new decree if he wanted the flat, and when Mr Bower had made further enquiries of the Housing Department Doctor Pachek had been obstructive, one might even say hostile, as if he had a spite at the Mission; he had made a point of insisting that Collins must not enter the flat without first notifying him and applying for a new decree. It would be safer, the Chief thought, to transfer the old decree and present Doctor Pachek with a *fait accompli*. That was the usual procedure among Embassy officials, he believed.

He had also enjoined Mr Collins to be tactful in dealing with Mrs Owen, since women, of course, could not be relied on to admit the logic of necessity, and in a fit of spite she might send the decree back to the Foreign Office. And that, if she did so, would cause a row, possibly a scandal, even though the flat were vacated. Tact, said Mr Bower, tact; Collins must really learn how to use tact.

Yet Mr Collins's self-esteem, trodden down by the Chief, began to revive after his departure and prompted the reflection that tact, on the Chief's lips, was a synonym for cowardice. One knew what a curious mixture the Chief was, a bland of ambitious theory and timid practice, of direct logic and devious policy. Mr Collins preferred to trust his instincts, which told him that Iris Owen could be bullied.

On the very day after the Chief had gone Mr Collins rang up Mrs Owen at an hour when he guessed she would be at home, and said: "The term for your occupation of the flat will be up a week today. I suppose my wife and I can count on getting in then?"

"Oh," said Iris Owen. "I don't know, Mr Collins. I haven't anywhere to go yet."

"I shall see that you get a room in the Star Hotel at Prsht, until you find other accommodation. But I must insist that you vacate the flat by next Saturday. And meanwhile I suppose we can at least park some things in your spare room?"

"I haven't got a spare room."

"What, is Miss Lidgard *still* there? The Chief assured me positively that she was to leave. You had better see that she does."

One point thus made, the next point was easy. Mr Collins sent on Monday, by hand, a memorandum to Mrs Owen containing an inventory of the furniture he expected to find in the flat when he took possession. The inventory included a bedroom suite which the Owens had borrowed a hundred pounds from the Mission to buy, during the last weeks of Rigg's incumbency.

This communication brought Mrs Owen in person to the office, protesting that the bedroom suite was private property, which the Owens had promised to pay for by instalments. The fact that they had not yet paid any instalments, emphasised by Mr Collins, Mrs Owen sought to cancel by offering to provide a cheque for the whole amount within a day or two. Mrs Owen also pointed out that the suite had been chosen by the Owens to please themselves, and might not please Mrs Collins, who would doubtless prefer to select her own bedroom furnishings. Mr Collins then wanted to know what the Owens thought they could do with a bedroom suite, since they averred that no flats or villas were available in Prsht, to which Mrs Owen returned that Bob thought they had a chance of an unfurnished flat in a few weeks' time, but that it might take months to get new furniture.

Mrs Owen's defensiveness, which was so ambivalent that it could turn into aggressiveness in the twinkling of an eye, stood her here in good stead; her instincts were as sure in their promptings as Mr Collins's. Her next move was to say that she would appeal to Mr Bower about the bedroom furniture. With exceeding haughtiness Mr Collins assured her that the Chief had no rights over the furniture, which was solely the Deputy's responsibility, and that she was not to move any of it without his permission. And why had she not brought the decree with her?

Mrs Owen, concluding that she stood a fair chance of securing her furniture if she did appeal to Mr Bower over Collins's head, retorted that she would hand over the decree only to Mr Bower, on his return.

On the day following, Mr Collins sent her another reminder which said: "The Star Hotel in Prsht has promised to give you a room. You are expected to be out of the flat by Saturday at the latest, and it is expected that there will be beds in it for the Collins family."

The jauntiness of this message, which suggested more than mere self-satisfaction, provoked Mrs Owen into making another visit to the office for the sole purpose of telling Mr Collins that there was one and only one Mission bed in the whole flat, and he could make what he liked of that.

One must infer that Mr Collins found it piquant to be wrangling with a pretty girl over beds, for he did not need to do it, well knowing that two beds of his, together with other much-carved furniture, after travelling overseas were now lumbering overland towards Slavomania, where they might arrive at any moment; while, as the whole Mission was aware, the Collinses, immediately on arrival, had bought a decoratively painted Slavomane cot for their son.

"And, Mission furniture or no Mission furniture, I'm jolly well going to take Rosemary's cot with me," said Mrs Owen to Mrs Russell, whom she encountered in the Tea-Room. "Collins doesn't need it and I do."

Mrs Owen, in fact, had arrived at the conclusion, long since reached by Miss Ballard, that Collins was a man at whom any spirited woman could cock a snook.

Mrs Russell, having finished her tea, spread out a double-page foolscap document covered with lines of small print and compartments for long-hand entries. It was headed: Application for Extraordinary Supplementary Ration of Heating Fuel, Section Three, Sub-section G, of Fuel Ministry Ordinance Number Two Hundred and One; which, in Slavomanian, seemed even more portentous.

"Just look at this," she said. "I think it must be the hundredth time I've written down my mother's maiden name. See the nice rubber-stamps? I've got Collins to put on the Mission one, and Martin the College one; don't you think I might get Claude to dab on a few library ones as well? Vladimir Mladski told me to get as many as I could, because it impresses Slavomane officials. And even then, he warned me, he couldn't guarantee anything."

"It's all sickening, isn't it?" said Iris. "Oh, Jamesina, I *am* fed up."

"So am I."

They sat silent.

Mrs Owen was wondering what Arch was saying at Headquarters to discredit Bob. She also wondered what Jamesina would say if she knew that Bob had excused himself to Arch for writing to the Foreign Office by pleading that he had done it on Mrs Russell's advice.

Mrs Russell was thinking that she had better not let Iris know how she had prevented Vladimir from obstructing Collins's entry into the flat. "Don't do it, Vladimir," she had said. "The Owens have caved in and it's no use carrying on war." Vladimir had not insisted. Doctor Pachek of the Housing Department would make a row anyway, he had said, and he himself was bothered about other things — Jamesina would be able to guess what. And she was to remember that he could guarantee nothing, nothing at all. And then he had hung up, leaving her staring blankly at the telephone.

"I've sent Bob a wire to ask him if the Star will really take us in," said Iris. "Bob's utterly fed up. I had *such* a miserable letter from him this morning."

"You will at least have the advantage in Prsht of being well away from Arch," said Jamesina. "And think how pleased Anne and Rosemary will be to have the family all together again. And Bob will be glad to have you beside him."

"I hope so," said Iris, looking like a forlorn waif. She has been wondering if Bob really wants her in Prsht, said Mrs Russell to herself, and added aloud:

"Of course he will. What's Jane going to do?"

"She's staying with me until Saturday, and I'm very thankful. She's found herself a room in the Small Town, near the river."

"The whole thing is too sickening for words," said Mrs Russell, thus completing the circle by returning to its starting-point.

The unhappiness of these two ladies, which filled them with anxiety both specific and vague, bore little conscious relation to the unhappy turbulence then beginning to agitate the capital city in which they sat. Had Mrs Owen been asked what she was worrying about, she would have answered: everything; but on being pressed she would have specified her furniture, her children, her husband, her future; she would not have mentioned Slavomania, even although Katja, her maid, had been bringing in rumours of impending trouble and she herself had no faith in the stability of foreign regimes. Mrs Russell, likewise, would have admitted that she was anxious about the possible failure of the central heating and about her husband, who had told her that he was haunted by nightmares in which Mr Bower, disguised as an octopus, pursued and strangled him in his tentacles, but she would have mentioned Slavomania only in passing, saying that it was a pity the Slavomanes let themselves be upset by baseless rumours, and it was difficult sometimes to know what to do with them.

And yet the world they were living in had become perilously unstable; waves of general apprehension, although they failed to realise the fact, were re-inforcing their own fears.

◆

Doctor Mladski, although he had moments of dumb distress during this week was usually simmering with exasperated incredulity. He found it difficult to believe that politicians could be such fools. Were they really deluded enough to fancy that if all the right-wing Ministers resigned *en bloc* from the Coalition, the President would re-instate them in a new Government that excluded the Communists? Was it possible that they thought they were still living in the nineteenth century, when a sovereign Emperor could well dismiss or appoint Ministers at his pleasure? By what conceivable means had they persuaded themselves that a Communist Prime Minister, representing the dominant Party in Slavomania, could be side-tracked by a political manoeuvre that was fifty years out of date?

"Yes, it's a mad idea, of course," said his Chief, to whom he was expounding these views, "and of course I won't have anything to do with it. But neither will the President. He'll simply refuse to accept their resignations. I still don't see why you think we're heading for an immediate smash. Granted that the Communists would like to stage a *coup*, and may be planning one to come off before the elections, they can't be nearly ready for it yet. They would need another month, at least. And I don't think their *coup* would come off even then. They're short on public figures, aren't they? Their key men come mostly from the Egon Erwin Kisch crowd, don't they, Hungarian Jews and German Jews who can't speak enough Slavomanian to show their faces in public?"

"They have the Cominform behind them."

"And the Cold War, granted. But do you think Russia would risk throwing in an army? I doubt it."

"Look at the way Agitprop is working overtime to frighten the people with rumours of war and invasion. Have you heard the latest one, by the way? The Yanks are supposed to have put all our expelled refugees into uniform and have got them lined up in arms, just over the western frontier, ready to invade us. That's calculated to make every Slavomane grab for a rifle if he's offered one. And I think he will be offered one. I think they mean mischief."

"They always mean mischief. But I don't believe that our people — the salt of the earth, Mladski, the salt of the earth — would follow these Moscow-trained theorists who haven't a decent human feeling among them."

Doctor Mladski turned down the corners of his mouth

and lifted his shoulders.

"Decent human feelings," he said, "when they come up against a totalitarian power system, have as much chance as fledglings in the track of an army tank."

"Oh, come, come," said the Foreign Minister, with his jolly laugh, "that's poetry, not politics. Cheer up, man, we're not dead yet."

◆

The Trade Union Combine, which was about to hold its annual Congress in the capital on the coming Sunday, was a powerful, massive body. Preparations for the Congress had been long drawn out and delegates were already beginning to arrive. The secret alliance between the Executive of the Combine and the central Secretariat of the Communist Party was as unknown to the Foreign Minister and to Doctor Mladski as to the world at large, but it was much in the minds of the Communist leaders when they consulted together about the measures they should take. It was like a deep organ note sustaining their deliberations.

The Right-wing conspiracy which was now a-foot was, of course, a Plot against the People, but it was a gift to the Party. That it should coincide with the Trade Union Congress was a stroke of sheer luck. It should be easy to put across the idea that the Communists and the Trade Unions between them could form a solid People's Government and save the country from the treachery of the Right Wing. This looked like the very opening that they wanted. In any case, they had their Master Plan ready; all that was needed was to speed it up.

Why not? Why not? Those rifles for the Works Militia could be distributed at once to the factories. Let them be taken out of store, anyhow. Just in case. The Action Committees could be constituted now, instead of later. Let the local secretaries be warned. Just in case. And then, of course, the Cominform . . .

Chapter XXIII

Mr Bower had brought back with him a Medical Officer, an Education Officer, and an extra young man who was to be called the Functional Officer. This extra young man was to be dogsbody in the Mission, to handle the transport of exhibition material and Distinguished Visitors and do any tiresome work the Chief or his Deputy had no time for. Even more than the punctual delivery of the two officers he had indented for, the bestowal of this extra young man delighted Mr Bower, for it was a mark of approval from Headquarters, almost a Present for a Good Boy.

Headquarters had been very sympathetic, he told Victoria. They fully appreciated his difficulties.

Victoria's anxiety began to lose its thin, fretful edge. Yet her voice retained some sharpness as she said:

"I hope you made them understand what a lot of trouble your Staff gives you. Unnecessary trouble, too. You've always had bad luck with difficult and ungrateful colleagues, haven't you, Arch? It's been the same everywhere. I can't imagine why the Organisation appoints such people. Do you think the new ones will be any better?"

Mr Bower, all complacency, assured her that the Education Officer was a man with up-to-date modern ideas.

"He agrees with me about the importance of science and technology rather than literature. He inclines to think, as I do, that until we achieve a more scientific approach to literature, its value for international exchange schemes in education is, to say the least of it, dubious."

"You mean that you won't need to bother about Doctor Russell any more?"

"H'm," said Mr Bower, shying away from this formulation of what was in his mind. "As regards Russell, I have warned him about Russell, of course. I had to tell him that Russell is somewhat old-fashioned in his attitude to these matters and that we may have to over-ride his prejudices. He made quite a *bon mot* about that; he pointed out that Russell probably needed streamlining to turn him into a more modern model. I ventured to repeat that at Headquarters, and I must say that it was appreciated. I found them most understanding at Headquarters, Victoria; most understanding. — By the way, I've asked the Education Officer to look in this evening. The Medical Officer too."

"What's he like?"

"I'm afraid the Medical Officer is a she. But I think she'll be all right. Where's Arthur?"

"Down at the Mission, I believe, practising for the concert. What kind of a woman is she?"

"Oh, nothing much to look at, not at all attractive. More like a fat boy than a woman. A keen officer, though, I think."

"A fat boy! Well, I'm thankful she's not one of these home-breakers," said Victoria, relaxing into skittishness.

Mr Bower thought, but did not say, that the Medical Officer's lack of apparent femininity was precisely what made her appointment bearable. He had strong objections to female executive or administrative officers, since he believed that they could not be impersonal, or, as he himself put it, could not achieve impersonality; but he did not air these objections in his wife's hearing.

It was years since Mrs Bower had seen her husband so sure of himself, so happy. On that evening she began to feel, as he did, that everything would now go on oiled wheels. He would be able to make the Mission what he had dreamed it should be, to streamline it, as the Education Officer was just saying, into its new functional pattern.

"We shall have to re-distribute our space, of course," confided Arch to her later. "We are to lodge all the specialist officers and their secretaries on the top floor, beside me, so that we can keep in touch. These ornate rooms on the first floor are not really convenient as offices; they will do better as reception rooms, or specialised reading-rooms."

"That means turning Doctor Russell out of his present room, doesn't it?"

"Oh yes. We are to offer him Owen's old room upstairs."

◆

On Friday morning, Mrs Russell went into the library of the Mission to keep herself warm while waiting for her husband, who was attending a Grand Conference of Specialists called by the Chief. Despite her anxious unease, she felt that the library was a restful place, the more so since Claude was not in it at the moment. From her seat between two bookcases she could just see one of the two girls who were quietly busy in a far corner over the card-index files of the catalogue. Already more tranquil, she opened her own book, one she had read so often that she almost knew it by heart.

Presently Harold Pottle, the member of College staff whom no one ever noticed or recollected, sidled round a book-case to put back on a shelf a treatise on phonetics and to take out another work on phonetics.

"Good morning, Mrs Russell," he breathed.

Mrs Russell was one of the few people he was not afraid of.

"Icy weather, isn't it?" she said. "I'm taking refuge here because our central heating has given out at home and the flat's like a refrigerator."

"Oh, Mrs Russell, be sure you don't catch cold! There's twenty degrees of frost outside. I'm so afraid for my throat."

Mr Pottle carried formalin tablets for his throat, pastilles for his catarrh, and vitamin tablets for his general well-being. When armed with chalk and blackboard, as Athena with spear and aegis,[1] he was bold, able to face students and instruct them in phonetics; yet without his equipment he shrank from human beings as he shrank from germs. Mr Pottle never came to a social function at the College, nor was he ever seen in the Tea-Room; he lived in furnished lodgings, no one quite knew where. Even Miss Ballard and Miss Smith had given up trying to mother him, and soothed their consciences by putting about the theory that he lived in a nursing home.

"I bought some electric heaters," said Mrs Russell, "but they only make little puddles of warmth in the Arctic desert."

"This is a harsh climate, you know," said Mr Pottle, shaking his head. He tried an experimental cough.

"You should ask for a transfer, shouldn't you, to some warmer country?"

"But the language here is so *interesting*," said Mr Pottle. "And I am . . ." He swallowed once or twice, and then said: "There's no good standard work on Slavomanian phonology, Mrs Russell, and I am . . . I am compiling one."

"I do congratulate you, Harold. How satisfying it must be to have something definite to do."

"Very satisfying, very satisfying indeed," sighed Mr Pottle, and the next moment he was not there.

Really, thought Mrs Russell, Harold gets more and more like the Cheshire Cat.

The reason for his de-materialisation was now evident; Claude had come in and was advancing upon her. One had to be careful what one said to Claude; one had to parry his inquisitiveness; one did not mention Arch.

"Waiting for Martin, are you?" said Claude, after hearing the story of the Porter and the Coke. "What's that book

---

[1] The Greek goddess Athena's aegis is sometimes depicted as a shield, sometimes as an cured animal skin draped around her, in either case usually with decorations.

you've got there? Jane Austen? Oh, I can give you something better than that. There's a new parcel of books come from Headquarters; I've just been unpacking them. Some real new thrillers among them that I bet you haven't read."

"I will *not* have Dornford Yates," said Mrs Russell, giving back, like a mirror, Claude's emphatic robustness of speech, "even though he *is* your favourite author."

"Come into the boudoir and see the new 'tecs[2] anyway," said Claude, cajoling her into a low-brow conspiracy of two.

In the tapestried boudoir Claude's enormous roll-top desk, among the delicately scrolled settees and arm-chairs, looked like a jolly but over-bearing financier among a troupe of ballet-girls.

"I didn't want to mention it in there before the girls," said Claude, his blue eyes popping, "but do you know that things in this country are going from bad to worse?"

The man who cried: Wolf! Wolf! must have been a comfort to the shepherds, thought Mrs Russell; he gave them a pleasant, re-assuring feeling that things were normal, after all.

"I've just heard from a Swiss friend of mine," said Claude, "that the Ministry of the Interior — the secret police, you know — has shoved a Swiss business man behind bars, and the Swiss Legation can't get him out. Can't even get a sight of him."

"What's he supposed to have done?"

"Oh, just what everybody does, helped some Slavomane to tuck away a nest egg abroad."

"You'd better be careful, or they'll catch you next."

"Get along with you, I wasn't born yesterday."

"I believe you. I'm sure you could wangle yourself out of anything, Claude. You're a great comfort to me."

"But it's a bit thick, isn't it, if they're beginning to pick up

[2] detective stories

foreigners?" said Claude, after accepting the compliment with gratification. "And his Legation doesn't seem to be able to do a thing. They're getting above themselves, these Communists."

Refreshed by this conversation, Mrs Russell met her husband with determined cheerfulness, which became more spontaneous when she saw that he was not bearing himself as one moving towards the condemned cell.

Yet no questions about the College could be asked within earshot of Claude, so she waited until they were in the street, picking their way over frozen ruts.

"How did the Cabinet Meeting go?"

"Not so bad as I expected."

They turned the corner into the Square, where a thin, icy wind sharpened their noses. Martin Russell pulled his scarf up round his ears and indicated that he was unwilling to talk until they were indoors again. His wife, who had an unfair advantage over him, because she was wearing Slavomane felt boots and had her ears well covered, smiled and slipped her arm under his; in silence they plodded up-hill against the wind with more warmth and stability together than separately.

On the other side of the Square, in the roadway, a dense knot of people, dark against the snow, stood shuffling and stamping their feet to keep warm as they watched a flickering white screen mounted in front of a large building. Above the screen, bright capital letters flitted across the façade in a tireless ribbon, spelling out softly radiant messages divided into words by points of light like stars.

Mrs Russell nudged her husband to make him turn his head and look. He gesticulated astonishment, and when they had pushed through the revolving door of the restaurant, he said: "What on earth's all that?"

"Propaganda for the West, as a counterblast to the

Communist shop-window on this side. The Communists haven't thought of a cinema-screen for their cartoons; the West seems to be one up."

"Do you mean to tell me that East and West are now facing each other across the Square?"

"Not exactly facing; the Communist window's farther down, darling, don't you remember? Facing diagonally, if you like. Looking askance at each other."

"Facing," insisted Martin Russell. "East one side, West the other. I don't like it. Was there a crowd at the East window, did you notice?"

"A fairish crowd. Not so big as the West crowd, though. Not so much free entertainment."

They sat down at a table in an alcove, from which they could see, dimly, through the steam clouding the restaurant's great window, the restless flickering and flitting of the cartoons and capital letters. The building which had mounted this show was the headquarters of a large publishing firm that supported the National Party, a Party which in any Western country would have been described as pink or Leftish, but in Slavomania was called the extreme Right.

"I don't like it at all," repeated Russell. Another situation ceasing to be fluid, I suppose, thought his wife.

"But they've been Easting and Westing for a long time already," she said.

"Yes, but it's coming into the open now. A bad sign."

"What makes you think so?"

Martin Russell sat crumbling a roll and dividing the crumbs with one finger into two separate camps on the table-cloth, but he made no answer.

"I sometimes wonder, Martin, if the trouble you've been having with Arch hasn't made you too ready to see trouble everywhere."

"Well, I'm getting more sensitive to it, that's all. Beginning to recognise the symptoms. Or, rather, the technique."

"Technique, what of?"

"Aggression, to use a fashionable word. Forcing people to do your will."

He smoothed his two heaps of crumbs into a level mass, and said:

"The queer thing about it is that Arch doesn't need to use the technique of aggression. He's the Chief. He could govern the Mission with kindness and understanding. At least, he could if he were a different sort of man, if he *had* any understanding. He holds the real power. And instead of using it to combine people so that they work happily together, he uses it to divide and discredit them, simply because he wants the appearance of power, I suppose, rather than the reality. He wants personal domination ... You should have heard the Cabinet Ministers all yes-yessing today, Jamesina. They little know what's coming to them."

"Why, what's coming to them?"

"Trouble. He'll keep them divided. Not one of them will be able to trust another. They'll have to compete for his favour, you see."

"But, my dear Martin, they may have more sense than you think."

Russell began to smile.

"The Education Officer," he said, "keeps telling me that our major task in the College is to evaluate the overall statistics of something or other."

"Doesn't he know that you always reach for your gun when you hear the word major?"

"He doesn't even suspect it. He sees me as a major problem, that's all. A brash and half-baked young man. I'm going to have my work cut out to keep him from ruining the

College. But I'm still the Director of the College, Jamesina; I haven't dwindled yet into being the Literary Officer."

"Oh, Martin!" said his wife, half-laughing.

"I'm going to be turned out of my room, though. It's to be a Small Reading Room for science and technology, I understand, when it's not a Small Reception Room for the medicos. We're to have a field day tomorrow, changing over."

To Martin Russell's surprise, his wife took this information more seriously than anything he had yet said. She was indignant.

◆

That same evening, while the College was rocking with laughter at its Brains Trust, the news was broadcast on the wireless that twelve Ministers of the Coalition Government had offered their resignations to the President. Only the Social Democratic Ministers were left in office, together with the Communists.

On hearing this, Dick and Eleanor Zelezny packed their joint suitcase immediately and, although the roads were treacherous, came back to the capital by taxi.

CHAPTER XXIV

Next morning the news of the resignations was in the Slavomane press, and Annushka brought it back to the Russells from the milk-shop.

"They shouldn't have done it," she insisted. "One should never give the Communists the slightest opening. They should never have done it."

"Is the fat going to be in the fire now, I wonder?" said Martin Russell.

"It might only mean a change of Government," said Jamesina, still unwilling to doff Utopian habits of thinking.

"I don't know. I wonder why the Social Democrats have stayed in?"

"That man who leads their minority fraction, that man with the long, foxy nose, I forgot to tell you, — I've seen him every day nearly, in the past week, walking down our street to the Russian Embassy. He's a fellow-traveller, isn't he? But Dick could tell us. When's he coming back?"

"I don't know," said Martin, looking troubled.

"Doesn't he join in the change-over today?"

"No, he still keeps his own little office."

"I do think it's a shame, your being turned out of your room."

"It doesn't really matter."

"And this is the day Iris gets turned out of her flat, too. What a Black Saturday!"

With Mr Bower's car waiting at the gate, Martin Russell was unusually hesitant in his movements. He wavered on the threshold of the flat and came back to say: "Will you be all right, Jamesina?"

"The kitchen's very warm," she assured him. "We've got the gas oven turned full on and the door of it wide open."

"I only hope the coke comes today, for if it doesn't . . ."

"Yes, the whole weekend without it would be terrible."

Russell had been on the point of saying: for if it doesn't, it may never come at all; but he still hesitated to voice his fears.

"Buy another heater or two," he said.

"And plug them all in at once, and fuse the whole system," said Jamesina, laughing.

Doctor Russell hesitated again before climbing into the Black Maria, for the seat beside Mr Bower was vacant and he had to nerve himself to occupy it.

"Where's Merrion?" he asked.

"Merrion's resting this morning, because of the concert."

Mr Bower's voice was cold and prim, signifying disapproval, and Russell, with some vague intention of defending Merrion, put extra warmth into his reply:

"Very wise of him. Though I shouldn't think he'd be likely to have stage-fright."

"I believe even good artists are liable to stage-fright. But Merrion, I fear, is inclined to seek courage in undesirable ways. He partakes rather too freely of the kind of courage one finds in bottles."

"Oh, I don't know," said Russell, still fending Arch off, "lots of good artists do that."

"Do you think so? I confess I am a little worried about tonight's concert, since the Ambassador has accepted our invitation and is bringing Lady Thring with him."

"Merrion will probably come up to scratch all right."

"You're coming to the concert, I take it?"

"I don't know. I hadn't thought about it."

"With the Ambassador there, it might be advisable for you to attend," said Mr Bower in his most distant manner, feeling put out by Russell's evasiveness. "Black tie, of course."

Russell shifted a little in his seat and said with some abruptness:

"Have you heard about these twelve Ministers resigning from the Government?"

"Which twelve Ministers?"

"All the Ministers there are, I believe, except the Social Democrats and the Communists."

"Indeed? Some political crisis?"

"I don't really know. But it might mean big trouble."

"Oh, I should hardly think so," said Mr Bower, who was little disposed at the moment to accept any suggestion made by Russell.

And yet, thought Russell, shrinking farther away from his Chief, you should know, if anyone, that after a split there's bound to be action.

This was one of the mornings when his flesh crawled with dislike of the Chief, and his stomach turned over if the man inadvertently touched him.

Dismissing the political crisis, Mr Bower began to discuss the College's future programme.

"We had better draw up a new syllabus," he said. "The Education Officer naturally wishes to give a course of lectures in the College, and he has suggested as a subject the working of the new Education Authorities in Utopia. I believe he is himself an authority on their administrative set-up."

Russell sat rigid on the extreme verge of his seat, thinking: Brute administration. How am I to save the College from brute administration?

Yet, on arriving at the Mission he discovered that brute administration had its comic relief. Mr Collins was now transformed into General Collins commanding Operation Change-over. To those concerned he was issuing a detailed time-table, together with instructions that all watches were

to be synchronized with the telephonist's. The two chauf-
feurs and the messengers were standing by, almost at
attention, presumably waiting for zero hour, which was,
Russell perceived on his time-table, at 9.10 hours precisely.

At 9.10 hours, he read, Miss Ballard's larger cupboard to
be moved into B7.

"What's B7?" he asked Miss Ballard.

"The Education Officer's room. See the list at the foot of
your time-table. Your new room's B8."

Skipping several items, he read further on: 10.03 hours,
Doctor Russell's books and papers to be moved into B8.

Well, that gives me time, he thought, to get my papers in
order.

"Operation Coffee," said Miss Ballard in his ear, "will
take place as usual at 11.03 hours precisely, in B.F., the usual
cubby-hole."

Doctor Russell went to his room smiling. Jane Lidgard
did more than smile when she came in presently to report
lack of progress; she was doubled over with laughter.

"Karnet's got stuck at the corner of the stairs with Mary's
big cupboard. It's wedged tight under the cornice, and
Collins is dancing with rage and pointing to his wrist-watch."

"The incalculable human factor, God bless it," said
Russell.

He went on sorting his papers into irregular bundles. As
he brought order into the chaotic mass of his lecture notes,
letters and memoranda, he found that the disorderly
resentments in his mind were fading, and that a plan was
emerging for saving the College from the Education Officer.

It was the Friday night audience he was most concerned
about, he realised. That lyrical phrase: "saving the College,"
when one looked at it calmly, really meant: "saving the
Friday night audience." The Friday night audience was the
very heart of the College. Sandford, who had not had the

benefit of the full Friday night audience but had talked only to a small group hastily collected from among the Friday regulars, had remarked how friendly and stimulating he found them; he had said he envied Russell the atmosphere of his College.

Well, it was an audience that had learned much during these last two years. It had learned, for instance, to give a quick response, to laugh openly without malice, to ask unembarrassed questions. And the College Staff, on their side, had trained themselves to give direct talks rather than read essays, to improvise coherently without scripts. Only a few special programmes were now written down before-hand, like the Winter Symposium. And even with a set programme one was aware of a spontaneous flow from speakers to audience, from audience to speakers. Between them, the College Staff and the audience had created something alive, a give-and-take of affectionate goodwill. To hand that audience over to the Education Officer would be like maltreating a live thing.

Brute administration, he repeated, slapping papers to-gether; brute machinery.

He would not do it. A specialist officer, he would tell Arch, should have an audience of specialists. The Education Officer could impart his mechanical information to selected bureaucrats from the Ministry of Education. He had a right, hadn't he, to be judged by his peers? The Friday night audience, Arch should be told, was merely a general audi-ence, a mixed lot, an assortment of all ages and occupations, not a suitable audience for a course of specialised lectures.

After this interlude, the rest of the day was bustle and confusion. About midday Jamesina rang up to say that the miracle had happened; the coke had come, and was being shovelled into the cellar by the sulky house-porter, under the eye of Mr Rychlik.

Martin had better come home for luncheon after all. Iris and the children, by the way, would be there too. Bob had wired that the "Star" in Prsht couldn't give them the promised room till Sunday, and Iris had begged for a night's shelter.

"Of course I told them to come along," said Jamesina. "Iris doesn't believe she'll get a room tomorrow, either; Prsht seems to be more Balkan than the Balkans, she says."

Naturally enough, among so many private events, including a lively bout of gossip concerning the change-over in the flat and in the office, the Russells learned nothing of the day's public events. In the evening Doctor Russell, unwillingly got up in dinner jacket and black tie, went off alone to the concert, quite unaware that the Prime Minister had spoken for over an hour that morning to a large concourse of Slavomanes in the Old Town Square, despite the parching cold, or that the President had later broadcast a message to the country emphasising his refusal to accept the Ministers' resignations or to allow any change in the composition of the Government before the spring elections.

◆

Doctor Russell's unwillingness to go to the concert, his attending it under constraint, as it were, may have limited his perceptions when he first entered the ball-room, so that he did not see all he might have seen. He noticed with a shade of malice that the four rows of arm-chairs ranged in a grand semi-circle — the palace's best arm-chairs, with seats and backs of purple satin embroidered with golden stars — were going to be largely untenanted; the people standing about would occupy less than half of them. He was aware of Sir Edward and Lady Thring, to whom he dutifully paid his respects, even although Arch and Collins were hovering in their neighbourhood; he was aware that Merrion looked formally correct, and wondered with an inward smile what he had been up to on the previous evening; but he did not come out of himself until a young girl touched his arm and said: "Doctor Russell." This was Sonia Beran, a member of the College, one of the Friday night regulars, and the welcome he gave her was positive and spontaneous. But he did not see Dick Zelezny, neither then nor immediately afterwards, when the big chandelier was switched off and he sat down in the back row with Sonia, who seemed downcast and inclined to cling to him. Not until half-way through the third item on the programme did he catch sight of Dick, and then only because he was fidgeting, glancing round idly instead of listening to Merrion.

Dick Zelezny was standing inconspicuously with his back to the wall, near the door leading into the corridor. Russell had the impression, at first glance, that Dick was looking queer. It was perhaps an effect of the dim lighting from the wall candles that shadowed his face. Russell glanced at him again, and, before he knew why, felt an oppression at his heart. He scanned Dick intently, and saw that he *was* looking queer, unlike himself. His skin seemed blotched and patchy over the cheek-bones; his eyes, flickering unsteadily, appeared to see nothing; his mouth twitched from time to time. One could have thought that he was in a high fever, almost delirious, and hardly knew where he was.

Yet Russell suppressed his first impulse to make for Dick and lead him out. He did not wish to push past Sonia or to disturb the audience; the ten-minute interval was coming soon, he thought, and he would speak to Dick then. It did not take long for these scruples to vanish when he noticed that between one glance at him and another, Dick had slipped away.

Muttering excuses, Russell dashed to the door and shut it behind him as quietly as he could. The short corridor was empty. He ran down it and turned off towards Dick's office. To his surprise, the door of the office was locked. He squinted as best he could through the key-hole but could see nothing; the little room seemed to be in darkness.

Well, Dick must have gone home, down the other passage. Perhaps he was only feeling ill; influenza or something.

Russell retraced his steps slowly, wondering if his painful agitation were foolish. Yet the impression remained strong that the fever Dick was suffering from could be described as political fever; that Dick, in fact, was beside himself with panic because of the political crisis. For the first time in hours Russell remembered that Slavomania was possibly on the verge of a political catastrophe that might well drive Dick Zelezny frantic.

He waited in the corridor outside the ball-room until he heard clapping, and then went soberly in. The lights were just going up for the interval, and he joined Sonia again with apologies for his abrupt excursion.

"I wanted to catch Major Zelezny," he said, "but he was too quick for me."

He now studied Sonia's face, covertly, for it occurred to him that he had seen flickering in her brown eyes, too, something that looked like fear. "Is your father here?" he asked, recollecting that her father was the conductor of the orchestra at the National Theatre.

"No, he was not able to come. I came without him. Yes, you may wonder why, Doctor Russell, but I wanted to be here. And I hoped very much to see you . . . Oh, please excuse me, I have been feeling so frightened at home, and I thought I should feel better here. And I do, I do. Please excuse me, Doctor Russell."

"My dear child," said Russell, piloting her towards a window seat, "come into this corner and tell me; what is it?

What is happening?"

"My parents say there will be a Communist Government, and my brother says it will perhaps be a good thing," said Sonia, beginning to tumble out a medley of fears, surmises and rumours. But then she said: "And the Prime Minister this morning did not mention the West, and did not mention the President, as if for him they did not exist."

Russell elicited from her that she had attended the Prime Minister's open-air meeting, with her brother, and had heard him pleading with his countrymen to open their hearts and minds to the great joy of brotherhood with Russia, in order to build the new People's World in which plots against the workers would no longer be possible.

"He said the National Party was plotting against the people. And it's not true, Doctor Russell, it's not true. My father is of the National Party, and he doesn't plot against anyone."

Sonia's eyes filled with tears.

"My father was four years in a concentration camp, and we did not, all of us, live through the Occupation for this, for a Communist Government."

"But you haven't got one yet," said Russell, feebly, as he himself was aware.

"My mother fears that we shall have. And my father says it may depend on what the Trade Union Combine decides tomorrow, but he too fears that we shall have. The President, I know, said this afternoon that he will allow no change in the Government, but, Doctor Russell, the Prime Minister spoke as if the President did not exist."

"The President is, after all, still the President."

"Yes," said Sonia, without conviction. "But my father says it is all because of the Marshall Plan, which Slavomania wants to join, and the Russians do not want her to join, and that the Communists will stick at nothing. They might even kill the President, he says, for the President is a very sick man and it would not take much to kill him."

"My dear Sonia! Don't let your imagination quite run away with you."

"Do you think I am a little fool, Doctor Russell? I want to hear that. I hope I am just being a little fool. I do feel better now than I did at home . . . I have been so frightened today, so frightened."

Almost the last thing Sonia Beran said to Doctor Russell was: "You will not shut up the College? You will not go away from this country? Please do not leave us, Doctor Russell, whatever happens; please not."

When Doctor Russell got home, Mrs Owen and the children were presumably asleep. His wife, exhausted by hospitality, was in bed dozing over a book, enjoying the regained pleasure of a warm bedroom, glad to see Martin again, but expecting merely perfunctory remarks about the concert and some reluctantly yielded gossip. She was shocked into wide-awakeness instead by a passionate harangue.

"The dreadful thing is, I feel Sonia's right," concluded Martin Russell, unwinding his black tie and throwing it on the floor. "And if I were Dick, I'd be panic-stricken too."

He wrenched off his collar and threw it after the tie.

"Eleanor did tell me that when Dick was acquitted Sova heard a man from the Ministry of the Interior saying: "We'll get him yet." Poor Dick. Poor, poor Dick. What a nightmare to be in," said Jamesina.

"That's just what he looked like, as if he were in a nightmare. But, I tell you, it's a nightmare that may come true."

"Oh no, Martin, don't say that."

"But if the Communists seize the Government — Blast and confound these blasted studs."

266

"Come over here and I'll take them out for you . . . How can I get them out if you don't stand still?"

"I'm too much worked up by all this infernal, bloody nonsense."

Martin Russell wrestled with his stiff shirt and emerged from it to say: "What's gone wrong with the human race? Where have we got to, Jamesina, that all we can think of is brute violence and grabbing power by force?"

"But how *can* the Communists seize the Government? How does one seize a Government, anyway? It isn't as if the Slavomanes were oppressed with grievances. They all have enough to eat now, and enough to live on. Vladimir once told me that a tram driver gets more money than he does . . ."

"Grievances! What have grievances to do with it?"

"But, Martin . . ."

"Didn't you hear what Sonia told me? It's a naked question of which power *bloc* Slavomania is to join, the Russian East or the Marshall Plan West. The split is there already, and the Communists want to force Slavomania on to the Russian side of it. That's all. That's all. That's why people are going to be driven frantic and have their hearts broken . . ."

"But they needn't be, they needn't be!" cried Jamesina. "Why should they be forced? How can they be forced, if they don't want to?"

"Because the people who have made the split will force them. The split has gone so far now that there's bound to be violent action. I don't see how any other conclusion is possible. I hate and detest pushing things to extreme conclusions, but that's just what Communists insist on doing."

"Grievances *do* matter, all the same," said Jamesina, "or the Communists wouldn't spend so much time trying to stir them up. They keep on telling people that they have grievances and ought to hate this, that and the other. But I don't believe, I simply don't believe that the Slavomanes are chock-full of hatred and grievances."

Martin Russell began to brush his teeth, and under the influence of accustomed routine found his agitation subsiding. He made more or less orderly preparations for bed, remembered to turn out the main light, and even kicked his discarded shirt and collar into a corner. Then he climbed into bed and said: "Give me a cigarette, Jamesina, will you?"

"The Slavomanes would much rather stay as they are, Martin, I'm quite sure," said his wife, passing him the cigarettes.

"Well, maybe," said Martin. "But it's like this, Jamesina. Let's suppose that here are your people, content to stay as they are." He picked an ash-tray from the bedside table and dropped into it a little heap of cigarette ash.

"Now, you want to move them, say, in this direction." He pushed the heap of ash with one finger.

"That's your purpose, your plan, and all you need is a line of action. Call it a Party Line, or a line of argument. A line, anyhow. So you put a dilemma before them, here. You make a point of it. Make an issue of it, is what's usually said, I believe. Your first point may be a small one. It may even concern a genuine grievance or a genuine loyalty. But you divide people on it; that's what matters. You tell them they must be for it or against it, they must go *this* way or *that* way. You don't give them time or room to realise that they needn't be for or against, that they can be indifferent because they're thinking of something else, or because they just don't care; you insist that they must divide. Of course you try to discredit the side you don't want them to take. You make it look as if justice and morality are on your side.

"Then a little later you make another issue, a larger one

this time, and you divide them again, pushing them a little farther along your line and abusing the other side a little more violently. You go on doing that, strengthening your ascendancy over them at every fresh point. It you can advertise your plan as being some kind of orthodox dogma, that makes it easier to discredit non-followers; you can call them deviationists, or heretics, or rebels, and you can set up as an authority on the dogma. And so you go on, from point to point, along your line of action, until you have made a split. When the split is large enough, when you think you have sufficiently discredited your non-followers, you hound your followers on to attack them. In the end, you liquidate them. You carry out your plan. You are the dominant power.

"That's the technique of aggression. It's as old as the hills, Jamesina. Divide and rule. Only the catchwords differ now-a-days and there's overwhelming power behind the threats . . ."

He sat staring at the window as if what he saw scared him.

"But can you do it to people if they're not unhappy, if they're contented?"

"No one is ever completely happy or contented. It's always possible to find a chink, to magnify or invent a grievance, if you want to split people. It's the will to split that counts. And you can split people through their loyalties too. Before they know where they are, people find themselves pushed a little way along your line, and then they're unwilling to draw back, hoping against hope that they're doing what's right. And you don't scruple to tell them lies — anything that will move them. It isn't truth you're thinking of; it's emotional effects you're after, to bring about action. That's what we call propaganda, these days."

Again he said: "It's the will to split that counts. But, of course, your followers will learn the technique themselves, and as one can't separate the doing of a thing from the way of doing it, they'll go on practising it, even after you've gained your power. They won't abandon the way they've been following — and neither will you, I should think. Imposing a dogma, making an issue, violently abusing opponents, that's the way to split any situation, any organised body, any community. It's like a sword, that line of action. Your followers may even use it to split *you*, instead of turning it against someone outside. Then you will need all the apparatus of repression, to keep down your own followers, after you've gained your power. Yes, that's how it happens. That *must* be how it happens. The splitter is bound to become the tyrant if he ever gains power . . . And that accounts for Arch," he concluded, unexpectedly, with a ring of satisfaction in his voice.

Later, when the bedside lights were out and all was dark, he said: "I ought to be grateful to Arch, Jamesina. I've learned a lot from him."

CHAPTER XXV

Although preoccupied next day by Iris and the children, who were finally seen off at the railway station, where Katja joined them, the Russells made an effort to find out what was going on at the opening session of the Trade Union Combine's annual Congress. The milk-shop at midday had no news of it; the only rumours there concerned a Plot against the People which the National Party was said to have prepared, with secret stores of arms hidden away in readiness for a treacherous *coup d'état*. But Eleanor Zelezny, when rung up in the afternoon, told them, speaking with audibly controlled distress, that Dick did *not* have influenza, and that the Trade Union Combine had called a token strike for an hour at noon on Tuesday, to support the Communist claim that the Party and the Trade Unions together could form a Government which the country would welcome.

On Monday morning, as if dragon's teeth had been broadcast in the night, armed police sprang up everywhere. They were on guard outside all banks, Ministries, and foreign Legations. As there were three Legations in the Russells' street, besides the magnificent palace at the park end of it which housed the Russian Embassy, Mrs Russell that morning kept encountering policemen, with wicked-looking shiny leather holsters on their hips and the black snouts of wickeder-looking rifles peering over their shoulder-straps. These were the new Security Police, and not one of them, so far as she could see, looked a day over twenty-one. They were strolling by twos along the edge of the pavement, laughing and chatting like boys out on a spree.

The sight of so much lethal and arbitrary machinery carried so casually by mere boys shocked and confused Mrs Russell more than she would have cared to admit. To compose herself, she paused at the last big lime tree in the avenue, to read one of the new Proclamations that had broken out on walls, hoardings and tree-trunks, headed, in bold capitals, by the unfamiliar words: Action Committee.

Thus she learned that a Central Action Committee, with subsidiary District Action Committees, now took all responsibility for maintaining law and order during the political emergency. No one, she read, was to leave the country without permission from the Ministry of the Interior. Here her eyes blurred so that she could read no farther, for an inner voice began to cry: Dick's caught in a trap, Dick's caught in a trap.

While she was standing before the big lime tree, armed police were raiding the offices of the National, Catholic and Agrarian Parties, impounding papers and clerks with equal zeal. Martin Russell reported this when he came home at one o'clock; he added that Eleanor Zelezny had sent Ruzi to his office with a written message begging them not to ring her up again; her telephone, she was sure, had been tapped.

"Tapped!" said Jamesina. "How can she know?"

"Jarmila tells me that it was common enough in the Occupation, and quite easy to spot. When you lift your receiver you hear a faint extra click in the distance."

"Ours isn't tapped," said Jamesina a moment later, coming back from the hall.

"Not yet," said Martin. "But you'd better not ring up any Slavomanes; it mightn't be healthy for them."

"Not even Vladimir?"

"Especially not Vladimir."

Now that it was clear which side of the fence the Trade Union Combine had jumped to, a Communist Government, said Martin, was inevitable. His wife, whose response to any situation was vaguely enveloping rather than precise, persisted in hoping that the President would prevail, despite lines of action, lines of argument, or any other lines. Yet the whole of Monday passed without any sign from the President, nor was there any on Tuesday.

"Of course the Prime Minister's putting pressure on him," said Russell. "And the Communists won't let him near the radio till he says what they want him to say."

"I still can't quite believe it," said Jamesina. "Everything's been quiet enough round here this morning, although these police youngsters are infesting the street. The token strike hasn't made any difference. People stop work from twelve to one anyhow, for dinner."

"There's been plenty of excitement down town," said Russell in an irritated tone. His wife felt that she was being foolish and said no more. Martin, she noted, was looking fagged and troubled.

He was troubled; he had been hearing rumours about a student demonstration.

"I must try to find out about the students," he said. "I heard that they were going to insist on seeing the President."

The buzz of gossip and rumour in the Mission had now swelled into roar. Utopian wives of Slavomanes darted in to complain that their husbands were being dismissed from Ministries, schools and business offices, or were being grounded, if in the Air Force. Members of the College brought news of high Government officials, even Ministers, being forcibly dragged from their desks. The Minister of Transport had been thrown out of his Ministry. The Minister of Posts and Telegraphs, too. The Social Democrats had now been raided as well as the other political parties and their chairman had been roughly handled; his arm was broken. A Minister had been carried down to the street, chair and all, and dumped on the pavement.

Among this confusion Doctor Russell succeeded in calling up on the telephone the Librarian of the University

Utopian Department, one of the men who had been haled to Police Headquarters and let go again on the evening of Dick Zelezny's arrest. Yes, yes, he said; the students had gone in procession that morning to the Castle, to demand an interview with the President. They wanted to tell him that rather than surrender the liberties of Slavomania they would prefer to die, as some of them had done in the November rising during the Occupation. But the Security Police had blocked the main street leading up the hill, and they had had to make a detour through by-lanes to the gates of the Castle. A detachment of Army soldiers was drawn up there, and the officer commanding lifted a rifle to warn them back. Then they stood at attention and began to sing the national anthem; the soldiers stood at attention too; they might have got through, after all, had not a shot been fired from behind them, by some of the Communist Works Militia in a side-street. One student was certainly wounded, perhaps dead; some said that several had been wounded; he did not know. Perhaps it had been an accidental shot that started it off, but there had undoubtedly been shooting and arrests.

Poor lads, poor lads, said Russell, feeling acutely miserable. As the afternoon wore on, it became clear even to him that he was in for a bout of the prevalent influenza. He went home and took his misery to bed.

During the night he was feverish and insisted on telling his wife that people must be individuals and not dividuals. "We mustn't let ourselves be split, we're not dividuals," he kept saying, starting up in bed with his hair on end.

◆

In the morning Annushka brought back a full load of gossip and rumours with the milk. All the officials in the Ministry of Justice had been arrested. The Prime Minister had seen the President, but there was no mention of that in any paper, nor had it been mentioned on the radio. Worst of all, there were no newspapers except the Communist Daily, the Trade Union Daily and a minority Social Democrat paper. People said that the workers had refused to supply paper for any others.

In the milk-shop they had said that a list of suspended officials was to be seen in what newspapers were available.

"I'd rather burn my hand than touch the Communist Daily," said Annushka, "so here's the Trade Union paper."

Mrs Russell spread it out on the kitchen table and went through it carefully until she found the list, inconspicuously printed, very small, in a corner. Vladimir's name was not in it. "The Security Police have been arresting people everywhere," went on Annushka. "And they say there's been incidents in Prsht, where Mrs Owen's gone. And incidents here, in the Square. Why do the Western Powers *allow* it, Mrs Russell?"

"How can they stop it?"

"They could send soldiers to stop it, surely."

"But that would mean war!"

Clearly Annushka considered war the lesser evil.

"But you Slavomanes are doing this yourselves," said her mistress. "How can anyone interfere from outside?"

"They should stop it," insisted Annushka. "I am angry with them if they don't stop it."

Mrs Russell carried in her husband's breakfast and told him as much of the news as she thought good for him. His fever was gone, but he looked limp and wan.

"I do believe," she said, "that the stoppage of the newspapers has caused more indignation in this quarter than anything else, to judge from what Annushka tells me. Lots of the women have only just realised that something's up."

About midday the rumour spread that the suppressed newspapers were now to be had, after all, and Annushka secured a couple. They looked much the same as usual, with the usual headlines and lay-out, but their contents and the composition of their editorial boards had been completely changed. One might as well read the Communist Daily, said the disgusted Annushka.

Having tucked her husband up for an afternoon nap, Mrs Russell, feeling tired and dispirited, put her head into the kitchen, thinking to beg Annushka to run out for some electric bulbs, since one of the bed-side lights had failed and there were no spares left. But Annushka had a visitor, a young girl who sat sobbing at the kitchen table.

"This is Marta, whom I have known from the cradle," she said, "and she has just been sacked from her factory, where she is a typist. Think of it; she has been sacked simply and solely because her father belongs to the National Party. Now, now, Martushka, now, now . . ."

The girl's face, which was rather like a kitten's, looked woe-begone. She was what would be called a Slavomane type, broadly built, with a broad head, a round bumpy forehead meeting wide strong cheek-bones that left little room for the nose, and a wide, soft mouth, now quivering.

"Make her some good, strong coffee, Annushka."

"That's the very thing."

Annushka began to grind coffee beans, turning the handle of the coffee-mill so fast that its grating clack rose to an angry whirr.

"And do you know what she tells me?" she said, desisting for a moment from her instrument. "All the men in her factory have been given rifles and told to march to the Square. Rifles! Jesus, Mary, Joseph, rifles! Whether they want to or not. Go, they are ordered, go or you are sacked."

The coffee-mill whirred furiously again.

This is a revolution, said Mrs Russell to herself, muffling her body, if not her heart, against the cold.

She went out of the familiar door, the familiar gate, expecting the street to look different. Yet, except for the strolling Security Police, everything looked startlingly the same.

At the last big lime tree in the avenue, where the shops began, she paused, as she had paused yesterday, determined, this time, to read the Proclamation right through. No one was to leave the country without permission from the Ministry of the Interior; yes. And then came an appeal for a National Front of Unity, to be embodied in a reconstructed Government. All very legal, she thought, all very constitutional in appearance.

Beside the Proclamation a fresh notice had been pasted on, a little askew, a smaller notice. It was signed by the Minister for National Defence and announced that this crisis was merely political and did not concern the Army, which stood at the disposal of the President.

Meant to be reassuring, thought Mrs Russell, finding that she was not at all reassured. Everyone knew that the President was not the man to grasp a club held before his nose and accept the responsibility of smashing his own people with it. The Minister of Defence must know that too.

The girl in the radio shop, where she bought her electric bulbs, looked much the same as usual, but Mrs Russell, feeling guiltily that she herself was not the same as usual, wondered if the girl did not know that a revolution was in progress, or simply did not care. The apparent indifference with which electric bulbs were taken down from a shelf, recommended and sold, instead of calming her increased her sense of uncertainty, so that she could not even venture, as she might have done on an ordinary occasion, to ask the girl what she thought of it all.

Outside the shop, she was just going to turn back down the avenue when she heard the tramp of many feet, and looking over her shoulder saw a body of men come marching, in straggling order, along the tram-lines, heading down-town, men in ordinary working clothes, each with a rifle slung over his shoulder.

These are some of the revolutionary forces from the factories, she thought, and stood staring.

There were about forty of them, some young, some middle-aged, one or two elderly. Some marched eagerly, with pride; but many, very many, were walking half reluctantly, falling now and then out of step. One elderly man in especial caught her eye, because he seemed an embodiment of uncertainties like her own. His knees were bent, so that he shambled rather than marched, and he looked as if he wanted to hang back yet could not help going on, as if he were ashamed of what he was doing yet did not know how to get out of doing it.

He's like a nice dog with the tin can of the revolution tied to his tail, thought Mrs Russell, and found to her concern that her cheeks were wet with tears.

All the way home tears welled involuntarily into her eyes and fell down her cheeks; she had not summoned and she could not stop them.

"It's my eyes that are crying and not me," she said aloud, over and over again. "It's my eyes. I can't help it."

The people who passed her did not look at her twice. No one, apparently, on this day was surprised to meet a woman walking down a street in the capital of Slavomania talking to herself with tears streaming down her face.

Yet the procession of armed workers which was to march at four o'clock from the Square to the Castle did not, after all, march. The Prime Minister in person came to the Square and announced that the President had formally accepted the new Government.

After hearing this news on the wireless, Mrs Russell went to bed, she, too, feverish and shivering with influenza.

CHAPTER XXVI

It was all over.

Dick Zelezny, who came to the Mission early on Thursday morning merely, it seemed, to make this statement, stepped out into the street and vanished.

And next morning, by the first post, his wife Eleanor received a letter from him.

She must now do what she had promised him she would do: convince everyone that his suicide letter was genuine, that he had really made away with himself.

Fingering the letter, she stared at the daffodils glowing softly on her breakfast table in a beam of sunlight, diffused through delicate muslin curtains. For the moment, she felt almost incapable of going through with the plan.

Yet she had already set it in motion on the previous evening when she had reduced poor Ruzi to such straits of fright and alarm because Dick had not come home. That had been horrible. It would be still more horrible now to tell her that the Major had disappeared for ever.

Yet Dick had insisted that not one friend of theirs must be left to feign an unfelt grief, for the Ministry of the Interior would spy closely on all of them. And if it came to questioning, Ruzi would be the first victim, after herself.

The Ministry of the Interior will be suspicious, Dick had said, for it was a well-known trick in the Occupation, but you must convince them, Eleanor. If they think it's only a trick to cover my escape, they won't give you a permit to leave. They might even keep you as a hostage to lure me back. And I should certainly come back if I knew that they had got you. I couldn't bear it, if you were held for questioning. It would be only a living death without you, he had said, and escaping would lose all meaning; so you *must* convince them, for both our sakes. You must make them feel that I am really dead. And then they'll let you go back to Utopia.

She read some passages again. "The only real happiness I have ever had has been with you, Eleanor. I thank you for it. If there is another life, I shall be waiting for you."

Dear, dear Dick; he had put that in to hearten her.

"Do not look for my body; I shall take care that it won't be found . . . God be with you."

She sat staring at the familiar, flowing signature, with the little line sloping up from it and a final dot, as Dick always wrote his name. With an abrupt movement she held the letter to her breast. It might well be the last contact she would ever have with him. He had told her that escaping now would be easier than escaping later, but he could not make her believe that there was no danger in it. Of course there was danger. Frontier guards, ready to shoot; police dogs, ready to spring. That was why he had forbidden her to try the escape route. God be with *him*, she prayed.

Reluctantly she then thought: Now I must do it. She rose from her chair and gazed round the room, letting her eyes linger on each object. This has been happiness, she said to herself. Everything in this room has felt our happiness and perhaps will keep the memory of it.

She dressed herself with her usual care and adjusted a veil over her eyes, which had deep black rings under them. First the Mission, she thought, and then the local police, and then the Ministry of the Interior.

So Eleanor Zelezny set out once more to fight, in her own way, for love and liberty, clasping a crumpled letter in one gloved hand, since she could not bear to let it go, even to drop it into her handbag. She had no need to simulate distress; the effects of shock and calamity were genuine and she carried them with her.

Whether the Ministry of the Interior was really convinced, or someone in authority was gallant, the permit to
leave the country was granted within forty-eight hours, and
by Monday afternoon Eleanor Zelezny was on her way to
Utopia by air. The moments before she climbed into the
plane were perhaps the most dreadful of all. She felt that she
could not bear it if some last-minute intrigue were to prevent
her from leaving, yet she found it equally intolerable to say
goodbye to Honzik and Ruzi. Honzik was to hold the flat
against confiscation, if he could, and had promised to look
after Ruzi; yet she felt that she was saying goodbye to them
for ever.

What lay in front of her, she did not think about. She
would stay with her brother, that was all. Until she heard
from Dick again, her life would be suspended.

Nearly three weeks later, news of Dick's successful
escape trickled through, by devious ways, to the Ambassador, who alone had been in his confidence. As soon as Sir
Edward knew that Dick and Eleanor Zelezny were together
in Utopia, he sent for Mr Bower and asked him to tell Dick's
friends in the Mission, privately, keeping the news as quiet
as possible.

In the Embassy, Mr Bower said little, but he was angry.

"I shall never forgive Eleanor Zelezny for the wild way
she went on," he said to Victoria, remembering how uncomfortable he had felt while Eleanor dropped tears on his desk.
"It was quite ridiculous to carry on in that theatrical way. I
don't believe that they ever wanted to get hold of Zelezny;
they were probably only too glad to have him out of the
country. And now he wants our Organisation to send some
things after him! That's all the thanks we get."

A few days later, thirty-six members of the Skrs Utopian
Society were re-arrested on a charge of treason and espionage. The name of Major Zelezny was included in the

published list of the accused. Still later, he was condemned, *in absentia*, to a long term of imprisonment.

◆

Not long after the news of Dick Zelezny's escape became known, the telephone rang one evening in the Russell's flat. Doctor Russell was sitting silent in an arm-chair, an open book lying disregarded on his knee, while Mrs Russell was carefully giving water to some pots of cyclamen.

"You go, darling," she said; then, almost at once, she repeated in a louder tone: "You go, Martin."

"Go?"

"The telephone. Ringing its head off."

"The telephone?"

"Go and see who it is."

Martin Russell went out to the hall. His wife could hear him talking; she looked anxious, but went on watering her pots.

In a moment he was back. "That was Michael Grey speaking, and he said: I'm coming to see you in about three-quarters of an hour, I'll ring you again. And then he said: Will Jamesina be in too?"

"Are you sure that was what he said? I mean, did he actually say: Jamesina?"

"Yes, he did. Will Jamesina be in too? I thought it a bit queer."

"More than queer. Michael Grey and I have never been on these terms. I should have expected him to say: Mrs Russell, or: your wife."

Russell sat down again in silence.

"You didn't ask him what he was coming to see us about?"

"To see us about? No, he seemed in a dreadful hurry and rang off."

Mrs Russell went out to the verandah with her watering-can, and presently came back to say: "Perhaps he's bringing us news of Vladimir."

"Vladimir?"

"It just came into my mind. He and Vladimir were always very friendly; they used to go round together a lot."

When the telephone rang again, nearly an hour later, Mrs Russell answered it.

"This is Michael Grey speaking," said a hurried voice, which she recognized, at once, as Vladimir's. "Yes," she said, on a full, reassuring note, "this is Jamesina."

"I shall be at your front gate in about five minutes. Will you see that it's unlocked? I must be able to slip in without being seen."

"Yes, I will."

This news roused her husband. Of his own accord he donned greatcoat and scarf and went out to unlock the front gate and watch discreetly for his friend, the first positive action that he had undertaken, without prompting, for days past.

When they both came upstairs, Jamesina was at the flat door and shut it quickly behind them.

"Oh, Vladimir! I'm so thankful to see you. I've been wondering and wondering about you."

"There's far too many policemen in your street, Jamesina, or I'd have come to see you sooner. There's no moon tonight, thank goodness."

In the drawing-room, Vladimir would not sit down until he was assured that the windows were shut. He made Jamesina pull the curtains together, tightly, so that not even a chink could be divined. And when he did take a chair, he could not at first sit still. He kept turning his head, as if listening to the silence on both sides of the house. "Are you sure the verandah window isn't open?" he asked.

"I'll make certain," said Jamesina.

The verandah window and door were both shut, she told him, when she came back, shut and bolted.

"Now!" she said, pouring out glasses of wine.

"Now!" said Vladimir, with a sigh, leaning back. "I've given my policeman the slip at last."

He had a policeman all to himself, he said, a special, told off to watch him from morning till night. He wasn't left alone for a moment.

"The first one I had was just a boy, and I made friends with him. 'Look,' I used to say, 'I'm going in here for dinner, and I'll come out in about an hour's time; you go and have some dinner yourself.' We had a very good working arrangement. But they must have grown suspicious of our friendly relations, for not long ago they took him off and put a tough guy on my tail, a different kind of man. I've had the devil's own job shaking him off tonight."

"I saw a figure scurrying down from the park like a blown leaf," said Martin Russell, "and somehow I knew it was you."

"The last time I rang up was from the kiosk beside the other park gate. Your telephone isn't tapped, is it?"

"No," said Jamesina.

"I hoped it mightn't be. And your house-porter wouldn't see me coming in?"

"No," said Martin. "Even if he did, he couldn't tell who it was, but I'm sure he didn't."

"I have to be extra careful for the next few days, because this weekend I'm going to escape. That's what I've come to tell you."

"Escape?" said Martin.

"Yes. I'm safe till I've finished sorting my Chief's papers — I'm his executor, you see — but once that job's done, they'll put me away. I'm carrying too much information in my head. Well, Monday and Tuesday of next week are both holidays — good old Saint Cyril and Saint Methodius; they haven't got round to liquidating the church calendar yet — so it will be Wednesday before I'm missed at the office. I'm going to take the chance. I only fear there may be a mass exodus this weekend, for that very reason, and the guards may be extra vigilant. Pray that it rains hard, will you?"

"Is rain a help?" said Martin.

"Yes, the guards can't see so far, and they're not so likely to range abroad."

"I'll pray for a deluge," said Jamesina.

"Do. And if I get through, Michael Grey — the real Michael Grey this time — will ring you up and say: That play of Shakespeare's you were asking for has come to hand. Will you remember that? I'll get in touch with him as soon as I'm in my concentration camp."

"What concentration camp?" asked Jamesina.

"Didn't you know they put refugees into concentration camps until they're screened? I believe they feed them on frozen turnips," said Vladimir, beginning to smile. "It'll be pretty horrible, I should think. But when I get out of the camp, I'll make for Utopia and trust to luck. I'm to stay with Michael's people for a bit."

"What are the chances of getting through the frontier, do you know?" asked Martin Russell.

"About one in five, I am told."

"One in five!" echoed Martin, staring at him in concern. "My dear boy!"

Martin's coming alive, said Jamesina to herself, and was aware that her eyes had begun to cry again. She hardly breathed, hoping that Vladimir would not notice.

"But I'll get through all right; don't you worry," said Vladimir. "My mother's psychic, and she says I'm going to get through. I went down to see my father and mother, to say goodbye to them, on Sunday — why, Jamesina!"

"Don't mind me; it's only my eyes; I can't help it," said Jamesina. "They've been doing this at intervals ever since the *coup*. Just shock, I think. It takes people in different ways. It drives Martin in on himself and brings me out in silly tears."

"Oh, the *coup*," said Vladimir. "Yes, we've all been suffering from that."

"You look as if you'd been bleached and shrunk, yourself."

"Sheer lack of sleep, Jamesina. I've been working in the office by day and conspiring by night. Well, the *coup* happened, as I said it would. Didn't I? You must allow me the pleasure of saying: I told you so."

Martin Russell sat up. "You were right, Vladimir, astonishingly right . . . What a long time ago it seems, that evening."

"And yet, you know, it happened much sooner than I expected. I hadn't allowed for the utter stupidity of our politicians. They made things only too easy for the Communists."

"The President should have stood out," protested Jamesina, dabbing at her overflowing eyes.

Vladimir raised one hand and let it fall.

"It wouldn't have made any difference in the long run."

"It seems such a long time ago," repeated Martin Russell. "Long, long ago. There were so many things I didn't see then. I don't suppose the President saw them either."

"I don't know what he sees now," said Vladimir, grimly.

"One rarely sees things in the middle of an action, I should think. Once started on a line of action, most people follow it blindly," said Martin.

"Oh, Vladimir," said Jamesina, with a hint of desperation in her voice, "Martin's inclined to think now that all lines of action end in disaster."

"Is that so, Martin?"

Martin Russell looked embarrassed, hesitated for a moment, and then said: "I find that I have a natural preference for contemplation, these days."

"Well, you should turn refugee," said Vladimir, lightly. "When I'm a refugee, I shall have plenty of time for contemplation."

"My dear boy," said Martin Russell, suddenly getting up, "you must have another drink." He picked up the bottle of wine. "We must drink to your successful escape. That's a line of action I can well approve."

Martin's more like himself again, thought Jamesina.

"How's my friend Mr Bower?" asked Vladimir, presently.

"The blasted Bower? Wet-blanketing everything, of course. We are all to be very careful, very cautious. No more careless, unscripted talks. Nice little lectures on cathedral towns, with nice magic-lantern slides," said Martin Russell. "Nothing that could possibly annoy the Government. But the amazing thing is that people come crowding into the Mission, to see the newspapers and magazines they can't get anywhere else. In spite of two policemen stationed at the gate to take down all their names . . . It's heart-breaking, Vladimir."

"Wait until they start really tightening the screw."

"Nobody speaks to or even looks at anyone else in the trams," said Jamesina.

"There are spies and informers everywhere, of course. In the College, too, I suppose, Martin?"

"I should think so. It's easier to spot them in my University lectures, where they take down every word I say. My two Communist spies nearly had a fit last week when I lectured on John Stuart Mill's idea of Liberty, — and so did Arch, when he heard about it — but the rest of the class was delighted. Poor things, the outlook's bleak for them. An

Action Committee is testing each one of them for political reliability. 'Why have you not joined the Party? Can you prove that you are progressive?' That kind of thing. And if they don't get a certificate from the Action Committee, they won't be allowed to sit their degree exams. It's a dreadful atmosphere. And students keep begging me privately to warn Kodichek to be more careful what he says. He's a brave man, Kodichek. He's refused, so far, to sign the loyalty formula."

"Oh yes, that's the latest joke, the people who sign the loyalty formula. They're called the radishes. Red outside and white inside, Jamesina. Good for purging."

"But they've sacked Kudera," went on Martin, growing more lively, "and for a comic reason. Our Literary Group told me why. You know old Vitamvas, don't you? The Grand Old Man of Communist letters? He hasn't written anything for years, apparently, and he's losing his memory. Well, last year he came on a manuscript in his desk, obviously put together by himself, and when he read it over he thought it pretty good and had it published under his own name, as an original work. But Kudera, that incorruptible scholar, wrote to the newspapers pointing out that it was a translation of Prescott's Conquest of Mexico, and a translation of a German translation, at that. So the Communist papers abused Kudera for a liar and a scoundrel, and set him down as a public enemy. That's why he's been sacked now."

"The usual dreary tyranny," said Vladimir. Presently he told them he had reason to believe that the Trade Unions were beginning to feel the pinch already, and added: "It'll take our people sixty or seventy years to grow out of it. Perhaps they'll learn something, meantime."

"I've been learning a lot myself," said Martin. "And our Literary Group — some of them, anyway — are learning fast. Four or five of them are idealistic young Communists, you know, expecting a new earth, if not a new heaven. They still approve the economics of Communism, but the rest of the Communist pattern is beginning to give them the horrors already; the dictatorial repression, the mass treatment. They've been telling me that they wish Communism had grown up in France rather than in Russia, where it was isolated from Europe for too long. And they've already grasped the fact that it's no use trying to exercise goodwill within the Communist Party. But they don't yet see, I think, that violence and repression are in the very bones of the Communist structure. They passed some fine resolutions in favour of the artist's inner freedom at their Young Writers' Conference last week, and now the Party Secretariat has stamped on them, hard, and they're very cast down, poor young things."

"Havran was telling me that if he gets to Paris on some delegation which may be allowed to go there, he won't come back," said Jamesina. "This is his country, he says, and he can't write well except in Slavomanian, but he can't live here, where his roots are, he says. In France he might be rootless, but he would be free."

"The dilemma of every refugee," commented Vladimir, looking into his glass. "But if I were to stay here, I shouldn't live at all, or not for long. It's hardly a dilemma for me, is it?"

"Dilemmas, dilemmas!" said Martin Russell, opening a fresh bottle of wine. "Who cleaves all the cleft sticks, I wonder?"

Vladimir laughed a little.

"No, it isn't the wine," said Martin, also laughing, "Or not entirely the wine. I'm very glad to have this evening with you, my dear boy. And I shall be seeing you again in Utopia, sooner or later, for I don't really think that I can do much more here."

"Oh, Martin!" cried Jamesina, reaching out her left hand to clasp his. "Are you going to ask for a transfer, after all?"

"Well, I've come to the conclusion that the double burden of Communist tyranny and Bower tyranny is more than I can be expected to shoulder, at my age. I've helped to keep something alive here, but now I'll have to leave it to grow. Yes, I'm going to ask for a transfer to another country."

"Fine!" said Vladimir. "Fine! I didn't want to say it, but now you've said it yourself. There's no use in your waiting here till you're thrown out. You would simply go to pieces, Martin. When will you be leaving?"

"At the end of the summer term, I should think."

◆

When Doctor Mladski finally rose to go, saying that it was high time he got back to his conspiracies, Mrs Russell said: "Do you know that the Zeleznys are safely in Utopia, Vladimir?"

"That's good news."

"Dick escaped over the frontier, just as you're going to do, and Eleanor got out legally, because he sent her a suicide letter. You're not sending a suicide letter, are you?"

Young Doctor Mladski smiled.

"I suggested to my father that I had better write a suicide letter, for his sake and my mother's, and do you know what he said? That it would be telling a lie. Telling a lie!" He shook his head. "My father wouldn't accept any protection that meant telling a lie. I had to promise him that I wouldn't escape with a lie on my conscience, Jamesina. I promised him, Martin, that I wouldn't tell a lie. I promised him!"

He began to laugh, a little wildly.

THE END

Ingram Content Group UK Ltd.
Milton Keynes UK
UKHW011815100323
418392UK00001B/97